The wisp of periwinkle silk drifted to the floor. Jessica was as lovely as Bret had thought she would be; her body was a pale, curving shape against the charcoal quilt of his bed. He thought of how long he had waited to have her like this, of the years he had burned for her. And as Bret first touched her, feeling, as he had so often ached to do, the creamy satin of her leg, the ivory rose of her breast, for a hard, racking moment, he wasn't sure he could wait any longer. . . .

And Jessica herself wasn't prepared for how she herself would feel. The first stirring tightness had been familiar. She'd felt it before. Sometimes, pausing in the wings, listening to the crowd roar their impatience for her, she felt an electricity, an energy. But performing had never deepened the tightness into pleasure, the kind of pleasure Bret was giving her right now. . . .

*Dear Reader,*

It is our pleasure to bring you a new experience in reading that goes beyond category writing. The settings of **Harlequin American Romance** give a sense of place and culture that is uniquely American, and the characters are warm and believable. The stories are of "today" and have been chosen to give variety within the vast scope of romance fiction.

This time Kathleen Gilles Seidel takes us into the glitter and sometimes realistic world of a recording star. Childhood incidents and the compelling magnetism of Bret Cavanaugh make Jessica Butler a heroine you will not soon forget.

From the early days of Harlequin, our primary concern has been to bring you novels of the highest quality. **Harlequin American Romance** is no exception. Enjoy!

*Vivian Stephens*

Vivian Stephens
Editorial Director
Harlequin American Romance
919 Third Avenue,
New York, N.Y. 10022

# A Risk
# Worth Taking

## KATHLEEN GILLES SEIDEL

# *Harlequin Books*

TORONTO • NEW YORK • LONDON
AMSTERDAM • PARIS • SYDNEY • HAMBURG
STOCKHOLM • ATHENS • TOKYO • MILAN

For Becky, Kit, the boys
and the warehouses

———————◆◆◆———————

Published August 1983

First printing June 1983

ISBN 0-373-16017-8

Printed in Canada

# Chapter One

The red "Don't Walk" sign flashed on. Jess Butler forced herself to wait patiently as the Los Angeles traffic started up and surged by her. She was late, she thought unhappily, and she hated being late. She didn't really mind waiting for other people, but she loathed making them wait for her. She always imagined them getting impatient, then restless, and finally apprehensive, wondering if they had come to the wrong place or managed to show up on the wrong day. She didn't like making people go through that on her account, but ever since getting back from her latest concert tour, she couldn't seem to do the simplest things.

Maybe it was the sunshine. She glanced nervously around her, peering over the top of her sunglasses. The early afternoon light was pale and straw-colored, the bright edge of the California sun filtered by the smoggy haze. Maybe it was this business of being outside during the day that was the problem, the reason that she couldn't get places on time.

For months and months she had been living in the world of the night. Only at night had she ever been awake or alert; only at night had she ever felt capable of doing anything. After a concert, still charged by the music and the adrenaline, all the musicians would drive the dark streets of some town whose name only the road manager knew, looking for the neon lights of a still-open restaurant or an all-night movie. Failing that, they would go back to the hotel, and if the night were warm, they would persuade the night manager to unlock the fence around the pool, and there they would sit, in lounge chairs, surrounded by flat cartons of half-eaten pizza, immersed in the sweet magic of the night, waiting to board the bus again.

Daylight was something they had all slept through— the black-out curtains of the custom bus turning the vast sweep of America's highways into perpetual night. In the afternoons the two buses would pull up at some Holiday Inn, and the musicians, the crew, the technicians, would stumble across the motel parking lot until they could get into their rooms and close the curtains, restoring the world to comfortable darkness.

Light was electricity, something you hired a technician to produce from a light board.

The tour had been over for nearly a week now, and she wasn't adjusting. She wasn't sure what to do with herself in the daylight, how to plan her day when there was no concert scheduled for the evening. She felt tired all the time, but she couldn't seem to sleep. Today was nearly the first time she had ventured outside, and already she was late and wishing that she had stayed indoors. So far it hadn't been much of a vacation.

A little gust, perhaps of wind, but more likely just a current stirred by the rush of traffic, lifted a few strands of her hair and blew them across her face. Patiently, Jess smoothed them back into place.

Her hair, falling sleekly down her back to below her waist, was black—such a pure color, so fine and straight that from the back, people occasionally thought that she was Oriental—although with her fair skin and deep blue eyes Jess Butler was as Southern as a mint julep on a hot afternoon. But as bright as her eyes were, it was her hair that people remembered her by; it was how people recognized her on the street, what they looked for on album covers.

It was hair to be proud of; "a fine head of hair" it would be called down South: shimmering, floating, enticing. Men were tantalized, women envied it, and Jess was sick of it. It was exhausting to take care of; even the most expensive cream rinse did not make it easy to comb out after a shampoo, and it took her hours to dry it. But she did not dare neglect it. A bright back light would pick up every split end.

The traffic signal finally changed and Jess started to step off the curb, waiting only for the last few cars to sweep by in defiance of their red light, when she sensed an almost sickeningly familiar scurry behind her shoulder.

"It is, I know it is." A man's excited whisper reached her ears. "You can tell by the hair. It is Jess Butler."

"Hey, Jess!" It was a second voice, louder, more confident, its Southern drawl slithering through the air. "Hey, Jess, we're from Georgia too."

Jess intended to cross the street, to smile and wave once she got started, but she felt a hand close on her arm, stopping her. The grip was moist and felt contaminating. For a moment, she just stared ahead at the white light ordering her to "Walk" and then slowly she turned her head to face her assailant, her jailer, her fan.

"Now see here, Jess, we didn't like your last album so much." She could smell the tang of bourbon that was giving the man—no, he was really only a boy—the courage to stop her. "Why don't you sing real country anymore?"

Why didn't you sing real country anymore? She had heard that so often and she was tempted to give him the "freeze"—that haughty look of flaring nostrils, a stiffened back, and cold, narrow eyes that had earned many Southern ladies the reputation of being much too proud. Whether or not the freeze had actually, as often rumored, saved several plantations from the torches of an advancing Yankee army, Jess knew that, if she tried, she could get this person to let go of her arm.

But he was a fan, and he and his friend were probably on vacation. It didn't seem right to send them back to Georgia with memories of being humiliated by someone they apparently thought of as a hometown girl who had made it big. If she handled it right, they'd go home and every memory of the California beaches would be overshadowed by meeting Jess Butler. "Guess who we saw?" they would brag. "Why, she's just the nicest little thing." Or "thang" as they would pronounce it.

And Jess understood why they were disappointed with her music. She had started out eight years ago as a country singer, singing simple songs about broken-hearted girls, about wives waiting for husbands to come home, about the heartache of living without enough love, money, and respect.

She had done well singing country. What set her apart from every other eighteen-year-old with a beautiful voice was that she understood the way other people felt. It wasn't any sort of rational knowledge that she had learned from a textbook; it was a raw instinct that she simply couldn't explain. She didn't know how she did it, but she could easily—automatically—see the world through someone else's eyes. While, for example, she hated scary movies and never went to them, she knew exactly how it felt to crave that kind of thrill.

Because she could understand experiences even if she hadn't had them herself, because she could know what something would feel like, Jess Butler could sing just about any country song and sing it with such sincere understanding, with so much honest feeling, that anyone would have thought that the troubles in the song were her own. Jess Butler made you feel things, that's what her fans said about her. When her rich alto voice would smolder with a story of loneliness, even the toughest truck driver would duck his head, blinking back an unfamiliar tear.

Jess had been perfectly content singing the country circuit throughout the South, but her manager and her producer were both more ambitious than she. When she was twenty-three, three years ago, they had brought her from Nashville out to Los Angeles and changed her material and her image.

Her voice kept its lazy country rhythms, and her arrangements were still dominated by the whine of a steel guitar, but she had added electric lead and rhythm guitars; the bass line became more complex, more melodic; and the drums beat out a stronger accent. Everything was more vigorous, more driving and energetic, moving toward rock and roll.

And the lyrics of her songs changed. The women in the new songs seemed older; they had made mistakes. They were more openly admiring of men, doing foolish things to attract them, proving incapable of holding them. "It ain't right," a disapproving fan had once told her. "That's the way men sing about women; women aren't supposed to sing that way about men."

Her onstage manner altered to fit these new songs. Jess was no longer eighteen, and she knew what yearning was. Her producer taught her how to project the magnetism that her country-bred modesty had always told her to hide.

Her allure was not the raucous, earthy frenzy of rock and roll. Instead she was almost languid, her manner whispering of long, lazy afternoons, with the summer heat swelling into passion. Her voice promised sleepy secrets, and the sometimes fragile stillness of her body was as provocative as movement. Her appeal seemed subtle, but few men heard her sing without being stirred.

Her California music had won her a place on the popular charts and a new audience, younger, more urban, better educated, but sometimes Jess felt like she was betraying the people who had started listening to her first, the sort of people who worked with their hands and went to church on Sunday. They were confused by the more complex arrangements and disapproved of the more provocative album covers, the more sensual performance. Although they continued to buy her records and come to her concerts, they felt like she had sold out and moved uptown where the money was better.

So as much as she now longed to be free of this man's grip, as tired as she was, she wasn't going to embarrass him. She owed people like this too much.

"Whereabouts in Georgia are you all from?" she heard herself say. Jess's speaking voice was low and rich, charged with a lush resonance, quivering as if simple speech were too small a container for such abundance.

"Outside Atlanta, ma'am."

This was from the other boy. Jess glanced at him; he was clearly starting to feel like they shouldn't have stopped her. She smiled a warm, although rather practiced, smile.

"I've got a brother going to school at Emory," she said, hoping that this would make them feel like the conversation were a personal one. It was true—Tate was at that Atlanta university—but she might have said it even if it weren't.

"What's his name?" he asked. "Maybe we know him."

"Tate," she returned pleasantly.

"Tate Butler...." They both shook their heads. "Don't know him."

It was hardly surprising. Tate's last name was Cavanaugh.

"Well, that's sure too bad," she lied. The light had changed back to red, and she was forced to keep standing on the curb, although this would have been a good moment to get her arm back and cross the street.

The first man let his hand slide up as if he were about to hook his arm around her shoulder. "Well, as long as—"

"Any problem, Jess?"

Jess turned with relief at the sound of that familiar voice. It belonged to Cade Hunter, the bass guitar player in her backup band. The other two men eyed Cade suspiciously. The guitarist was lean, almost bony, with long blond hair scraped into a ponytail and a small gold hoop in his left ear. But when Cade touched the arm that was gripping Jess, the man let go of her.

"This is my bass player, Cade Hunter," Jess introduced although, of course, she didn't know the other men's names.

Cade nodded, but did not extend his hand. "You all will have to excuse us," he said; his accent was Southern too. "We're meeting some people for lunch, and one of them is a lady who is going to skin me alive if we are any later than we already are."

Cade had much less respect for traffic lights than Jess did, and so he took her arm and started to cross the street as he spoke. She threw the two Georgians a soft, apologetic smile.

Once they were across the street, Cade let go of her. "What was that all about?" he asked.

"The usual," she replied. The plaintive pleas for Jess Butler to please sing some nice country songs had been heard by all of them.

They stopped in front of the restaurant so Cade could do up the pearl-covered snaps on the front of his black cowboy shirt and stuff the shirttails into his faded jeans.

"Well, wait until you start singing straight rock," he said as he opened the restaurant door for her. "Then they'll really be mad. They'll still buy your records," he acknowledged, "but they'll be mad."

"I'm not singing rock." Jess had let a number of rock influences creep into her music, but she still thought of herself as a country singer, and she planned to stay that way even though her manager, her producer, her band, seemingly everyone but herself and her original fans, wanted her to abandon country music altogether.

"Oh, sure you will," Cade said with a confidence that would have irritated Jess if she weren't so used to it. "You just aren't going to get any bigger in country music."

It wasn't that Jess was on top. Certainly any list of the

top ten female country singers would include her name, but if the list were narrowed to the top five, she wouldn't be on it. Her manager and her producer, even at their most optimistic, never saw her easing out Dolly, Loretta, Tammy, or the others. Even if she had never left the South, she wouldn't have been able to do it.

The reasons were many, starting with the fact that she didn't want it badly enough. Equally important Jess Butler wasn't living the sort of life one needed to be a country superstar.

Country-music fans like to suffer with their singers; they like to share in the musicians' troubled lives: the drinking problems of the men, the difficult marriages, and the heartbreaking divorces of the women. The fans wanted to read about these things in the magazines and then find traces of autobiography in the songs.

But Jess Butler's private life did not spill over into her music. She didn't have one to spill. She had given at least two hundred concerts a year for the last eight years—some years more than two hundred fifty. She barely had time to keep her hair washed, much less have an affair with another woman's husband.

The only people she knew were the ones she worked the road with; they were almost all men, but she was, by choice, romantically involved with none of them. The magazines, try as they might, had nothing to write about on that score.

And of her past, her press releases only told how she had grown up with her family on a smallish, but by no means impoverished, farm in north Georgia, a story that was as boring as it was untrue. But by the time that Jess realized that certain bits and pieces of her past would make thrilling reading in the tabloids, she had enough sense to keep quiet about them.

Sometimes she thought that her very ambitious manager, Nathan Geer, was going to insist that she switch over to singing rock, whose audiences were younger and cared less about a singer's private life. If she refused to do that, he would probably demand that she thrill the hearts of her country fans by having a series of well-publicized affairs with married steel-guitar players who had terrible drinking problems. She thought that either alternative sounded a little too exhausting for a woman who couldn't get herself to lunch on time.

The restaurant that Cade was now ushering her into was typical of chic California restaurants. It was bewilderingly bright with white stucco walls, hanging plants, bentwood chairs in pale, natural woods. It was not a particularly good restaurant; the food was unimaginative and certainly overpriced, but a fair number of successful musicians ate there. The absurd prices kept the tourists out, which the performers liked, and the restaurant had a phone jack at every table, which the managers and the agents all liked.

The maître d' knew instantly who Jess and Cade were and ushered them to a round white-covered table where Sally Daniels, Cade's girl friend, was waiting patiently while Jess and Cade's manager, Nathan Geer, was talking on a yellow phone that had been brought to the table.

Jess apologized for being late.

"Don't be silly," Sally said immediately. "We expected it."

Sally was in a sleeveless kelly-green dress, which she wore with some bright cloisonné bracelets. Draped over the back of her chair were a white blazer and a print scarf. Sally owned several health-food stores and needed to look businesslike.

Jess admired Sally's dress and silently wished she had put on something more bright and springlike. She was in a pair of gray silk trousers that she never wore on the road because they were too hard to take care of, and with them, she wore a plum-colored, loose-knit pullover. She looked all right, but perhaps she would feel better if she were in a dress as cheerful as Sally's.

But Sally's scarf had the same colors as her bracelets. Finding bracelets and a scarf that matched—Jess couldn't imagine herself managing to do that.

Cade carelessly pulled out a chair for Jess. "I would have thought that you would make us all eat outside, Sal."

"I was already on the patio when Nathan showed up and insisted that we move inside. There aren't phone jacks on the patio," she explained.

Nathan finished his call and slipped some notes in the breast pocket of his linen blazer. "If I weren't so great on the phone, the two of you would still be singing in low-rent bars in central Mississippi." He gestured for the waiter to take the phone away.

"But we are inside, Jess," Sally said.

Jess looked at her blankly.

"So you can take your sunglasses off," Sally explained. "Unless you are on drugs," she added cheerfully, obviously teasing, "and your pupils are so dilated that you can't take any light."

"Oh, no." Jess pulled the glasses off so quickly that one of the earpieces tangled her hair. She bent her head and started to work it free.

"Jess, you look terrible," Nathan exclaimed.

Too proud to hide herself behind the curtain of her black hair, Jess lifted her head and looked directly at them all, knowing perfectly well that she did look haggard, with dark circles marking the fair skin around her eyes.

Nathan was clearly concerned. After all, he had a great deal of money riding on Jess Butler's continued good health.

"You do look peaked," Sally agreed. "Maybe you should try vitamin B in megadoses. Shall I send you some?"

"Thank you, but no," Jess replied. "I think I will try eating and sleeping first. I haven't been doing much of either lately." She opened the heavy parchment menu. The thick, italic letters blurred. She pushed the menu aside wearily. "Will someone please order for me?"

"Sure," said Cade. Like the others on the bus, he had gotten used to what happened to Jess on the road; during each tour she would gradually lose her capacity to make any sort of decision, right down to what she wanted to eat for lunch. Cade thought nothing of it, but Nathan and Sally stared at her curiously.

Jess sensed their regard and wished that they would stop watching her. She was a reticent, self-contained woman. It wasn't that she was shy, but she felt so exposed onstage, that offstage she didn't want to be the center of attention.

Jess didn't like to talk about herself. She didn't see the point of it. Either a person understood you or he didn't. When she first became successful, she had tried to explain herself to reporters, answering their questions as best she could, but she had long since decided that it was pointless. They always got it wrong; no matter how carefully she spoke, it always came out differently in print. So she quit trying, just accepting the misinterpretations, the strange stories, as her lot in life.

However vibrant and provocative she was onstage, the rest of the time she tended to be silent, sitting back, watching other people with a gentle understanding that turned her blue eyes almost navy. This quiet poise gave her an elegance and a dignity that was rare among country musicians.

So she did not want this lunch to be devoted to a discussion of her troubles.

"Tell me how things are going with the band?" she asked Cade, deliberately changing the subject. "Are you really getting a saxophone player?"

"We sure are," he answered. "Roger's going to take his steel guitar out to the desert and shoot it between the eyes. And me—I'm never going to play another chromatic bass line as long as I live." He started humming one of the maddeningly mindless bass lines that he had had to play when backing up Jess Butler's country songs.

The band had decided to try to make it on their own. Jess Butler might not be the best, but her backup band definitely was. When she had come to California, Art Laurian, her producer, had scoured Los Angeles to put together a band for her. With her Nashville successes behind her, she was able to pay very well, and Art had hired the best musicians around. Now they were the standard by which all other backup bands were measured, for they were indeed excellent.

And they were bored. Although Jess's California arrangements were more elaborate than the ones she had been doing in Nashville, her music was still too simple, too country, for their tastes. They wanted to do more ambitious work, and finally they all decided to try to make it on their own. Although Jess still owed the record company one more album under her current contract, and in turn the band had a contract with her, she, with typical generosity, wasn't holding them to it.

Art Laurian, who concentrated on the music while Nathan Geer tended to business, was so busy with the band that Jess knew it would be some time before he would start auditioning a new band for her. That was the reason that she was now able to take some time off. It couldn't have happened at a better time. Clearly she needed a vacation.

"Have you chosen a name yet?" Jess asked Cade. Once the band had decided to break from her, they had whiled away the tedium of traveling by thinking up names for themselves—the majority of which involved words that disc jockeys were not allowed to say on the air.

"They are going to stick with 'Jess's Boys,'" Nathan said. "If you don't mind, that is."

"Of course not." She looked at Cade, surprised. His lips were twisted in a bitter smile. Clearly in the struggle over the group's name, he had lost.

"That's how people think of us now," he said. "And as everyone keeps telling me, it's what we will get called, regardless of what we name ourselves."

"He feels like he's hiding behind a woman's skirts," said Sally disapprovingly. "He's being silly and proud."

"Or Southern," Jess said lightly.

The four friends had ordered and were talking about Jess's Boys' first recording sessions when a waiter brought another phone to the table. "You are to call your service, Mr. Geer."

While Nathan phoned, Jess picked at her food, some

strange concoction of alfalfa sprouts, herb cheese, and
seven-grain bread that Sally had insisted would make
her feel wonderful. So far it hadn't. The bread seemed
so hard to chew, and the sprouts kept slipping off her
fork. It was just too much trouble to eat.

Nathan's message proved to be for her. "Bret is
looking for you," he said.

"Bret?" Surprise lifted her out of her lethargy. Why
was Bret calling? He only called her on her birthday.

"Listen, if he invites you out to Minneapolis, you
ought to go," Nathan said emphatically. "It would do
you good to get away and have some family looking out
after you."

After Nathan had given the operator a credit card
number, Jess took the phone from him. Nathan was
perfectly capable of saying, "Please put Mr. Cavanaugh
on the line for a call from Miss Butler." Managers
seemed to love those elaborate telephone games, who
comes on the line first, who puts whom on hold. They
struck Jess as incredibly pointless. And she certainly
wasn't going to have Bret put on hold waiting for her.
Just knowing that she was going to talk to him made
her feel much better.

"Cavanaugh–Buchanan," a pleasant female voice
said into her ear.

Jess had to smile at the woman's accent. She rarely
heard the rounded vowels and curious up-and-down cadence of the upper Midwest, and such accents always
conjured up images of Royal Canadian Mounted Police
and ice fishermen drinking Moosehead beer—although
this girl was clearly a receptionist in an ordinary Minneapolis office.

"May I please speak to Bret Cavanaugh?" Jess
asked. "This is Jess But— Jessica Cavanaugh."

"I am sorry, Miss Cavanaugh. He's on another line. Will you hold, or may he call you back?"

"I'll hold," Jess replied, thankful that she no longer had to worry about long-distance phone bills.

Cade was looking at her interestedly. "Bret Cavanaugh..." he mused. "Didn't he quarterback for Georgia Tech a few years back?"

Jess nodded.

"Was he ever great!" Cade reminisced enthusiastically. "Do you remember that pass against Georgia? It was the fourth quarter and the ball was on the—" Cade broke off, realizing that no one shared his interest in a college football game that had been played nearly ten years ago. "What's he doing now? Why didn't he turn pro?"

"Pro?" Jess was surprised. When she had been a teen-ager, she and the rest of the family had always thought of Bret as simply the finest quarterback in the history of Southern college football, but Jess had long since dismissed that as family prejudice. "Why, I don't know. Could he have?"

Cade nodded emphatically, his mouth full of food he had commandeered off Jess's plate.

"He's an electrical engineer now," Jess told him, switching the phone to her other ear.

Cade swallowed. "An electrical engineer?" He shook his head in disappointment. "That seems like an awfully tame sort of career for someone who used to play like he did. The chances he'd take on the field...he was just amazing."

Nathan suddenly laughed. "No, Cade, that man is still taking risks that would curl even Jess's hair if she knew about them."

Jess glanced at Nathan. "Do you know him?" Although she had worked with Nathan and Art for eight years, neither of them had, as far as she knew, ever met any of the Cavanaugh family.

"I've never met him," Nathan explained. "But we've talked on the phone several times. Once he was getting into some deal, and for a lot of reasons, he wasn't setting up a corporation so he could have lost his personal assets if it went sour. It was quite a risk, and he wanted to make sure that no one could touch any of your property."

"Why did he call you, not me?" she asked.

"Probably because he wanted the answer," Nathan returned. "Could you have told him?"

"I guess not," Jess shrugged. "What was the answer?" she asked, only mildly interested.

"It's complicated because you are a resident of California, which has community property laws, but we've got you so sheltered that at the very worst someone might try to attach your car and they probably wouldn't even get it away from you. So I told him that you wouldn't want him to be worrying about your car."

"I should hope not." Jess gently massaged her ear. She was getting a little tired of waiting for Bret to answer the phone.

Sally suddenly looked up. "I don't understand. Why was he worried about Jess? Siblings aren't liable for each other's debts. Good heavens, if someone could attach my assets to pay my brother's debts, I would have to move to Brazil this afternoon."

"Oh, no," Nathan said very smoothly. "Bret isn't Jess's brother. They are married."

## Chapter Two

"Ticketed passengers only.... May I see your ticket, ma'am.... No, sir, only for unaccompanied minors.... Ticketed passengers only."

Bret Cavanaugh grimaced at the security guard's routine chant and moved out of the line of people waiting to go through the metal detector.

He probably should have tried to get through. The security guard was a young woman and when Bret Cavanaugh smiled, his gray eyes glowed with a warm light that women had been known to have trouble resisting. But Bret never thought about how much better he looked than most men, and it certainly wouldn't occur to him to try and get special treatment in an airport because of the golden glints in his brown hair or the clean lines of his features. So he folded his arms, leaned against the tile wall, and waited, a tall figure in jeans and a sportcoat.

At least, he thought, trying hard to be patient, she'd be flying first class and would be off the plane first.

In a few minutes an irregular line of people started to stream up the concourse, and one of the first was, just as Bret had hoped, his wife. From this distance she looked lovely and chic in the way of a California celebrity. Her jeans hugged her slender legs, and she was wearing a warm-up jacket, the kind baseball players wear, except that this one was made of apricot satin. The expensive satin gleamed with a fluid sparkle somehow suggesting that among all the dark business suits of the other passengers, here was someone only a visitor to the everyday world, a glittering fantasy creature just on a brief stop in reality.

Bret smiled. Two women standing nearby self-consciously adjusted their collars and wondered if they still had lipstick on.

But as the apricot satin came nearer, his smile faded and the alert look in his eyes darkened with concern, then worry.

She looked thin, pale. The sun streaming through the plate-glass walls of the airport bleached her skin to almost a paper white and sent blue lights dancing through her long hair. It was as if all the energy and life had been sapped out of her by the cascade of hair, as if all the shimmer and vitality had gone into the swath of black silk, leaving nothing for the rest of her.

He hadn't seen her looking so weary, so completely drained, in years, not since she was fourteen, walking down a narrow country road when his pickup surged by her, hazing her figure in a cloud of red dust. Her hair hadn't been so long then nor did her body have the richness of today. But one thing was the same as it had been that spring evening so long ago: She was Jessica and she needed him.

Although her movements had their usual lithe grace, she was walking very slowly. Other people hurried around her. As the first passengers reached the ropes of the security system, the satin of Jessica's jacket—its sleeve was now all Bret could see of her—was still only halfway up the long hall. As more people emptied out of the concourse, Bret realized why she was no nearer.

She was trapped, surrounded by people rummaging through their pockets and purses, searching for something to get her autograph on.

Silently cursing the security that had kept him from meeting the plane, Bret motioned to one of the guards. "Excuse me, sir," he said, his Southern accent giving his words a lazy politeness he was far from feeling. "That woman down there is a bit of a celebrity and I think she's very tired. Could you go help her?"

Bret watched as the guard set off to rescue Jessica. For such a nice, thoroughly ordinary sort of girl, he thought, Jessica did seem to take a fair amount of rescuing.

Then he smiled ruefully. By what possible stretch of imagination and nostalgia could Jessica be called a nice, ordinary sort of girl? She might have been once, but she certainly was no longer. He would have to remember that while she was staying with him. Not only was she twenty-six and a woman, not the girl he had known back in Georgia, but she was Jess Butler, with several platinum albums, a string of seven straight number-one country singles, most of which had also been in the top ten on the pop charts.

She would have changed, but then so had he.

They had both grown up in north Georgia in what often seemed like a completely different world from this one. Minnesota was a land of sweeping prairies and clean, dark-scented forests, while that part of Georgia was marked with lazy hills, straight dirt roads, and sluggish treelined rivers. They had lived in farm country where the earth was rich clay and the sunlit fields glowed red after spring plowing. Once sprawling cotton plantations, the land was now broken into small farms, farms that were generally much too small to support the large families that lived on them.

The Cavanaugh farm wasn't much bigger than anyone else's, but that family seemed to do better by it than their neighbors did. The white frame farmhouse got painted regularly; the wire around the chicken coop didn't sag; the barn doors closed tightly, not hanging loosely on their hinges as so often happened in places where things didn't get attended to.

Clayton Cavanaugh attended to things. He was an excellent farmer, cautious, hardworking, meticulous, never taking the easy way out, and one of his sons was bidding to be just as good at working the land.

But it wasn't his oldest son. For all that one might say about Bret Cavanaugh—and that little farming community did say a lot about him—it could never be said that he was, by nature, a farmer. At eighteen, he had a charm, an unpredictability, and, above all, an arrogance that would ever keep him from entrusting his fate to nature as a farmer must.

Of course, Bret had a great deal to be arrogant about. Tall, good-looking, with eyes as gray as a Confederate uniform, he had a smile that made women soften and glow. His manners were easygoing, almost lazy, and they only barely concealed a hot temper that he never bothered to control. He was strong from years of working his father's fields, and from some unknown ancestor he had inherited an alertness, a quickness, that gave him lightning reactions. His eyesight was excellent and the movements of his hands sure and instinctive. His mother used to sigh and joke that Bret had been born a hundred years too late. A century ago he could have gone west and made a living as a hired gunfighter.

Instead he played football, finding in the violent competition something that satisfied his need for intensity, for an urgent focus. The best quarterback his high school had ever seen, he was starting Georgia Tech next year on a football scholarship. This was not a town that usually sent her sons to college, and people were proud of young Bret.

But that spring, the spring of his senior year, he was putting some strain on the image the town had of him. Football was an autumn sport, and Bret found himself restless during the rest of the year. He missed the fierce concentration that he had so far found only in competition. The farm work that absorbed most of his free time, while it was demanding physically, didn't give life the edge that Bret craved.

He tried to like farming. He was the oldest son and for generations the Cavanaugh farm had passed from father to son, but as each month passed in a haze of wearying, monotonous routine, the spring inside him coiled tighter and tighter.

The sultry nights stirred something in him, a yearning, an aching that he didn't understand. The heavy air that blanketed the fields felt close as if it were oppressing him, stifling him. The sun's glare lit off a spark in him, restless, rebellious, dangerous, a spark that was fanned by the hot breezes that seemed to be carrying a message to him, always promising that something exciting was just about to happen. He grew tense and expectant, waiting for what the heated winds promised, but it never came. And Bret knew that if he ever did finish college, if there ever was a way out, he wouldn't come back.

But in the meantime he knew no other way to vent his restless longings, his gnawing impatience, except through anger.

It didn't help that his next brother, fifteen-year-old Luke, loved the farm, finding every little detail of its routine important. Luke was continuously curious about new fertilizers and hybrid seed. He talked to other farmers with a fascination that Bret simply couldn't share.

Understandably, Luke, already sick of being known around school as "Bret Cavanaugh's little brother," resented Bret. He coveted the responsibilities that Bret chafed at. He knew that although no one was going to inherit the farm for a good, long time, in the end it would be Bret who did.

The easy camaraderie that the two brothers had shared as boys dissolved as Bret grew more restless and Luke more envious. They shared a room in the unheated bunkhouse, and the proximity irritated them. Both had strong quick tempers and many times only respect for their mother kept them from coming to blows.

Bret's relationship with his father wasn't much better. He respected his father, knowing full well that in the twenty years the family land had been under Clayton Cavanaugh's control, it had become much more productive, and that if the Cavanaughs didn't have six children, they would have been considerably more comfortable than their neighbors.

Despite this respect, Bret found it hard to work for his father. That's how he felt it was—that he was working for Clay, not with him. He resented the orders his father gave him and the quick way Clay made decisions, not consulting Bret, never explaining his reasons. Bret believed that his father treated him like a hired hand, and unconsciously he had even quit calling his father "Dad," using only "sir" when he had to speak to him. Sometimes Bret would swear to his friends that he might as well go hire himself out to someone who would at least pay him and who would have no say about what he did when he wasn't working.

When he wasn't working, Bret was wild: drinking too much, hanging around bars in the fading twilight, getting in fights, driving his pickup too fast on narrow country roads. His friends were like him, restless and bored, simmering caldrons of temper barely controlled by the polite manners their Southern mothers had drummed into them. Their movements, their speech, were slow, almost sleepy, but they turned dangerous quickly, and it was often only Bret's smile that kept him out of serious trouble.

Clay would hear about his son's exploits, and the fields and outbuildings would often seethe with tension as father and son moved toward the angry confrontation that seemed inevitable. Bret challenged his father on nearly everything; in response, Clay would turn stony, refusing to explain himself or listen to Bret at all.

Finally the tension couldn't be kept out of the farmhouse any longer. One humid, unusually sultry spring day, when the weather had everyone at the supper table on edge, a low sarcastic remark from Bret earned a sharp "Not in front of your mother, boy."

A pointless, bitter quarrel followed. It was brief; Bret saw the tightness in his mother's face, the fear in his sisters', and almost as ashamed as he was angry, he stormed out, his chair falling against the floor with a sharp clatter.

He flung himself into his pickup and in a moment

was speeding toward town, resolving never to go back. He swept by a pedestrian walking along the dusty road. Only in the rearview mirror did he notice that it was a girl. From the black hair swinging down to the middle of her back, he knew it was Jessica Susan Storey.

The early evening light was a yellow-gray and the air was heavy with an impending thunderstorm. They were more than a mile from the Storey place; the girl had little chance of getting home before it started to rain. Quickly Bret reversed the truck and backed up to her.

He had known Jessica Storey all her life. Their mothers had been girlhood friends and as women had lived only a few miles apart. In the way of many rural Southerners, they had both married young: Amy Brett married Clayton Cavanaugh when she was sixteen and her friend Susan Butler had married two years later. But Susan's husband had died just as her baby was learning to walk. Distraught and exhausted by the demands of a toddler and a farm, Susan had married again too quickly. She herself had died a few years later, leaving seven-year-old Jessica in the hands of her stepfather, Rafe Storey.

After Susan's death, Amy Cavanaugh had wanted to take Jessica into her home, but Rafe Storey refused. He loved her, he said, as much as if she were his own child. He'd be able to give Susan's daughter a good home.

But by the time she was ten, if anyone was making the Storey place into a home, it was Jessica herself. Rafe Storey was drinking and Jessica was nearly doing a woman's work. If cooking, cleaning, and laundry were done in that ramshackle farmhouse, Jessica did them. Naturally a lot of people felt sorry for Jessica, thinking that she wasn't having much of a childhood, but they knew Storey was not mistreating her—he was too dreamy and vague for that—so no one thought to worry about her.

Jessica was four years younger than Bret Cavanaugh and less than a year younger than his brother Luke, but Bret knew her better. Last summer Rafe Storey had lost his hired hand, and Clay Cavanaugh had, without asking Bret about it, sent his oldest son over to the Storey place to help out some.

Bret had always liked Jessica with the same sort of easy affection that he gave his three little sisters. But the contempt he now felt for Rafe Storey's shiftless, drunken ways made him look at the skinny thirteen-year-old girl with a more respecting eye. He admired her for how hard she worked, for her complete absence of self-pity. Since his mother had begged him to be especially nice to the girl, Bret started spending a little bit of time with her before and after his work. She was a kid, of course, but she wasn't shy and nervous.

One day, on an impulse, he had tossed onto the seat of his truck an old guitar left at the Cavanaugh farm long ago by some hired hand. Neither of them knew the first thing about playing it, but it took Jessica less than a week to teach herself.

He had known that she was musical. She sang solos at church almost every week, and even before she had started ninth grade, the high school choir director kept "borrowing" her from the lower grades. But even so, Bret had been surprised at how quickly she learned how to accompany herself on every song she knew.

She clearly loved the guitar, and because he had given it to her, Jessica simply worshiped Bret, and he knew it. He was flattered, certainly more than he would admit, but it embarrassed him because he knew that he was not at all the fine and perfect person she thought him to be.

At harvesttime Clay couldn't spare Luke, and Rafe Storey had to hire a regular hand. He found Cal Winsley, an emaciated, pockmarked man in his midthirties, for whom Bret had about as much use as he did for Storey. Then school started, and Bret, busy with senior-year football and often in the farmhouse only for meals, saw Jessica very little, catching glimpses of her in the halls of school and speaking to her only on the increasingly rare occasions when he went to church with his family.

Seeing her so rarely meant that he was one of the first to notice how she was changing. She wasn't skinny anymore. Her blouses fit more snugly, and her walk had lost its coltish awkwardness, taking on a light swing she was entirely unconscious of. But the changes were just promises of what she would look like later. There was still enough of the child about her that Bret noticed how she was growing without responding to it or being excited by her.

But he certainly liked her, and no matter how angry he was with his father this spring evening, he wasn't going to let her get soaked in a spring thunderstorm. He reached across the cab of the pickup and thrust open the passenger door.

"Hop in," he said, expecting that she would be grateful for a lift.

She hesitated for a moment, almost as if she didn't recognize him. "Oh, Bret, hello," she said. "Thank you, but I am out for a walk."

Bret looked at her carefully. She seemed tired, somehow pinched and strained. "Not in this weather," he said abruptly, a little confused by his concern for her. "My mother would roast me whole if she knew that I let you walk through a thunderstorm."

Jessica smiled wanly, unable to say no to him, and slid into the truck.

He put it in gear and started toward her house. "What were you doing taking a walk when the weather's like this?" he asked casually. "It's going to storm any minute."

And to his complete horror, Jessica started to cry.

Bret Cavanaugh liked girls, he liked them a lot, but he still had a young man's healthy terror of feminine tears. Nonetheless he quickly pulled to the side of the road and stopped the truck. He turned to face her, stretching one arm along the back of the seat. "Now, Jessie, what is it?"

The evening was rapidly darkening, and finally it started to rain, fat drops splashing little circles across the windshield.

Jessica was trying to pretend that she hadn't broken down. "I just wanted some fresh air, that's all...because—" She faltered and could not go on.

"Because why?" Bret asked. And when she didn't answer, he moved his arm and, just as he might with one of his sisters, put it around her shoulders.

Her reaction astonished him. She stiffened at his touch, and in her dark blue eyes he saw a look of terror, reminding him of some small animal, frightened and cornered, but too young to know how to fight.

He immediately let go of her and reached for a pack of cigarettes on the dashboard and slowly lit one, cracking the window to let the smoke curl out, wondering what to say. He was tempted to take her to his home and let his mother try to sort it out, but he had stormed out in the middle of supper, and he knew that the house would still be lively. His mother would be busy trying to get the dishes washed, the little ones to bed, and things organized for the morning.

He tilted his head, looking at her. "Jessie, are you afraid of something?"

He could see pride wash over her, giving her strength. She straightened, brushing the stray strands of black hair off her face.

"I can't talk about it," she said, her voice low, charged with a resonant tremor.

That was enough for Bret. The Cavanaugh household was not a modern one, and Bret certainly believed that there were plenty of things females couldn't talk to men about. That was fine with him. If a girl didn't want to talk about something, he figured he probably didn't want to hear about it. So he would leave her off at her home—as wretched a place as it was—and ask his mother to go see her in the morning.

As he leaned forward, grasping the keys to restart the engine, a flash of lightning sent a sharp white light into the truck, momentarily illuminating the girl he was still watching—the redness around her eyes, the swath of long black hair, the new curves of her soft body. With an insight he had no idea he possessed, Bret thought suddenly of the pale glittering eyes of Rafe Storey's new hired hand. Tomorrow morning might just be too late.

"Has Cal Winsley been bothering you?" he demanded bluntly.

Jessica covered her face and shook her head.

He knew she was lying. "Tell me," he ordered. "What's he done to you?"

"Nothing," she said, her voice muffled by the hands

covering her face. "It's just the way he looks at me; it scares me sometimes."

The rain drummed on the roof of the truck, and Bret wondered just how much she understood, if she had any idea just how scared she should be.

Her next words answered that. "And, Bret"—she turned her soft eyes to his—"I don't...my bedroom door doesn't have a lock on it."

He could almost see it—Jessica lying in her bed, sleepless and afraid, waiting for her doorknob to turn. His stomach turned.

"I'm taking you home," he said abruptly, and in response to her gasp, added quickly, "No, Jessie, *my* home. My parents will know what to do."

Ever after, Bret believed that when he opened the door for Jessica to walk into his family's home, that moment marked a turning point in his relationship with his father.

The whole family was still gathered around the table. As their curious eyes turned toward Jessica, he knew that he couldn't embarrass them or her by explaining.

"Jessica Susan's come to stay with us for a few days," he said instead. He looked straight at his father when he spoke, not with an angry defiant look—Bret had entirely forgotten about their earlier quarrel—but a direct man-to-man look which said, "I hope you understand, because I can't explain in front of Mother and the girls."

Clay Cavanaugh understood immediately. Bret saw his father's gray eyes darken and his lips tighten, but his voice was even when he spoke to Jessica. "We'll be glad to have you. Amy and the girls are always saying they don't see enough of you." Then he turned to his wife and in a low voice said her name, and then she too understood.

Her face pale, a weary, exhausted look in her eyes, Amy Cavanaugh pushed her youngest daughter off her lap and stood up with a smile on her lips. She came over and kissed Jessica. "What a lovely surprise. And you are just in time to help with the supper dishes." Amy Cavanaugh, with the spirit of the true country woman that she was, believed that hard work was the best, the only, way to relieve troubles.

Silently, almost as if she were in a stupor, not even taking off her jacket, Jessica started to clear the table, and as the other girls jumped up to help, Clay Cavanaugh looked at his oldest son and with a quick jerk of his eyes—a kind of wordless communication they had never shared before—indicated that he wanted to talk to him on the porch.

Once they were alone, Clay didn't waste any time, never doubting for a moment that his son understood everything. "Her stepfather or Winsley?" he asked without preamble.

"Winsley," Bret answered.

Clay cursed. "Has he hurt her?"

"Not yet," Bret replied. "But she's scared."

They were both silent for a moment, staring across the white porch railing to the darkened fields. "How did you get it out of her?" Clay asked. "Your mother says she is as proud as they come."

"I just guessed, and when I put it to her, she finally admitted it."

"Good for you," Clay said in a flat even voice. "You did the right thing bringing her here."

Bret couldn't remember when his father had last praised him, and for a moment, a red angry flame burned in him, and he was almost furious with himself for being pleased, for caring what his father thought.

With the resilience of most fourteen-year-olds, Jessica seemed brighter and happier just by the next morning as she set off for school with Luke and the others. Amy asked Bret to stay home and go with her to the Storey place so that they could get some of Jessica's clothes and her guitar.

They went over in the middle of the morning, assuming that the unlocked house would be empty, as it indeed was. Bret had never been in Jessica's bedroom before and he found it astonishingly neat. As Amy opened the drawers gathering up a few things, he could see that the drawers were far more than just neat. Jessica had arranged her belongings with extraordinary precision; her clothing lay in stacks as straight as the walls of a building. Obviously she had tried to keep her own room in a rigid order as a defense against the confused squalor that must have often threatened to engulf her.

Suddenly Amy Cavanaugh burst into tears.

Bret looked at his mother with dismay. He had, he felt, had more than his share of teary females in the last day.

"Just look at this," she sobbed. "That poor, poor girl. I am so glad that Susan doesn't know about this."

"This" was, as far as Bret could see, just a little plastic case with soap, toothpaste, and a toothbrush, sitting on top of a neatly folded towel. He was hard pressed to see why it was worth crying over.

"Now, Mama," he said awkwardly. "We could have guessed that Jessica brushes her teeth. It's nothing to cry about."

"But don't you see? She doesn't leave her things in

the bathroom. It's not right. A young girl ought to be able to leave her things out in her own home, knowing perfectly well that no one else will use them. Even her soap—she doesn't want to use the same soap those men use.''

Suddenly his mother stood up briskly. "Go get a box or a feed sack out of the truck, Bret. We are taking all her things. She is never coming back here. Cal Winsley or not, Rafe Storey can't take care of her like he ought.''

Saying that Jessica was never going to return there was easy. Keeping her was not. Before a week had passed, Rafe Storey was getting tired of not having his meals cooked and his laundry done, and Cal Winsley, with the aid of a few bottles of bourbon, persuaded him to get Jessica back. Storey had shown up one evening to bring her home, and Clay had ordered him off the property before Jessica had even known that he was there.

The next evening the local lawyer came to the Cavanaugh home as they were finishing supper. It was such an unusual visit that Amy and Clay abruptly ushered the guest into the front room, a parlor so seldom used that it had not needed refurnishing since Clay's mother had done it as a bride.

Suspecting that the visit was about Jessica, Bret followed them. He didn't sit down with the adults; one part of him still expected his father to order him out of the room. Instead he folded his arms and leaned lightly against the tall mahogany secretary, one of the few relics the Cavanaugh family still had of the wealth that had been theirs before the Civil War.

After a few polite preliminaries about the weather and everyone's health, the lawyer, Jack Barnes, got to the point. "You know that Rafe Storey thinks that you all have got something that belongs to him."

"Well, we do," Clay said evenly. "And we aim to keep her."

"Is she here"—the lawyer's eyes flicked over to Amy apologetically—"for the reason I think she is?"

"Yes" was Clay's firm response and the two men exchanged the glances of decent men sickened by the behavior and appetites of a man less honorable.

"She simply can't go back there," Amy insisted.

"I understand that, ma'am. That's why I'm here." He outlined the situation briefly. Cal Winsley had persuaded Rafe to go to a judge to get Jessica back; in order to keep her, the Cavanaughs would have to prove that it was an unfit home.

"Well, it is," Amy said emphatically. "I'll testify to that. So will Grace Talbot or Corrine Mayhugh."

"Excuse me, ma'am, but what are you going to say?" The lawyer looked at Amy. "No judge is going to keep her away from her home just because she doesn't have a mother and has to do all the housework. Lots of girls in these parts work hard. But if you all say one word about Winsley, he can just say that she's a confused teen-ager who made it all up."

Amy gasped and Bret started to speak, but the lawyer continued. "In fact, he'll probably say that she was pestering him."

"No one will believe that," Bret scoffed.

"Maybe not, but she won't forget hearing it."

Bret saw what he meant. "But if the only alternative is to send her back there—" He stopped; the lawyer was looking at him carefully, examining him as if they were sitting across a poker table. Bret didn't understand what Barnes was trying to find out, but he didn't flinch or look away.

"Isn't there something we can do?" Amy's voice was tight. "There has to be some other way. She's Susan's daughter and I'll never forgive myself if anything happens to her." Amy's hands were gripping the arms of her chair, crumpling the white crocheted doilies that protected the garnet upholstery.

"There may just be one other way out." The lawyer's gaze swung away from Bret to Clay. "Is your boy over seventeen?"

Bret bristled, not liking to be referred to as a boy, but he let his father answer.

"Sure. Why?"

The lawyer's white head turned back to Bret. "What would you do for this girl?"

"Name it," Bret said tersely.

"Would you marry her?"

Bret stared at him. He couldn't have heard right. Marry? Marry whom? Surely not Jessica. She was a kid.

"But she's just fourteen." Amy's gasp echoed his thoughts.

"I know," Mr. Barnes said. "But in Alabama that's all a girl has to be if she's got her parents' consent."

"But how would you get that?" Clay asked slowly.

Bret now stared at his father. With the quick decision that so often irritated his sons, Clayton Cavanaugh had already considered this extraordinary plan and found it a good one.

"I think we can manage it." The lawyer coughed discreetly and Bret knew that he simply planned on getting Rafe so drunk he wouldn't know what he was signing.

"An old friend of mine is a justice of the peace just across the state line. He won't ask any questions. So it depends on your boy here."

Then Bret heard from his father words he had never heard before. "It's your decision, son." Clay's gray eyes were flat and respectful, genuinely letting Bret decide.

"When do we leave?" Bret heard himself say.

The lawyer stood up briskly, clearly pleased. "I'd like to take care of it tonight. Clay, if you and your son will come with me, we'll start...ah, talking to Rafe. Mrs. Cavanaugh, if you could say something to the girl and get her ready, we'll be back for her as soon as we can."

The men stood as Amy hurried out of the room, and with an eye on the door, Lawyer Barnes spoke to Bret in a low voice. "We might just have to tell him that she's having your baby. Will that bother you?"

Bret blinked. It had never occurred to him that Jessica was old enough to have a baby, although he supposed she was. "It will sure as hell bother her."

"I know," the lawyer said sympathetically. "We'll try to avoid it." He suddenly put out a hand to Bret. "It's a fine thing you're doing, young man. I hope that this isn't going to disappoint some other young lady."

"No, sir," Bret answered as he shook the lawyer's hand. The girls he'd been spending time with were not the sort that he would ever think of marrying or who even got described as "young ladies" too often.

His blank expression hiding a flash of parental pride, Clay Cavanaugh watched the lawyer shake his son's hand. As they left the front room, he stopped in the hall at a corner cabinet that was rarely unlocked outside hunting season. Pulling some keys out of his pocket, he opened it and took out a rifle and a box of shells.

"Son, there's no need to be saying anything to your

mother about this," he said to Bret, jerking his head toward the gun.

"No, sir," said Bret.

Bret knew that his parents kept little from each other. If there were matters that Clay had thought a woman shouldn't know, he hadn't told his son either. But things seemed to be changing.

The two Cavanaughs waited outside the Storey house while Jack Barnes went in to "speak" to Rafe Storey alone.

As they waited in near silence, Bret looked at his father, who was idly wiggling a rotting fence post as if disgusted that a man would keep his fences in such poor shape.

Clay was such a familiar figure that Bret hardly ever looked at him carefully, but in the shadowless evening light, sensitive to something new in their dealings with one another, he examined him.

His father was a young man. That surprised Bret. He had never thought of it before, but some of his friends' fathers were getting paunchy and bald; Clay wasn't. There was no gray in his sun-streaked hair, and the wrinkles at the edge of his eyes were caused more by long hours in the sun than by age. His legs, encased in jeans, were as lean and hard as Bret's.

Bret thought back. He gathered that his parents had married young and that his father had been eighteen when he was born. He must be thirty-six now; yet when he was in town, he dealt as equals with men in their fifties, apparently having long since earned their respect.

"Hard thoughts, Bret?" he heard Clay ask. His father was obviously willing to listen, but not planning on prying.

"Actually, I was just thinking how young you are, sir."

Clay scuffed at the dirt of the Storeys' drive with the toe of his boot and then squinted unnecessarily at the light of the sinking sun. "It might be easier on you if I were older."

Bret raised his eyebrows questioningly.

"You know Big Bill Jefferies?" Bret nodded, and Clay continued. "Young Bill's just a year older than you, but Jefferies is probably ten, maybe even fifteen years older than me. He was saying in the bank the other day how glad he is to have Young Bill taking over so much for him, and it occurred to me he was talking about decisions and responsibilities I am sure not ready to be turning over to anyone, not even you."

"I am not complaining, Dad."

"I know that," Clay said quickly.

They were now both leaning against the pickup, staring out across Rafe's poorly plowed fields, both automatically noting the too straight furrows that were inviting erosion. They were not looking at each other.

It was easier that way. They had been raised in a tradition that valued straightforward dealings between men, but not intimate confidences. Everything about their demeanor, their folded arms, the hats pulled low over their eyes, suggested the most casual interchange; yet never before had they spoken so honestly to each other.

"There's still so much I want to do with the farm," Clay went on. "I've got plans; your mother"—he smiled—"she calls them dreams, and I just hadn't figured on sharing them. But it's something I can get used to."

Bret waited for a moment and then spoke in a careful tone. "You ought to be saying this to Luke, not me."

Clay turned and knelt down in the red clay, examining the treads of the truck's tires. "You're the oldest."

"He's the farmer." Bret looked at his father, squatting like a catcher, his forearms resting on his knees. "He loves the place as much as you do. I wish I could, but I can't." Nothing like this had ever been said before.

Clay stood up in one easy swift motion. "That's why your mother wanted so badly for you to go to college. She knew that you'd never be content here."

"Then, Dad, don't you think we owe to Luke to let him know how things stand? It's eating at him and unless things get straightened out soon, you'll have two very wild sons on your hands, not just one." And in those last few words, Bret came as close as he ever would to apologizing to his father for his behavior.

Clay smiled at his son, a quick, flashing grin. "Well, we'll cross that bridge when we come to it. Right now, we've got that little girl to worry about."

In a moment Jack Barnes emerged from the house and came over to the truck.

"How are you making out?" Clay asked in a voice so laconic that it might have been a question about some Saturday fishing trip.

"He wants to talk to the boy," the lawyer said. "I think he expects him to come ask for her hand, all polite and humble."

"Humble?" The word snapped out of Bret. "To him?"

His father's voice was crisp. "You will and you—" Clay checked himself, apparently trying to break the habit of barking orders at Bret. When he spoke again, his voice was mild. "The stakes are pretty high here, Bret; maybe we should do whatever needs to be done."

Bret tried to swallow down the angry spill of temper that had swelled at the sharp command that had first been in his father's voice. But it was hard to stay calm when he crossed into the house, the heels of his boots setting off hollow vibrations through the uneven floorboards. Obviously nothing had been done since Jessica had left. Newspapers, dirty clothes, muddy boots, lay everywhere. The table was cluttered with dishes encrusted with remains from several meals. It was so different from the cleanliness he had always seen here before. For the first time he realized just how hard Jessica had had to work here.

Why did they have to ask this man for anything? Hadn't he forfeited every right he might have had to his stepdaughter?

Then he remembered his father's words. "The stakes are pretty high here." They were.

Rafe Storey was sitting at the cluttered table. He had obviously swept a place clear for himself, a jumble of beer cans and chicken bones ringed the place where he sat. With one hand curled around Jack Barnes's bourbon bottle, he had a dreamy, abstract look on his face.

This was a different kind of competition, Bret thought to himself slowly. He wanted to beat the man without him even knowing that there had been a struggle going on, certainly without him knowing that he had lost. Always before when Bret had beaten someone, he wanted them to know it and know it well. But maybe that was because the stakes had never been important before. The competition had been an end in itself. In football games or fights in tavern parking lots, there hadn't really been anything at stake. Not like now.

"Sir, I've come to ask for your daughter's hand," he

said carefully, falling back on the old-fashioned formula the lawyer had used.

"She's my little girl," Storey sighed.

Then protect her from your hired help, Bret wanted to snap at him. "I know, sir," he said instead. "It can never be easy for a man to give up his daughter."

These were just words to Bret; he had no idea what it felt like to have a daughter, much less how it would feel to have one getting married, but his glib clichés seemed to strike Rafe as profound truths.

Rafe sighed again. "That's just so true." He laced his fingers over the top of his glass and leaned over, resting his chin on his hands. "So why do you want to take her from me?" He rolled his head and stared up at Bret fisheyed.

Bret hesitated and then remembered the rest of what his father said, "Maybe we should do whatever needs to be done." And that obviously included lies. "I love her," Bret said smoothly. "I want to take care of her. I want her to be happy." At least the last one was true.

Rafe's eyes went dreamy and Bret suddenly realized that the man was a romantic. He wanted their hardscramble world to be easy, polite, and rose-colored. When it wasn't, instead of trying to change it or at least see it as it really was, he drank.

Bret felt a surge of confidence. He knew what to do; he had a game plan.

He pulled out a chair, flipping the stack of newspapers onto the floor, and sat down next to Rafe. He started talking about Jessica, her beauty, her generosity, her voice, things about her that he had hardly realized that he knew. Tears filled the other man's eyes.

"But she's so young," Rafe sniffed blearily. "Can't you wait?"

Bret drew up short, not sure how to reply. To buy himself some time he poured the man another shot of whiskey, trying frantically to think of something to say, but everything he could think of just sounded like he was eager to get Jessica into bed. Or that he had already done it.

Finally, just as he heard his father step forward, obviously about to cover for him, it came to him.

"You know, don't you, sir, that I am going to college in the fall?" Normally Bret didn't talk much about his autumn plans. He was a little embarrassed that everyone thought them all so wonderful. But he'd talk about them now if it would help. "Jessica's such a beautiful girl that I want to be sure she's still here when I get back."

"College ..." Rafe mused. "Jessica Susan's mother would have liked her to marry an educated man."

"Yes, sir," Bret agreed immediately. "It is the very least that she deserves."

He felt like a fraud. He wasn't going to college to get an education; he was going to play football. He didn't plan on learning one thing if he could avoid it.

They were both quiet, and Bret felt very sure that he had won. Now it was just a matter of waiting out the clock.

"Why is your father here?" Rafe asked suddenly.

Bret felt Clay start to step forward and he gestured quickly to stop him. He had this under control. "Although I love Jessica Susan and want her with me," he said smoothly, "I don't think she's ready to go to Atlanta next year. So with your permission, sir, I'd like to leave her with my parents. My mother would have come too to tell you how welcome Jessica is, but she had to stay home with the children.''

Mentioning Amy clinched it. "Ah, your mother!" Rafe sighed. "She and Susan were such good friends."

"And she will take as good care of her as Mrs. Storey would have."

Bret felt the man relax and he knew with a sharp thrill of pleasure that he had won.

As they walked toward the pickup, Bret heard a soft "Well done" in his ear.

It was his father.

Bret shrugged, trying not to be pleased. "I just didn't want to say she was in trouble. Enough people will probably think it for a while at least."

Clay smiled. "I didn't bring the gun for you."

"Don't tell me you wouldn't have pointed it at me if that's what was needed," Bret returned lightly as the tension in him eased, "because I know you would have."

"Perhaps, but I wouldn't have actually shot you."

"Only because it would have made Mama so mad."

Clay laughed and clapped him on the shoulder. Then he changed the subject. "Do you mind driving? I think we should take two cars to Alabama. We are going to have to keep Storey this drunk and maybe drunker, and I would hate for the girl to see that. You can take Luke to help with the driving."

"He doesn't have a license," Bret pointed out. Luke was just fifteen and wasn't supposed to do more than drive tractors in the fields for another year.

"Given everything else we are doing tonight, I wouldn't much worry about that," Clay returned.

They drove home, got another car and Jessica and Luke. Mr. Barnes had called the town doctor who opened up his clinic to give Jessica and Bret blood tests.

It was the doctor who spoke to Bret. After he had taken the blood samples, he sent Jessica out to the waiting room to sit with Luke. He pulled out two clean microscope slides and started to prepare the tests. For a moment he worked without speaking.

"Young man," he finally said, tilting back in his chair to look at Bret, "you'll probably turn out all right, but at the moment you've got a reputation for being just a little wild."

"I'm sorry to hear that, sir," Bret lied.

The doctor ignored him, giving this remark just as much attention as it deserved. "Jessica is a fine girl. She is going to be your wife, and nobody will have the right to question the way you treat her especially when you consider what her alternatives are. Of course, you'd be a sight better for her than Cal Winsley, but it would be best for her if she didn't have to deal, well, with any demands from you either," the doctor said delicately. "She's too—"

"She's fourteen," Bret interrupted. "What sort of man would take a fourteen-year-old to bed?" he asked bluntly.

"Well, there are some," the doctor said. "But the important thing for you to remember is that fourteen-year-old girls have this funny habit of not staying fourteen. That one is growing fast; she may well look eighteen by this harvest or next." He leaned back in his chair again. "You may not think it any of my business, but I do. The doctor in a town like this always gets asked to pick up the pieces. And I would like your word that you'll keep away from her for another few years."

"You have it," Bret said crisply.

The doctor looked at him long and hard, and Bret

returned the look, biting down the anger he felt at the doctor's doubts. Suddenly the man seemed satisfied. "You may find that promise a lot harder to keep than you know." He stood up, handing Bret the paper certifying the results of the blood tests, and surprisingly he put out his hand. "Let me say that I respect you for what you are doing. I'm a lot happier to be running this test for young Jessica than having Winsley sending her in for some other one."

For years after, a certain kind of warm night would ever remind Bret of that drive across Georgia. It was spring and the peach trees and dogwoods were in bloom, the pink and white of their delicate flowers shining bright in the growing dusk. Many of the fields had been plowed, and the rolling foothills were swathed by the curving furrows that turned the bright red clay of the north Georgia soil up to the sun.

Bret followed the two red taillights of his father's car as the evening turned into night. Jessica, who had said almost nothing, soon fell asleep. From the corner of his eye, Bret saw his brother lift his arm to settle her head comfortably on his chest. Bret glanced over at them curiously. At fifteen, Luke still wasn't comfortable enough with girls to make such a gesture casually.

He saw a defiant look in Luke's eyes as if the younger brother were daring the older to object.

Bret wondered how this strange marriage would affect Luke. He wasn't even a year older than Jessica, and for all Bret knew, he might be fond of her. Even if he weren't, Luke already so resented his older brother that he was probably capable of deciding that he wanted Jessica for no other reason than that it was Bret who had her.

Bret cursed to himself. Things were already bad enough between the two of them. They were brothers; it shouldn't be like this.

So uncharacteristically, he ignored the challenge in Luke's eyes. "Is she comfortable? I hope your arm doesn't go to sleep."

The justice of the peace lived on the edge of a small town twenty miles into Alabama. It was past midnight when they pulled in front of the stone house, but the lights were on. Lawyer Barnes had called, alerting his friend.

Luke gently shook Jessica awake and as Bret came around to help her out of the truck, she whispered his name shyly.

It was the first time she had spoken to him directly.

"What is it, Jessie?"

"Do you mind—" She faltered. "Do you mind sharing your family with me?"

So that was how Amy Cavanaugh had explained things to her, emphasizing not that she would be Bret's wife, but that she would be a part of the family. "Not at all," he said gently, brushing a strand of silky hair off her face. "I've got family to spare."

He thought about what he had said as they crossed the grassy lawn toward the lighted house. This sort of thing would never happen to any of his sisters because they had family to take care of them. Any man threatening one of those girls would have to face Clayton Cavanaugh and his three sons before the sun was down. Bret glanced at his brother: Any peril to their sisters would make them forget all their differences. But why did they have to wait for that?

And then he realized that he had been wrong in what he had said to his father earlier that evening. It wasn't

Clay who was remiss in talking to Luke; it had been Bret himself. He had known for at least a year that he would never settle on the farm, that he would never want to own it, but in his natural competitiveness he had never said the one thing that would have calmed Luke's anxieties and eased all his resentment. He had never said to his brother, "Look here, we both know it—this isn't for me."

He would do it.

Jack Barnes had prepared the justice of the peace and no one asked embarrassing questions about why the bride's guardian stayed in the car. The justice did ask if he and his wife could speak to Jessica alone, probably just wanting to be sure that she wasn't being used in some way. But that didn't take him long, and then he sent his wife and Jessica back to the living room and in a few quick words to Bret, delivered him a lecture that was substantially the same as the doctor's.

Amy Cavanaugh had sent word to keep the ceremony as little like a wedding as possible: otherwise Jessica would get nervous. So it was just a matter of saying a few words and signing their names: The justice's wife didn't sit at her piano, there was no ring, and Bret did not kiss Jessica.

# Chapter Three

So Bret and Jessica were married.

It was surprising how little difference it made. Jessica settled into the family so easily that only Amy could remember what it was like before she had come, and Amy only remembered because she had so much more help with the housework now that Jessica was with them.

There wasn't too much talk about it in town. The near-poverty of many of the small farmers and the tendency of people to marry very young often resulted in rather complicated family situations. If the outcome seemed respectable enough, people tried not to judge. When it became clear that Jessica was not pregnant, people soon forgot. They just thought of her as the oldest of the Cavanaugh sisters. When she sang in school plays and church recitals, the newspaper listed her as "Miss Jessica Cavanaugh, daughter of Mr. and Mrs. Clayton Cavanaugh."

It wasn't that the family was pretending that Jessica was Bret's sister. When strangers would seem surprised at how close in age Jessica and Luke were or when someone would marvel at her dark blue eyes in a family of grays and browns, Amy or Clay would explain, "She's our daughter-in-law." But unless it came up, no one thought to explain.

Bret was soon convinced that Jessica herself never thought about it. When she needed the signature of her legal guardian on her enrollment card for school that fall, she had, like the others, automatically asked Clay. It had surprised her when he had told her to go to Bret.

Shortly after he had signed all Jessica's forms for her, Bret went off to Atlanta to start college. He soon found that football was even better than it had been in high school, rougher, more intense, just the way he liked it. And to his surprise, he didn't mind his classes. The teaching in his small, rural high school had given him a pretty poor idea of education, but he found that at a university things were quite different, and he started to understand why people made such a fuss about going to college.

Unlike the rest of the football team, Bret had time to study. Some feminine grapevine, whose workings were a complete mystery to him, had informed all the decent girls that he was married to someone back home. So Bret found himself spending his Saturday night with check-out girls and cocktail waitresses who did not, as he put it to his teammates, "require so much courting time." It was a situation he was entirely content with.

He had gone home in the summers to work on the farm with his father and Luke, and during his second summer home, the summer that Jessica was sixteen, he discovered that the doctor was right. He had made a promise that wasn't going to be easy to keep.

He had taken the train home, riding with a teammate who lived farther down the line. As they pulled into the station and Bret was lifting his bag off the overhead rack, he heard his friend let out a low whistle. "Who is that girl?"

Bret bent over and resting one hand on the headrest of the seat in front of them, leaned forward to look out the window. He knew a lot about the girls of this town—more than he should have, in fact—and he marveled that any of them could merit such interest.

It was Jessica.

The wind, which was tossing her black hair and bringing a sparkle to her blue eyes, molded her light skirt to her legs, legs that were much longer and shapelier than Bret had remembered. Like everyone else on the platform, she had a hand tilted over her eyes, trying to reduce the sun's glare, hoping to see inside the train. The gesture lifted her breasts, calling attention to her graceful curves. When she took her hand away from her eyes to laugh at something Luke was saying, Bret was surprised to see her delicate features kissed with a vitality that turned her prettiness into beauty.

It was going to be, Bret thought as he could feel his senses stirring, a very long summer.

But as he stepped off the train he resolved that she was not going to know. And so the kiss on her cheek differed in no way from those he gave to his sisters.

It wasn't easy keeping it from her. The sharp sting of desire he had felt on the train fiercened under the hot Georgia sun. He found the smallest things about her arousing—the pulse he sometimes saw fluttering the smooth skin of her neck, the tip of her tongue against her white teeth, the soft curve of her arm where it disappeared into her sleeve.

He noticed a rich sensuality in her. The delight she had felt for sounds—all sounds, even harsh grating ones, had always fascinated her—had now flowered into an unconscious pleasure for the shape and feel of things. She didn't touch objects; she caressed them. Bret had seen her sewing a velvet ribbon onto a costume for a school play. As she held the ribbon in place with her left hand, her thumb had floated lightly back and forth across the velvet, luxuriating in the ribbon's softness, and he ached to have her touch him like that. Even in her daily chores, dusting, snapping beans, peeling peaches, her hands would occasionally break out of their light, efficient moves and linger over a curious shape or an unexpected texture.

No one in the family, including Jessica herself, noticed this at all. Except Bret, and it left him barely able to breathe.

The hardest times were when she was singing. The family had bought a used piano, and one of their favorite evening activities was listening to Jessica sing. Sometimes she would accompany herself on the piano, and Bret would sit across the room, watching her hair drift across her back as she moved to the music. Or she would play the old guitar he had given her, her arms curved around it as if it were a child, her hair falling forward, hiding her face.

Her voice had become even more beautiful than her face and body. She could do anything with it, letting it soar pure and clean on hymns, dropping it through the smoky twists of a country song, filling it with laughter on a children's song.

One time he had to leave the room almost before her song was over. His father followed, finding him out on the front porch, fumbling for a cigarette.

Clay lit it for him, the yellow light from the match briefly lighting Bret's face. "This isn't easy on you, is it?"

Bret stared at him in surprise.

His father smiled. "Your mother was only seventeen when you were born. I do understand a little of this, you know."

"I guess you do," Bret admitted shakily.

"People sometimes say it's something about the Southern sun that makes girls grow different," Clay mused, his voice almost dreamy perhaps in memory of how he had felt about the sixteen-year-old Amy Brett. "Anyway," he said abruptly in more characteristic tones, "your mother and I are both real proud of you, the way you are handling yourself. Jessica hasn't any idea."

"Thanks. I am doing my best." The low even tones of his father's praise, delivered in such a matter-of-fact voice that the words hardly sounded like they were praising, mattered more to Bret than all the cheers of a packed stadium.

Clay rested a booted foot on the lowest rung of the porch railing and looked out across the now green fields. "You know, son, the one thing I regret was how little time your mother had to be a girl. Jessica will make you a good wife someday if you let her, but every bit of time you give her now, I don't think you will regret. Look at the change in her over the last two years."

Bret knew that he was right. Jessica had blossomed in the security of a good home. She was laughing more, smiling, giggling with the girls, teasing Luke and their other brother Tate. She almost never lapsed into those profound silences that he had once thought so characteristic of her, silences during which she seemed to observe other people, curious about them and their feelings, seemingly believing that what she herself might have felt or said would have been of interest to no one. Those silences were rare now. For the first time since her mother died, she was loved, and she was starting to understand that she was an important part of the family, valuable for more than the housework that she did.

Bret hoped that she would continue to grow more secure. For he did observe one other thing that again the rest of the family didn't seem to notice.

During his sophomore year Bret had been required to take a psychology course. He hadn't expected to be the least bit interested, but he had studied his textbook diligently, hoping to remember everything in it until the final exam and then to forget it all the very next day.

But as he watched Jessica that summer, some of the ideas in that textbook kept coming back to him. This surprised him—he had never imagined that anything outside of his engineering courses would do him any good in real life. But these ideas seemed to explain Jessica.

Jessica desperately needed to be liked, to be approved of. Her first instinct at any moment was to please someone else, never herself. She always did what people wanted her to: She planted the flowers that were Amy's favorites; she made pies that she knew Luke and Tate liked best; she even sang only the songs that other people wanted to hear. In fact, she was so unused to consulting her own preferences that she could have hardly even said what her own favorite songs were.

It sometimes seemed as if she became a different person depending on whom she was with. With Luke and Tate, she was lively and teasing; with Amy, she was gentle and reflective. When she was with the girls, she was immediately absorbed by their interests—Betsy's new hairdo, Amanda's dolls. She was whatever the other person wanted her to be.

Bret knew that it wasn't conscious, that she wasn't deliberately manipulative. It was just her instinctive response; it was the only way she knew to relate to people. It bothered him. A lot.

It gave other people too much power over her, and he couldn't help worrying about the power that it could possibly give him.

He knew that Jessica was confused by him; she didn't understand what he wanted from her. It made her uneasy, uncertain of how to act around him. But, he thought almost bitterly, if she did know what he truly wanted—a long afternoon alone with her—she would be even more confused. And, in a thought that tormented his nights, he suspected that if she understood how badly he wanted her, she might, despite all her own inclinations, come to him. A stern, country morality would keep her from falling prey to the other men who might desire her, but she would, Bret knew, let him use her. She might even feel obligated to.

It did not make for an easy summer. But only at the end of it, when the family came to see him off at the train station, under the cover of the crowd and the noise, did he sling an arm around Jessica and pull her sharply to him, feeling her breasts flatten against his chest. But as much as he longed to circle her with his other arm as well, to mold the lower parts of her body to him, to feel her legs against, between, his—as much as he wanted to kiss her properly with a kiss that would leave her as shaken and hungry as he was—his lips just grazed her cheek.

A little breathlessly, Jessica stepped back. "I'm sorry, Bret, I must have stumbled." She smiled, apparently not understanding that he had pulled her.

Over her head Bret saw Luke's eyes burning.

Luke would have known exactly what had happened. He was seventeen, quite old enough to understand what his brother had felt all summer.

Luke was not envious. Jessica was completely a sister to him. As the two oldest children at home, they had a few extra privileges that tended to throw them together, and they had become very good friends. So he felt protective of her in a typically brotherish way. As a result, he was worried about Bret.

The Bret that Luke knew from his last year home was a dangerous one, hotheaded, impulsive, careless. Although Bret had grown out of much of his recklessness, whatever traces still remained were more evident to Luke than to anyone else. After once seeing a look of wide-eyed shock on Jessica's face, Bret avoided the farmhouse when he had been drinking or when his restless temper gnawed at him. So it was in the bunkhouse, with Luke as the only witness, that he would be like his old self.

So Luke was almost afraid for Jessica, concerned that Bret was capable of abusing her in a manner not all that different from what Cal Winsley would have done. Bret had soon realized that if he consummated his marriage with Jessica, his parents would be very, very disappointed. But his brother might shoot him.

So it surprised him that August afternoon on the hot railroad platform when Luke spoke lightly, "Really, Jessica Sue, people try to tackle him all season long, and they are an awful lot bigger than you will ever be. Whatever made you think you could do it?"

Jessica giggled, any possibility of embarrassment fading under Luke's joke. When Bret turned to shake his brother's hand in farewell, he said softly, "I see I am not the only Cavanaugh trying to learn to control his temper."

Luke threw him a twisted grin. "It isn't easy, is it?" Then he suddenly sobered. "But I've got no excuse for bad temper; I've got everything I want."

Bret ignored the last part of Luke's remark. "Well, I am obliged for the help."

Luke tried again; this time he looked Bret straight in the eye, almost the first direct look that had been exchanged between them as adults. "No, Bret, you've got no call to ever feel obligated to me. You've given me more than any man has a right to expect from another."

The Cavanaughs were not a family who talked about their feelings much, at least not the men, and Bret knew what it cost Luke to say this. "Well, little brother," he said lightly, "don't forget what you have given *me*. If I didn't have a brother like you, I'd still be on the farm."

"No way." Luke matched his tone. "If you had had to stay here, you would have long since wrapped your car around a tree."

"Luke," they heard their mother gasp, "what *are* you talking about?"

"Just about Bret killing himself, Mama, that's all." Luke picked up one of Bret's suitcases and moved with him to the line of passengers waiting to get on the train. Once they were away from the others, he spoke in their father's flat, even tones. "You'll be done with college the same time Jessica's done with high school. Have you made any plans for her?"

"Why, no," Bret answered, surprised. He had been

so occupied trying to get through the difficult present that he hadn't given much thought to the future. "Are Mother and Dad assuming that I will come home and claim her then?"

"I imagine," Luke returned. "I think they are real pleased with the way you've quieted down the last couple of years. I'd bet that was part of why Dad wanted you to marry her in the first place, thought she'd be a good influence on you."

Bret shrugged. "I doubt that it's her as much as being away from farming." Jessica's influence on him, he thought ironically, could hardly be called quieting.

They moved along in the line a little, silent for the moment. Then Bret spoke again. "Tell me, Luke, does she think about it, the future?"

Luke squinted up at the sun and then glanced sidelong at his brother. "Do you want the truth?"

"Sure."

"If she thinks about the future, I don't think she thinks about you, as being what's ahead for her, I mean. I suspect, although she'd probably die rather than admit it, she has all these fantasies about a recording career."

"A recording career?" Bret stared at his brother, amazed. "As a singer?"

"I am just guessing from a few things she let drop. But when she thinks about the future, I wouldn't be surprised if it isn't some notion about going to Nashville."

"How likely is it?" Bret asked.

"Well, not at all, I should think." Luke shrugged. "But what do I know? We all think her voice is wonderful, but it must take a lot more than that. Of course, she's got more determination and grit than any girl I've ever seen, but we don't know a soul in the music business and that sort of thing must take all kinds of connections. But, Bret, I wouldn't worry about it if I were you," Luke said with a confidence beyond his years. "All girls have their dreams, but I'm sure that she'll settle down and make you a fine wife if that's what you want from her."

Both men were too much products of a traditional background to think twice about this airy dismissal of Jessica's ambitions. It made complete sense to both of them that if Bret wanted to set up a home with Jessica in it, then that was what ought to happen.

And it almost did happen that way. In the fall of his senior year, Bret, having decided against a career in professional sports, was offered a position with a large Atlanta electronics firm to start as soon as he graduated. At Christmas he told his parents about it.

"And," he added, "I'd like to take Jessica with me." He hadn't really thought about her when he had been at school talking to the recruiters, but at home again, stung as ever by her beauty, he wanted to try and make a go of things with her.

"We'll sure miss her," Clay said. "But it is your right."

"She'll take good care of you," Amy added.

"Good Lord," Bret swore, "I am not taking her for her cooking." Which, he later thought, was quite a crude thing to say to one's mother.

"I know that," Amy said, her soft brown eyes twinkling. "But the next few months will be easier on her if we put it to her that way."

So Amy brought it up casually at the supper table that night, telling everyone about Bret's new job, pointing out how busy he would be, casually asking Jessica if she wanted to go to the city and keep house for him.

"I'll be glad to," Jessica answered politely, and only a quick startled glance at Luke had suggested that she realized that there might be a great deal more involved than cooking and cleaning.

Bret had had to return to Atlanta almost immediately. Georgia Tech was in one of the bowl games that year, and the team members had only been given a day or two to spend with their families at the holiday.

At the victory celebration that followed, Bret found himself cornered by several slightly drunken alumni, all of whom were delighted with his play. They felt some obligation to pay him back, encouraging him to turn pro, offering to help him get a job when he said he wasn't going to do that.

Bret tried to give them the coach's standard speech about contributing to the university—although his version of it was slightly muddled as he too had had more than a little to drink. Suddenly he noticed that one of the alumni's name tags listed him as Marshall Laurian and noted that he was a vice-president of a large record company in Nashville. Bret spoke without thinking.

"Sir, if you could listen to a girl sing, I'd be mighty appreciative."

The next morning Marshall Laurian might have shaken his head over having made such a tipsy promise, but he was a man of his word. So he called Bret, making arrangements to hear Jessica sing the next time he was in Atlanta.

Laurian soon had reason to bless himself for the half hour it took to hear Jessica Cavanaugh sing. He signed her to his label and turned her over to his son Art, who with a friend, Nathan Geer, wanted to start a manage-

ment company. Since then, not a year had gone by that
Jess Butler, as they decided to call her, had not made
money for both father and son.

The Cavanaugh family could hardly believe Jessica's
success. In fact if the decision had been theirs, Amy
and Clay might not have let her sign the contract, feeling that it was the path to certain heartache. But she
had been eighteen and to their mind, she only had to
answer to herself and Bret. When he seemed to think it
was a risk that she should take, they did not even murmur their misgivings.

Although he too was just as surprised by the career
of Jess Butler, Bret could at least understand why she
was such a successful performer. During the early days
when she was still doing little one-night stands in seedy
bars and high school gyms, she would come home full
of excited talk about what Nathan and Art had planned.
It was clear to Bret that she was surrounded by people
who were deeply ambitious, and Jessica would, of
course, do whatever she had to do to please the people
she worked with. Increasingly as she grew older and
more confident her attention shifted from her managers to her fans. More than any other young singer,
Jess Butler, Bret had read, felt a real obligation to her
fans. In the tradition of the older country stars, she
knew what she owed them. She felt a need to please
them; she wanted to be sure that they got their
money's worth. And Bret hoped that she had finally
found enough approval, enough people to please.

He himself had only stayed in Atlanta for a year. As
fast as it was growing, the town was too slow for him
and—he hated to admit this—too Southern. It still mattered too much who a man's grandparents were. Bret
didn't care about the country clubs and cotillions, but

he did want to make it in the business community, having found in capitalism the kind of thrill that until now he had only found in football.

He met another man, his age, in the same situation, and he and Walker Buchanan decided, to their mothers' dismay, to go north. They were both trained in electrical engineering and so they got jobs in the Minneapolis–St. Paul area, one of the centers of the nation's electronics industry. Within six months they had started their own company, manufacturing electronic equipment used in health care—digital testing devices and the like.

There was no hiding that they were outsiders in Minneapolis. Their liquid accents and Southern-sounding names made that all too clear in a city still largely populated by Scandinavian immigrants. But true to their hardworking heritage, Minnesotans judged a man on how hard he worked, not what regiment his great-great-grandfather was with, and Walker and Bret worked hard.

At first their competitors didn't take them too seriously. They were disarmed by their unhurried Southern manners, by their roundabout way of talking. Walker and Bret would always expect to pass the time of day before settling down to business and they called any man the least bit older than themselves "sir." They would ask about a person's family, professing themselves eager to see the pictures in his billfold, and then when the little snapshots were handed over, they would look at them with astonished, raised eyebrows as if they couldn't believe a man having a wife so lovely or children so healthy.

But behind their slow politeness, Walker and Bret had nerves they had inherited from riverboat gamblers and had honed on the football field. Neither of them had any family responsibilities and they took simply staggering risks. "What's there to lose?" they would laugh. And it was the knowledge that they could lose everything that made it all seem like such fun. Soon the people in the Chamber of Commerce were making jokes about Rebel Nerve.

They had made plenty of friends in the Twin Cities—Walker had recently married a local girl—but only Walker knew anything at all about the circumstances surrounding Bret's marriage. Being Southern, Walker could understand what had happened in a way that Bret just couldn't imagine the people of Minnesota doing. Their lives seemed so simple and uncomplicated, blown pure by the sharp Canadian wind.

Bret knew exactly what would have happened to a girl like Jessica in the Twin Cities. She would have been promptly placed in a good foster home, and a flock of social workers would have descended on her stepfather, filing reports on him, encouraging him to visit an alcohol-abuse center. Jessica would have eventually been entrusted to the Cavanaughs or some other good family. The state would have sent money to help pay for her board and her stepfather would have visitation rights. It would have all worked quite neatly.

Handling it that way made so much sense that Bret knew that these people would never understand what it was like in a poor rural community with almost no social services, in a place where change hadn't come so fast. The good people of these two bright, clean, healthy cities never thought to take the law in their own hands, but then they never needed to.

So Bret never tried to explain that perfumed spring night when they had driven to Alabama thinking it the only way to save this fourteen-year-old girl. He just said to people that he'd married young but didn't live with his wife anymore, not bothering to explain that he never had. When women would ask him hopefully if he were going through a divorce, he would say, "No, ma'am, that's just not the way we do things down South."

He had occasionally thought that he and Jessica ought to apply for an annulment; they were certainly entitled to one. But *he* wasn't going to suggest it. When she had first started singing professionally, he wasn't about to bring it up in case her career collapsed beneath her. Bret, who never bothered to provide himself with a safety net, wanted to be sure Jessica knew that he would be there to catch her if she fell. And now that she was so very successful, he told himself that he dreaded the publicity such an action might create—not even Walker knew that the girl he had saved from being abused was now Jess Butler.

He didn't see her much these days. She tried hard to be home for Christmas and for family weddings, but she couldn't always make it. When she was there, her stay was so short and the house so crowded and cheerful that he hardly had a moment alone with her.

Nor had he seen her perform in years. She'd never played Minneapolis. She had once come as far north as Fargo, North Dakota, and he thought about driving over there to see her, but it just hadn't worked out.

Except for one incident before she had moved to Los Angeles, the burning desire he had once felt for her had now largely abated. Part of it, he supposed, was his stubborn Southern pride. He just didn't like to feel as if he were standing in line. Particularly after her career had changed focus, when her image had grown more provocative, he knew that countless men and boys lusted after her. He wasn't interested in being one of the crowd.

It was strange, but her career since she had left Nashville seemed to bother Luke more than it did him. He had met his brother in Atlanta on some business the year before. When they had finished in the bank and were looking for a place to have lunch, they passed a record store.

In the window was a poster of Jess Butler. She was standing, her hands in the front pockets of her figure-hugging jeans. She was wearing a white T-shirt; the outline of her breasts was faint but visible through the thin cotton. Some unseen wind was lifting up the edges of her now waist-length black hair.

In some ways, the poster reminded Bret of the day he had seen her from the train window, the first time he had responded to her beauty. But there was something considerably more adult in her expression now. Perhaps it was a trick of lighting, but there seemed to be an invitation in her dark blue eyes, an invitation that any man could read, but that she herself didn't understand. Maybe it was something in the Southern sun. Northern girls didn't look like that.

"Lord," Luke cursed. "Bret, can't you do something about that?"

"Me?" Bret laughed. "What am I supposed to do?"

"You are her husband, aren't you?"

"Barely," Bret answered calmly. "Anyway, surely you don't think that husbands mean all that much out in California."

"Doesn't that"—Luke jerked his head at the poster—"bother you?"

"I don't let it," Bret answered. "Let's just be thankful that she's got her clothes on."

That was the secret. Bret didn't allow Jess Butler's new image to bother him, and in the past years, he had got almost as good at controlling himself, his temper, his feelings, his desires, as the best Norwegian immigrant. If he thought about it, he would have probably been able to work himself up into a violent frenzy. But that seemed pointless so he just didn't think about the invitation in those blue eyes or the thrill in her rich voice.

Once in a very long while, he would break out a bottle of good Southern bourbon and listen to her albums, thinking how it was just too clear that the girl who sang those songs was no girl; she was a woman who knew her way around a man. Bret would feel the swift familiar bite of Cavanaugh rage. He should have taken her while he had had the chance, he would think to himself. After he had spent two long, hot summers yearning for her, it didn't seem right that others should have her so easily, especially as legally at least she was his.

But in the morning he would remind himself—and his headache—that staying away from her hadn't been a matter of preserving some physical purity. She had been too young, still too insecure from her difficult childhood, too confused by Cal Winsley's hot glances to survive any encounter with a man. That Bret was her husband would have made no difference. But she was clearly now a fairly well-adjusted woman. If she could handle adult relationships, so much the better for her. It didn't have a thing to do with him.

Bret tried hard to believe that, and for the most part, he succeeded.

## Chapter Four

It was awkward. The shoulder strap of her purse kept slipping down the sleeve of her apricot satin jacket, trapping her arm, making it very difficult to sign autographs. On the road, there would always be someone with her, someone who could hold her things for her, who would take her arm, leading her through the crowd when she got tired or behind schedule. But here, in the Twin Cities airport, she was alone; she'd have to manage for herself. Nathan had offered to send one of his assistants with her, but she'd supposed that she could handle a nonstop, first-class flight by herself. Perhaps she'd been wrong.

People were talking, pressing in close. She could make out questions—what was she doing in Minneapolis, when would her next album be out? She just smiled and nodded and kept writing her name across envelopes, shopping lists, whatever people thrust in her face: "Jess-Butler, JessButler, JessButler, JessButler . . ."

Finally one deep voice penetrated the confused murmur. "Now, folks, let her through."

The blue sleeve of a security guard's uniform reached out for her. Jessica smiled apologetically at the people around her and returned the pen she'd been using although she had no idea if it were getting back to the person who had handed it to her.

The guard put his hand out, letting it hover near her back to move her through the people. He wasn't really touching her, not taking her arm possessively as so many men did if they had the least excuse. She appreciated that. Just as she also appreciated how respectfully the other people fell back, obedient to his commands.

"Thank you," Jessica said to him softly. "I am really grateful for the help."

The guard smiled. "Your friend sent me." He pointed up the concourse, past the security ropes and line of people waiting to go through the metal detectors, to a tall, brown-haired man, leaning against the wall, his arms folded.

It was Bret.

How normal he looked. How absolutely, completely, refreshingly normal. He wasn't wearing tight leather pants or a T-shirt with a lewd slogan spelled out in glitter. His hair didn't trail down his back, and although she couldn't really see from here, Jessica was sure that he wasn't wearing an earring.

He looked like the sort of person who worked during the day and slept at night, who was perfectly able to live without a vast collection of pills and drugs. He looked like he read real books and didn't take megavitamins. He probably always knew how much money was in his checking account; he certainly paid his own bills. He looked like he clearly understood the difference between men and women. And approved of it.

Jessica hadn't been around people like that in a long time.

Suddenly she touched the blue sleeve of the security guard. "Could you wait for just one second please?"

The guard stopped immediately. As she rummaged through her purse, he commented, "You are from the South, aren't you? You have such a pretty way of talking."

Jessica quickly slipped two straight-sided, brown plastic bottles in the trash container. The guard's remark made her smile. Her accent wasn't as thick as it had been. She thought of what she could have said: "Would you mind ever so much waiting right here for just one little second? Oh, Law, I would appreciate it so terribly. To the end of my days, indeed I would." Now *that* was a "pretty" way of talking. If she had spoken like that, the guard probably would have arrested her.

And in a moment, she was in front of Bret.

He had straightened and smiled at the sight of her. Moving to meet her, he slipped an arm around her shoulders and kissed her cheek. She felt the warmth of his lips, casually brushing across her face, and as he moved away, she looked up, meeting eyes that were a soft dark gray, eyes that you could drift into, with a color you longed to rest your cheek against, knowing it would be as comforting and warm as the cashmere flannel of a man's suit.

Then it hit her. This wasn't just any reasonably normal, healthy-looking man. This was Bret.

Thoughts of all that he had been to her, all that he had done for her, flooded over her, making her light-headed, almost giddy.

It had been Bret who had first made her believe in her voice, believe that it was something special. He would come to her, dusty and hot from working in her stepfather's fields. He'd swing himself down off the tractor and move across the drive with a lazy, rolling stride, stopping to dip some water for himself out of the pail by the pump. "Put that down, girl," he would say to her, shaking a cigarette out of a pack, "and sing something to me." She would drop whatever she was doing and sing. After a few bars, she would have to stop looking at him.

One day he had brought her the guitar. She had just stood at the kitchen window, not believing, staring at him coming up the walk, lightly swinging the precious instrument. It had been old, a little warped, with a thin sound, but she hadn't cared. If it had had no strings, it would have still been magical because it had come from him.

And then the winter day he had called from college. The family never made long-distance phone calls, and Amy's hand had flown to her throat when she heard it was him, fearing that something terrible had happened. But his message had been simple, a message so entirely unexpected, not even dreamed for, that Jessica had gone numb, unable to feel anything. "If Luke can bring Jessie to Atlanta, there's a man who wants to hear her sing."

And for a moment Jessica now felt like the rest of the world was all just trying to make money off her, trying to get her to record their songs, sign their contracts, endorse their products, promote their groups, sing at their clubs—everyone but Bret.

"I'm so glad I'm here," she breathed.

He smiled and she felt weak. "Good," he said softly, still so close to her that he could speak low. "On the phone, it sounded like you didn't want to come."

She tried to explain. "I was tired. I didn't think I could face another strange city."

*I had forgotten what it was like to be with you.*

He didn't hear the unspoken words and simply replied to those she had said. "Then let's get you home. The baggage claim is this way."

As they walked Bret lifted his arm around her shoulders. Usually she didn't like to walk that way. So often a man would settle his arm heavily on her, pinning her long hair to her shoulders so that she couldn't move her head. But Bret didn't trap her; his hand touched only her far shoulder, letting the black hair move easily across her back.

She couldn't take her eyes off him. He looked wonderful. Older, of course, but maturity had come without harshness or coarseness. Perhaps he was less massive than he had been in his football days, but he was still broad-shouldered, seeming just as vigorous and alert as ever.

Her regard seemed to embarrass him a little. "Come on, Jessie," he complained uneasily. "Don't look at me like that. I'm supposed to be looking at *you* that way."

Which would have been fine with her.

Even as they were riding down the escalator, she still kept peeping at him so she noticed when he smiled and nodded at someone on the floor below. As the moving stairs were flattening out in front of them, he asked her in a quick soft voice, "Are you here as Jessica Cavanaugh or Miss Butler?"

"Cavanaugh, please." What a relief it would be, she suddenly thought, if she could actually stop being Jess Butler for a while.

She watched curiously as he shook hands with two men. They were such a contrast to him and so unlike the people he used to know. Easily fifteen years older than he, one was starting to go bald and the other was spreading at the waist. A hand at her back nudged her forward, and she heard Bret mentioning their names to her and then saying, "Bill, Ralph, this is my wife, Jessica."

She went very still.

No one seemed to notice. The two men asked her if she had been on a trip; she explained that she was a singer and had been working in California; they shrugged and said that it must be nice to be home; she politely, if untruthfully, agreed.

"Well, we've got to get moving," one said. "It was nice meeting you, Mrs. Cavanaugh."

"I hope to see you all again real soon," Jessica managed to get out.

As the men melted into the crowd, Jessica glanced at Bret. He was grinning.

"It's your fault," she pointed out. "You introduced me as your wife."

"Well, you are, aren't you?"

"Yes, but Bret, it's been twelve years now, and you've never introduced me that way before."

"Look," he answered cheerfully, "it might be fun letting everyone think that Jess Butler is my current mistress who has come to Minneapolis for the sort of serious sex she can't get anywhere else, but this is a bit of a straitlaced town, so I guess we are better off telling people the truth."

Obviously done talking about this, he tilted back his head, looking up at the various signs. "They've posted your flight. Let's go."

As they moved toward the conveyer belt, Jessica wanted to go on talking with him. "Were those two men friends of yours?" she asked although she guessed that they were not.

"Who? Bill and Ralph? They aren't really friends.

We're on a Chamber of Commerce committee together."

Jessica blinked. "You? On a Chamber of Commerce committee?" What was Bret doing on the Chamber of Commerce? He used to be the sort of person the Chamber of Commerce formed committees *against*.

He guessed what she was thinking. "Now you can just hush up about my past," he said teasingly, "and tell me which bags are yours."

Jessica's bag was one of the first spit out onto the conveyer belt. It had been marked with an orange tag demanding "Priority Handling." Bret raised his eyebrows. "What's this?"

Jessica was so very used to such treatment that it took her a moment to realize what he was talking about. "Just the wages of sin," she said lightly.

"Then I will have to change my ways—go back to sinning. Don't you have some other luggage?" When she shook her head, he continued. "Now, Jessie, Mother said I have to keep you here until Memorial Day even if I have to hog-tie you to do it."

She had learned that Bret's phone call to California had been prompted by Amy Cavanaugh. She had been very worried about her daughter-in-law and had tried to get her to come back to Georgia for a rest. Jessica had refused, feeling incapable of traveling. So Amy had called Bret; she knew that Jessica would be unable to say no to him.

But Memorial Day was six weeks away, and Jessica couldn't possibly imagine that she would stay in the Twin Cities that long. She didn't think that since leaving home, she'd ever been in one place, even Los Angeles, for six straight weeks.

So she just smiled and said nothing.

As soon as they were settled in the car and out of the airport parking lot, she asked Bret about his company. She wasn't just being polite. That he was active in the Chamber of Commerce—something that seemed so very out-of-character—made her terribly curious about him. His home, his friends, what he ate, where he shopped—she would have liked to know about everything, but the company seemed to be the proper thing to ask about.

It was doing fine, he said. Things had gotten much easier in the last year or so. They had steady customers with long-term contracts; they no longer had to wonder where the next dollar of business was coming from. It took a lot of the pressure off.

"Are you getting bored?" she asked quietly. The Bret she knew adored pressure and uncertainty.

He sent her another one of those achingly familiar smiles. "I should be, shouldn't I? But, no, I am pretty content. Walker and I both seem to have calmed down a lot. We must have gotten a lot of the craziness out of our systems. But tell me about yourself. How on earth did you get time off?"

Jessica briefly explained about the band touring on its own and about how she needed to form a new one before she could do anything else. "But I need to decide if I want to change some things before I get a new band."

"You mean musically?" he asked

"Yes. I don't know, Bret." Suddenly she felt tired again. The golden bloom that had colored the air when she had first looked down the concourse and seen him had faded into a drab mist. She wished they weren't talking about her career. "I don't know," she repeated. "I can't seem to find any new songs. Of course, there are hundreds and hundreds—it seems every waiter and cabdriver in L.A. thinks he is a songwriter, but I can't get excited about them. The music is different, the words are different, but the feelings, the situations the songs are about, they all seem the same. I can't find anything that feels special. It's like I have sung everything there is for a country song to be about." She shrugged and leaned back against the headrest. She couldn't remember when she had last put together so many sentences offstage.

"Are you by chance worried that there won't *be* a next album?" His voice was gentle.

She sat up. "Oh, no. Not in the least." She explained about her contract, about having one more album to do to meet her legal obligations. "And Nathan says we can pretty much write our own ticket after that."

"Well, I would have been surprised to hear that your career was on the skids. Me and millions of other people. But I don't claim to understand the entertainment business." He flicked on the turn signal and, glancing over his shoulder, changed lanes. "I read somewhere that everyone's predicting that you will be doing straight rock next."

Pleased that he followed her career, Jessica had to shake her head. "I know that's what everyone is saying, but I won't."

He looked at her, his eyes leaving the road for a moment. "Why not?"

He seemed interested so she tried hard to explain although she wouldn't have bothered with anyone else. "I think that country music is, most of all, about loneliness, and that's something I understand quite well." She noticed his lips tighten in a brief grimace and she quickly continued. "But rock and roll, true rock, comes from anger, from rage and passion, and I don't think I understand those feelings well enough to sing about them."

"Come on, Jessie," Bret put in, "you grew up with Luke and me. That should have taught you enough about anger for forty albums." His short laugh was almost self-mocking.

When she said nothing, he went on. "You could do the watered-down commercial stuff. What you hear on AM radio doesn't seem so intense."

"Perhaps, but that seems faked to me, like the singers aren't sincere, that they are singing words they don't mean. I'm already cheating enough as it is."

Jessica jerked upright. She could not believe what she had just said. She hadn't told anyone that. Of all the things she had done, there was only one other that she was more ashamed of than the way she had started faking her songs. On this last tour she hadn't felt the songs anymore; she wouldn't become the person behind the lyrics. While she would sing one line, she would be thinking how she would sing the next. Or with some of the songs, she would just switch off; she wouldn't be there; she would be off thinking of something else with her throat and lungs doing the work, not her heart.

She had reasons—that she was tired, she was miserably sick of her old songs—but they weren't excuses.

Her whole career was built on sincerity. What if it got out that she didn't believe in the lyrics anymore? What if Bret told a reporter? What if—

She shook herself. What was she thinking of? No matter how much a reporter might cajole or a tabloid pay, Bret would never talk to anyone about her. That she could count on.

She looked over at him. Golden highlights danced

through his thick brown hair. He was driving like a
Southerner, his left elbow out the window and his right
arm almost straight, his hand resting on the top of the
steering wheel. It was a habit he'd picked up along the
empty country roads.

He glanced over his shoulder and started backing
into a parking space. "We're here," he said.

Jessica looked around her, her curiosity immediately
changing into surprise. During the drive she had hardly
paid any attention to where they were going, just re-
ceiving a vague impression of a green and pretty city.
But Bret had stopped on a street that was neither. On
one side, railroad tracks cut across a large vacant lot,
and on the other, in the shadow of a towering grain
elevator, huge dumpsters sat outside large, almost
grimy buildings. There was little life or activity on the
street although it was still early evening. The street was
every country person's nightmare of what an industrial
city would be like and Bret seemed to live here.

She glanced at him, very disappointed. He would
hardly be the first man who came up North and lied
about how well he was doing. She had recorded a song
about such men; "Write When You Get Work" it was
called. But it surprised her that Bret was one of them.
She would have thought that, above all, he would have
been straight about his failures, even laughing about
them, because he was so confident that successes were
to follow.

Well, she reminded herself, thinking of the Chamber of Commerce committee, how well did she really
know him? She had wonderful memories of him, but
that picture was undoubtedly a girlish one, much too
romanticized. Surely he was an ordinary man with ordinary human failings.

She got out of the car, waiting while he took her suitcase from the truck. He directed her toward a six-story, red brick building. It had obviously been a warehouse once; Jessica could hardly imagine that it housed anything but the cheapest tenements. She was so prepared to be confronted with elderly winos and scurrying rats that when Bret held open the glass door for her, she stepped inside gingerly.

The lobby was immaculate, with light oak floors, emerald carpets, wicker chairs, and billowing ferns. It was comfortable, inviting, even luxurious. The elevator was obviously new, and when its doors opened at the top floor, the little hall was carpeted with the same green and the brick walls were a fresh, soft cream.

Jessica felt like a fool.

She now expected Bret's apartment would be equally pleasant, but she was still utterly unprepared. As he unlocked and opened the heavy oak door and she stepped inside all she could look at were the windows.

They were vast sheets of glass set in walls of exposed brick. Mesmerized, she dropped her purse and floated toward them. Bret followed her, thrusting open the one that was a sliding door, his hand inviting her out onto the broad terrace.

From this balcony, she could see a wide river and across from it, a city. She drifted to the railing. The river looked—well, Jessica could think of no other word—it looked terribly American. It was more magnificent than beautiful, with a lock and several bridges, grain elevators on the banks and flatbed boats at the docks. The river was clearly the heart of a thriving, healthy city where people, vital and energetic, had gathered to make money under the big Midwestern sky.

Across the river, a commercial district gathered at the river's edge and then that tight cluster of tall buildings eased into residental areas, green and peaceful, with the occasional spire of a church breaking through the trees. It was still light out and the scene was sharp and clear, not blanketed with a hazy smog.

She felt Bret behind her. "Everyone does that," he said, "go straight for the windows. They were the main reason I bought the place."

"It's wonderful," she breathed. "What is it?"

"That's southern Minneapolis over there; there's St. Anthony's Falls and the first lock on the Mississippi—"

"The Mississippi?" Jessica said in surprise. "All the way up here?"

Bret laughed. "Yes, Jessica Sue, that's the whole point of the Mississippi—that it goes from all the way up here to all the way down there."

Jessica stiffened in embarrassment, just as she always did when her very real ignorance about ordinary things was exposed. "I guess I knew that," she acknowledged. "But I just think of it as a Southern river somehow."

"We share it with the North."

Jessica gave the Mississippi a respectful look and then turned back to look inside the condominium.

To get to the terrace they had crossed through a large room with sixteen-foot ceilings and walls of exposed brick that were softened by some interesting textile hangings and lightened, of course, by the sweeping windows. As in the lobby, the floors were oak, stripped and stained. Brass lamps and plants mingled with the contemporary furniture that was upholstered in pale, neutral shades. The room was warmed by the accent colors; the rich tone of the Oriental carpets were repeated in an occasional pillow or vase with an imagination and educated taste that Jessica suspected were not Bret's.

Divided from the living room by a broad counter was, Jessica could see, a kitchen, which had a lower ceiling. She then noticed an oak spiral staircase leading up to a gallery and a hallway. Clearly the rest of the apartment had been divided by a loft, making it two stories.

She turned to Bret, smiling. "From the outside, I thought you lived in a warehouse."

"I do," he returned with a lazy grin. "This used to be a blanket mill's warehouse; it was only recently turned into condominiums."

"It's beautiful. Have you been here long?"

"A little over a year. Walker and I lived in the most anonymous sort of apartments out by the company for a long time, but when he got married and bought a house in St. Paul, I decided it was time for me to get somewhere decent to live too."

"Is it convenient to the company?" Jessica asked. It was a wonderful apartment, but she still wondered why he had chosen such a tired part of town.

"Not particularly," he answered. "We're out in New Hope."

Jessica, of course, knew even less about the suburbs of Minneapolis than she did about those of Los Angeles and she knew next to nothing about them. "Then why did you choose this neighborhood?"

"Oh, the neighborhood's the best part of it."

"It is?" Jessica couldn't keep the surprise out of her voice.

"I know it isn't pretty yet"—Bret dismissed prettiness with an airy wave—"but it will be. Most of the buildings around here are being converted into condominiums or offices—that's partly why the street looks so gritty now. And remember that big empty lot with train tracks? That will be landscaped with trees and fountains and benches, and the old train shed will be enclosed with shops and boutiques. People here are really committed to keeping the downtowns alive, not letting all the money drift out to the suburbs as seems to be happening in every other city." Bret turned and looked out his windows. "This is such a great place, Jessie," he said, enthusiasm vibrating through his deep voice. "Things are happening here, and they are such good things—people trying to keep the Cities places families would want to live in. Did you know—" He broke off, a little embarrassed by his own enthusiasm. "You haven't even sat down and here I go on rambling about the quality of life in the north country. Now that was a dinner flight. Did you eat the airplane food or do you want something?"

"Thank you, but I am fine." Jessica hadn't eaten anything on the plane. In fact, she had had nothing but coffee and half a carton of yogurt since the alfalfa sprouts she had pushed around on her plate in the restaurant yesterday. She just wasn't ever hungry anymore.

With efficient and practiced ease, Bret made his own dinner, just steak, broccoli, and a salad. Jessica leaned against the counter, whose top was a warm persimmon color, watching him interestedly.

"I didn't know you could cook."

"I couldn't at first." The Cavanaugh family had been such a traditional one that the men cooked just as often as the women rotated the tires on the pickup. "But I learned how."

"Then we are even," Jessica said ruefully, "because I think I have forgotten how."

"One of Amy Cavanaugh's girls?" His eyes widened in mock disbelief. "Forgot how to cook? That will be the day. You used to be an angel with a rolling pin."

Her heart clutched at his words. Didn't he understand? She wasn't one of Amy Cavanaugh's girls anymore. Too much had happened. Forgetting how to cook was the very least of her failings.

To what extent she was no longer one of the nice Cavanaugh girls became absolutely clear to her that night—just as she knew it would.

Bret had taken her suitcase up to the second floor to what was obviously the guest room. It was a pleasant, quiet room, neither masculine nor feminine. The white wallpaper was sprigged with a small geometric pattern in a sand color. The carpeting was sand and the moldings and baseboards were painted in that color, a gentle contrast to the white walls. It had twin beds, an empty chest of drawers, a comfortable reading chair, and a private bathroom, but it did not, to Jessica's great relief, feel at all like a hotel. No hotel would dare use such light colors.

After saying good-night to Bret, she unpacked slowly and then showered, washing and drying her waist-length hair, a process that took, even at the best of times, several hours. And this evening she was perfectly willing to drag it out as long as she could, putting off the moment when she would have to turn out the light and try to go to sleep.

As she moved the dryer through her hair, she thought about her initial impression of the street where Bret lived. She had been wrong in thinking that it meant he and his company weren't doing well; clearly he was just as successful as they all had thought. But her point was probably still valid. He couldn't be all she remembered him being; no man could. Sooner or later she would have to pierce through the shimmering glow her memories had surrounded him with and discover that he was probably nothing at all like the exciting, romantic figure she remembered.

It was probably just as well if he weren't, she thought. Some of the things that had made Bret seem so exciting to her at fourteen—his quick temper, his unpredictability, his arrogance—well, all that might seem pretty thrilling to a girl, but a woman might find it just right tiring to live with.

With these thoughts came, just as she had expected, the beginnings of a headache. And gradually the rational thoughts disappeared and all she could think about was the headache. It was a strange and feverish ache, as if something in her brain was twitching, itching. No, but it wasn't in her brain, it was in her stomach, her arms, her legs.

Dear God, she thought frantically, what had possessed her to do that in the airport? Surely you don't do something so foolish, so impulsive just because a man showers regularly and keeps his hair cut. Why had she done it? And what *was* she going to do?

She was sure she was feeling worse by the moment. She tried to keep track. "Am I feeling worse? Do I feel a little bit better now? No, no, I feel worse."

She knew of nothing that would help, nothing she could do to pass the time until the misery, these aches, these tremblings, went away, *if* they went away.

Her heart was pulsing with quick, hard beats, like the sharp tattoo of a snare drum. She pressed her hand to it, hoping to keep it from leaping out of her body. What could she do with herself?

There were magazines. Someone had put magazines by the bed. She picked one up, but the words didn't seem to fit together; each word seemed to have nothing to do with the word before it, and after a moment the letters didn't have any reason for being where they were.

Maybe music. Maybe music would help. She'd have to keep it low; she didn't want to wake Bret. She couldn't have him see her like this.

The radio. She couldn't figure out the radio. Where was the knob? It had numbers and buttons, not a dial. She sat down on a bed and squinted at it. A little window kept flashing numbers at her: "1:15, 1:15, 1:16, 1:16." She didn't understand. Suddenly one of the buttons read "On/Off." It hadn't said that a minute ago; she was sure. Gingerly she touched the button, and a voice attacked her, "... a zero percent chance of precip—"

She punched the button again and the voice stopped.

But her hand was shaking and a little leather cup of pencils and pens fell to the floor.

A yellow pencil rolled across the carpet, and a blue ballpoint pen was lying under an emery board. She wasn't sure if this was important. She looked at it more carefully. The pen didn't move.

"Is everything all right?"

It was Bret, looking down at her, his face concerned.

She took a breath. "I couldn't work the radio, that's all."

"It's one of these new programmable ones. You can program it to do almost anything." And he was explaining, telling her how she could lock her favorite stations into the radio's memory and recall them by—

Memory? She couldn't remember anything. Why did a radio have a memory when she didn't?

"Jessie, are you all right?"

She tried to smile. "I just can't seem to get to sleep, that's all."

"The time change?" he asked.

"Something like that."

"In this bathroom there are some over-the-counter sleeping pills. Do—"

"*No*." Her voice was like a sharp shot. "I mean, no," she said, trying to sound calm. "No, I don't want any."

He looked at her curiously and then sat down next to her on the bed. "That's a pretty nightgown."

"Thanks, Nathan bought it for me."

It had been on a night almost as bad as this. She had finished her show and returned to the bus for an all-night drive, just the sort of thing she had done hundreds and hundreds of times over the last years, nothing at all unusual. But as she went into her little enclosed room in the back of the bus and opened her closet, she felt as if she couldn't face the road anymore. She had sunk on the bed, sobbing. When Cade and the others had heard her and come in, she was staring at the few clothes, hanging in the closet, swinging to the movement of the bus. And for all her anguish, her exhaustion, all she could think of was how sick she was of her nightgowns.

The road manager, frantic over this unusual display of temperament, had called Nathan back in Los Angeles. "Jess is crying because she hates her nightgowns." At the very next stop a department store had delivered to the bus a large package of elegant, expensive nightgowns.

They had helped but only a little.

Jessica bent her head and looked down at the folds and billows of white silk that surrounded her. It was so silly, she thought almost randomly, to have a nightgown that had to be dry-cleaned. Until she had started singing, even her best Sunday dress had been laundered at home.

Bret gently lifted a lock of her hair. "I heard you drying your hair. I can remember when we were kids, you used to let it dry in the sun; it would take all morning."

"It takes even longer now." She shrugged as she spoke and his hand dropped from her hair, brushing down her neck. He had already taken his hand away when suddenly his fingers returned to her neck, feeling for, then finding, her pulse.

"Have you just run a marathon?" he asked. "Your heart is going like it." He slipped his hand back to her neck, under her hair, feeling the tension there, and then with light, firm moves he started to rub her neck. "You are wound up tight, Jessie. What's wrong?"

She didn't say anything, just found herself leaning against him. She could barely feel his hand; her head, her heart, were pounding so, but it was reassuring to know that she wasn't alone. Maybe she wouldn't have to face this by herself.

"Lie down," he said, "we might as well do this properly."

She did, coiling her hair and tucking it under her shoulder. She felt him kneel over her, a leg on either side of her.

She tried desperately to concentrate on the way his hands felt on her neck and shoulders. They would be warm, she told herself, and strong and reassuring like the steady throb of a bass guitar.

But she couldn't feel a thing, not through the choking, engulfing fog that was circling around her, swallowing her. "You really don't have to do this," she murmured.

"I don't mind."

His voice was gruff, and despite the knots and thorns biting at her flesh, Jessica suddenly realized that he didn't mind. Not at all.

How odd, she thought idly, a space in her brain slowly clearing for these thoughts, that Bret should want her. Lots of the other men did, of course, but it was odd imagining that Bret wanted to touch her shoulders and arms, wanting to let his hands linger on her, wanting to brush aside the long, black hair and kiss the flesh beneath. It didn't make any sense that he would want that from her, but if he did...well, he was Bret.

She twisted under his hands, now lying on her back beneath him, between his legs, looking up at him.

She felt the muscles in his legs clench, and she heard him breathe a quick, sharp breath. And so that he would know for sure, she reached up and rested her hands on his thighs.

She could see his touch drifting down from her shoulder, past the disarray of her nightgown, probing inside the silk, gently touching her. She felt the warmth on her breast, but the weight of it was little more than vaguely comforting. Her body did not respond to him.

Bret was no fool, no inexperienced boy. He could tell. Abruptly he swung off her. "Jessica Susan, you had better tell me what is wrong."

"No, Bret, no," she murmured, turning her cheek on the pillow away from him. "Don't ask."

Then suddenly she wanted him to know, to know about this, the greatest shame in her life. She hated herself so much that she wanted him to hate her too. It would be her punishment; the revulsion, the contempt, that would be on his face, she would deserve it. She would have earned it. She had not deserved all that he had done for her, all the wonderful generous things. Well, she would deserve this.

She sat up and staring at the little green numbers spurting out the time on the radio's clock, she spoke in a bright, brittle voice.

"Don't you know? Can't sleep, no appetite, a pulse like...all the signs, can't you tell? It's pills, Bret, pills. Uppers every morning. Downers at night. I can't sleep without them; I can't get up without them; I can't do anything without them. I've got a pill habit, a nasty, nasty pill habit."

Warm arms closed around her body, pulling her cheek to a hard chest. "Jessie, my poor girl, my poor dear girl. What have they done to you?"

He held her. She had no idea for how long; she had lost all sense of time. Finally he eased her away and made her sit upright. He stood, pulled a chair to the bed, and sat down, facing her.

"Tell me. How long has it been? How did it start?"

"It's been years." She couldn't meet his eyes. "I just can't sleep after a show; I never have been able to. I'm just too charged up. So I started taking sleeping pills because I would have a show to do in another city the next night; I had to sleep. It didn't seem like a big deal. But I started feeling tense all the time and nervous. Not stage fright or anything, just nerves. So a doctor put me on Valium, and for a while that was great—I quit the sleeping pills and everything was fine...at least it was for a while. I don't know how it happened, but all of a sudden I was taking three a day and they weren't helping anymore. So they gave me something stronger too, but that made me so draggy and fagged out that I couldn't sing right. So then they gave me a prescription for a stimulant. I knew it was wrong, but I had to be able to get up there on that stage and sing: Nothing else mattered.''

"Who's 'they'?" he asked. "How do you get them?"

"From a doctor out in Hollywood. My name's on all the prescriptions; it's all legal, I guess. Lots of people have prescriptions in about four different names, or they just buy their pills on the street. I am not there— yet."

"I take it you didn't bring the pills with you."

She shook her head. "I did, but I threw them out at the airport. I don't know, Bret. I saw you, and you looked—" she hesitated. "I don't know; I just felt so ashamed, so abnormal. I didn't want to be like that when I was with you. But throwing them out was stupid; you would have never known otherwise." How she wished he didn't know.

"No, Jessie," he said softly. "You did just the right thing."

He was wonderful. He sat up with her the rest of the night and then the first thing in the morning parceled her up and took her to a doctor.

The doctor was young, apparently a friend of Bret's. He was sympathetic, but firm. As Jessica described exactly what she had been taking—the Valium, the Tuinal, the Dexedrine—his lips tightened, obviously disapproving, not so much of Jessica, as of the doctor who had written her the prescriptions.

Surprisingly he was also reassuring. "Don't get me wrong—you must stop and you have got a rugged week or so ahead of you, but you haven't done yourself any lasting damage. Once the worst is over, it may be easier than giving up cigarettes. As soon as your system readjusts, you won't go on craving the stuff.''

It was hard, sometimes a biting agony. At first, she couldn't sleep; she'd have tremors, feeling like she was shaking uncontrollably. She was listless and depressed; she'd hate herself and wonder if it was worth it. She wasn't ever going to be normal again; why go through all this? Each hour, each minute, was hard.

It went on for ten long, miserable days although when it was all over, she remembered very little of it, only that Bret was always there. At last she started sleeping, as much as twenty hours a day, and while she slept, her body slowly recovered.

## Chapter Five

Good health. Jessica couldn't believe it. She had forgotten how it felt to feel good, to have energy and an appetite, to wake up in the morning rested, to go to bed at night tired. It seemed like the most extraordinarily precious gift; she couldn't believe that she had once thought that performing was more important than this.

As she felt better Bret went back to work, at first just for a few hours, then for the whole day. Finally one morning at breakfast she too announced, "I'm going outside today."

Bret looked at her over his coffee cup. "Is it Groundhog Day?" he asked blandly. "Are you going out to see if you still have a shadow?"

She smiled. It felt so wonderful to smile. "It's been so long since I've been out I probably ought to check. Actually, I thought I'd get some clothes. I didn't bring many."

"I'd noticed. I was beginning to wonder if you singing stars spent all your time in nightgowns."

"Rock stars might, but I am a country singer and I had better get some clothes."

Jessica was pleased with herself. While this remark had been only the mildest pleasantry, it was the closest she had come to making a joke in years.

"Luke will be pleased," Bret commented.

"Luke? What does he have to do with it?"

"I think he's always afraid that pretty soon someone is going to decide that Jess Butler is such a success that she doesn't need to wear clothes anymore."

Jessica laughed. "No, one of the nice things about being a success is that people will come see you, clothes and all."

"Then perhaps you should go get yourself some." Bret reached into his back pocket for his wallet.

Jessica frowned. Surely he wasn't going to give her money.

"It will probably be easier if you took my credit cards," he was saying. "It will save you from trying to use out-of-town checks or using all your cash." He sorted through a stack of plastic cards. "Here are the ones for some local department stores. I don't have any for the women's shops, but I imagine most of them will take the bank cards."

"Can I use these? Doesn't my name have to be on the account or something?"

"Oh, probably," Bret said casually, "but I imagine if you sign 'Mrs.' no one will give you any problem."

He drew her a little map, saying that downtown Minneapolis was only a ten-minute walk, but that she should be sure and take a cab home if she got tired. "And you know," he said as he opened the front door to leave, "as long as you are going to be out, why don't you pick yourself up some sort of ring?"

"I don't understand."

"You never did get a wedding ring. My friends will think it odd if you don't wear one."

"Well, they'll just—" Jessica stopped, astonished to realize she had been about to tease him, saying that his friends would undoubtedly think he had hocked her ring to start some new business. Such lightheartedness felt too new to be trusted, so instead she just quietly agreed to get herself a ring.

Just before ten that morning she left the apartment for the first time since she had visited the doctor almost two weeks before.

The neighborhood did seem quite different than her first impression of it. The morning sunlight gave it a vibrancy that was reflected in the lively bustle of the people on the street. Bret was right: It wasn't pretty, but it had vitality; this was a street that was going somewhere, not like so many crumbling streets in other, more tired downtowns.

No wonder Bret liked it here, Jessica thought. Suddenly a surge of energy pulsed through her in the kind of response she thought came only from performing. High spirits, a sense of well-being, vibrated through her walk, giving it a bounce she had thought was lost forever. She felt relaxed, radiant.

She was glad the day was warm, that she hadn't had to wear her apricot satin jacket, the only sort of coat she had brought with her. She had always liked the jacket; it was cut like a baseball player's, and she could slip her hands in the pockets just under the rib cage and feel safe and self-contained. But here on the streets of Minneapolis, the jacket's apricot satin coupled with its unusual cut would stand out. The people passing by her were dressed neatly and conservatively without the extremes of exotic high fashion or rag-picking poverty. It was not a town for an apricot satin baseball jacket.

How lovely it was to blend in, to be an utterly anonymous woman, happy, healthy, and ignored, walking through these safe, light streets. How many women must take this bliss utterly for granted.

Suddenly the peace was shattered.

"Hey, look, it's Jess Butler."

Jessica tensed. The voice continued. "It is, sure it is. You can tell by the hair."

Jessica forced herself to relax. This was bound to happen; the Twin Cities weren't a big market for country music, but they weren't on another planet. Anyway, the voice was coming from above her; she wouldn't have to sign autographs or talk for long.

She stepped back on the sidewalk and waved up to where three or four young construction workers were gathered on a beam at the edge of a still wall-less building.

"Hey, Jess, what are you doing in the Cities?"

"I'm on vacation." Jessica knew all about projection and her voice reached them easily.

"Are you having a good time?" another voice called.

"I am. It's a nice place."

"When are you going to give a concert here?" the first voice asked.

"Would you all come?"

"Sure."

"Then maybe real soon." She waved and moved off.

It had been an exceedingly easy encounter, not at all awkward, as pleasant for the fans as it would have once been gratifying for her. But she wished it hadn't happened.

Jessica glanced at her reflection in the plate-glass window of one of the shops. Of course, her fans recognized her: It was her hair—the shining black length of it made almost everyone look at her twice. Jessica lifted its weight off her neck for a moment. Maybe she should cut it off.

She dismissed the thought immediately. Art and Nathan would probably strangle her, and even if she didn't care what it would do to her career, she couldn't just walk into a random beauty parlor and tell them to cut. Abundant, fine hair was the most unforgiving hair; every mistake, each waver of the scissors, showed. Jessica thought that she wouldn't mind having shorter hair—people wouldn't recognize her, she wouldn't have to spend hours drying it—but she would, like any woman, hate having a bad haircut.

Bret's map led her to the Crystal Court, a square block of shops and arcades that had been closed in against the cold of the Minnesota winter. From the complex radiated the skyways, which were glass corridors one story above the street that connected many of the buildings. Bret had told her that in perhaps five or ten years there might be a skyway connecting even his building to downtown.

The Crystal Court was a delightful place, light and airy, with banks of flowers and plants. The arching skylights were made of faceted glass that caught the sunlight, sending bluish-green reflections glittering through the air. In one corner was a little coffee shop with small wrought-iron tables and chairs. Jessica sat down and, with deference to her still fragile metabolism, ordered juice instead of anything with caffeine in it. She wasn't really sure that she was going to shop for clothes as she had told Bret. She was a little afraid that she wouldn't be able to make up her mind about anything—she had had so much trouble making decisions lately. This would be her first shopping trip in months and months; she didn't want it to be as depressing as shopping trips are when you can't decide what you like.

She was just going to sit here, listening to the people around her talk to one another.

Their conversations seemed wonderful to her. Two elegantly dressed women were talking about fund raising for the symphony; some men were discussing business in their shoe stores; three young mothers were talking about toilet training. The talk was very everyday, just the daily conversations of ordinary people with reasonably satisfying lives—unremarkable, unexciting, and infinitely precious.

Suddenly the two ladies stopped talking about their committees and were talking about hair. One of the women had just gotten a permanent. "And your hair is so fine and you have so much of it...."

Jessica immediately looked at the other woman. Although her white hair was far more formally done than Jessica would ever want hers, it did seem to be beautifully cut. If it truly was fine and abundant, well....

Celebrity had given Jessica confidence for any kind of casual encounter. She stood up swiftly and moved toward the table.

"Excuse me." The ladies looked up politely. "I apologize, but I couldn't help overhearing what you were saying, ma'am, about having hair like this...." Jess lifted a lock of hers. "And I am new in town."

"Oh, yes." The lady was quite pleasant. "It is a nuisance, isn't it? Do you want the name of my beautician?" As the woman took a gold pen and a little notepad out of her purse, she glanced at the jeans and cranberry-colored T-shirt that Jessica wore. "She is rather expensive, you know."

"That's all right." Jessica had to smile to herself. Her jeans had been custom-made for her and probably cost more than the ladies' two silk shirtwaists put together. The French-cut T-Shirt, with its three cranberry buttons across the shoulder, was a designer shirt; Jessica had paid a tailor to remove the insignia.

As Jessica moved to find a phone, she marveled at how simple that was. In the South, they would have spent forever passing the time of day, not stopping until they could prove that they were all related, and in California, well, Jessica would have never asked a stranger the name of her hairdresser. Maybe Bret was right; maybe Minneapolis was a good place to live, an easy place.

It was a Monday and so the salon said they could take her right away. The shop was a quick walk down Nicollet Mall, a pretty treelined street closed to cars and filled with clocks, fountains, and benches. In just a few minutes she found herself sitting in a line of swivel chairs in front of a long mirror.

The beautician, Rhonda, a pleasant-faced woman a little older than herself, did not recognize Jessica as anything but a woman with long, lovely hair. "You take beautiful care of your hair," she said. "You must spend a lot of time on it."

"I do." One day, several years back, Jessica had been nominated for one of the Country Music Association's awards. She had won before, but she had no chance at all of winning that year and they all knew it. But Nathan and Art had wanted her to get her share of television attention so they had sent her off to have her hair cornrowed in a hundred tiny braids clinging close to her scalp and then falling down to her waist in beads and feathers. Not only had she hated it, but it had taken two beauticians—they called themselves hair designers—an entire day to do, and Jessica was hard pressed to believe that three grown women couldn't find something better to do with their day.

That was another reason why she would have been

reluctant to go to one of the fashionable hair designers in Los Angeles. They would want people to notice their work. They would want everyone to look at her hair first, and who knows what sort of strange concoction they might have deposited on top of her head.

Rhonda did not aspire to be such an artist and simply began by asking Jessica what she wanted, a question that some hair designers felt beneath them.

"Something different," Jessica answered.

"Different from what you have now or different from everyone else?"

"Oh, no," Jessica assured her, "just different from this."

Rhonda's eyes met hers in the mirror with some sympathy. "Are you tired of being the girl with the hair?"

Jessica sighed. "More than you know."

Three hours later, when she looked in the mirror, she was pleased. Of course, when Rhonda had braided her hair in one thick braid and with great confidence sliced it off, Jessica had thought she would faint; she was sure it was all a terrible mistake, that she would regret it to the end of her days, that it would take her years and years to get her hair back.

But like many women whose appearance is part of their profession, Jessica was able to be objective about hers. She could look at the whole effect, not just focusing on what was new.

And the whole effect was good. Her hair still touched her shoulders, but it was layered with the top and sides much shorter, and a soft permanent had given Jessica something that she had never had before, curls. Her hair was very pretty, but it no longer called attention to itself; it was no longer the first thing a person would notice about her. And Jessica was so pleased with it that she left Rhonda a tip that so staggered the other woman that she tried to return it.

Out on the street again Jessica was surprised at how much freer she felt without her hair. It seemed easier to move without all that weight, and the curls tickled her cheeks and caressed the back of her neck. Not so many people looked at her; no one recognized her.

And when she started trying on clothes, she was delighted to find that she was able to decide whether or not she liked something. Maybe it was the softer hair that made deciding easier, but whatever the reason, this shopping trip was going better than she could have ever hoped.

Dayton's, Minneapolis's biggest department store, was the first place she bought anything—a pair of pleated white poplin slacks. She never wore white on the road; it got too dirty.

"Sign here please."

Jessica took the pen and the credit card slip and nearly wrote "Jess Butler." She checked herself and gingerly, for the first time in her life, traced out "Mrs."

However much her ideas and habits had been changed by her years out of the South, Jessica's manners were still pure country. Where she came from, "Mrs." got followed by a man's name. Awkwardly she completed the unfamiliar signature—"Mrs. Bret Cavanaugh"—and promptly felt like a forger.

But the salesclerk, instead of calling the store's security staff and having her arrested, barely glanced at the signature and handed Jessica the tan-colored shopping bag with her new clothes.

Her moment of uneasiness reminded her of Bret's

instructions to buy a wedding ring. So when she finished at Dayton's, she strolled through the Crystal Court again until she found a jewelry store.

She stepped inside and looked around her with pleasure. It was a small shop with soft lighting, dark blue carpeting, and antique walnut cases, beautifully polished. It felt like such a warm place, a very friendly place to shop. She could imagine customers getting personal service from a smiling white-haired jeweler—a young couple coming to buy an engagement ring, a man buying his beloved wife an anniversary gift, or all sorts of people coming in with all the other deliciously private reasons for buying jewelry.

Suddenly Jessica felt shy. She couldn't march into a store like this and buy herself a wedding band. Perhaps she could do it in some big, impersonal store with an arrogant, disinterested clerk, but not here.

She was just turning to leave when someone came out of the back room. He was hardly the portly, white-haired gentleman of her imagination, but a younger man, in his late thirties and blond.

"Can I help you?" He looked at her curiously, his eyebrows drawing together.

The man's regard was so intent that she felt she couldn't leave. Perhaps he thought her a shoplifter.

"I'd like to look at earrings, please," she said in her low, rich voice, "if you don't mind."

He looked at her for a long moment. "Of course not. They're over here." He went behind one of the walnut cases and started to unlock it. "Did you have anything in mind?"

Jessica still felt on edge over her silliness about the ring. "I don't know, but I think something smaller than

I have on. I just got my hair cut." Jessica started to look through the tray of earrings.

"I see that. It's a nice change."

Jessica swiftly raised her eyes to meet his. He knew who she was.

"I mean, haircuts usually are," he said immediately, obviously willing to let her be anonymous if she wished.

She smiled at him, sincerely, warmly. "The whole purpose of this was so that people wouldn't recognize me."

"It was your voice actually. When you came in, you just looked vaguely familiar."

"Then perhaps I should get my voice changed." Jessica smiled.

"Don't do that."

She laughed and easily found two pairs of earrings, as pleased with this newfound ability to make decisions as she was with the earrings. She handed them to the jeweler with Bret's American Express card, having noticed the familiar blue decal on the front door of the shop.

The man did not take the card. "Will you let me give you those? Your music has given me a lot of pleasure."

Jessica's blue eyes sparkled. She was used to compliments, to people trying to give her free merchandise, but this, for some reason, seemed particularly nice. "That's terribly sweet of you, but no, I can't take them. Your *wanting* to give them to me is enough."

"All right," he said and ran Bret's card through the machine without looking at it.

As Jessica signed the pale blue slip, he said, "At least I'll have your autograph."

"Actually," she apologized, "I signed it with my husband's name."

He glanced down at the slip and then his eyes widened. "You're married to Bret Cavanaugh?" He sounded as if this weren't a pleasant surprise.

"Yes. Do you know him?" When the man didn't answer, she went on, his silence forcing her to speak more than she would have normally. "Obviously I am not in Minneapolis very often, but we've been married for some time."

"I didn't know that he was married." The jeweler shook his head slowly. It seemed clear to Jessica that he was not so much surprised that Jess Butler was married to a local man, but that Bret Cavanaugh was married at all.

He still seemed shaken when she left although the farewells they exchanged were pleasant, and Jessica left enormously curious. Bret had told her that most people knew that he was married—why was this man so disturbed?

When Bret came home that evening, Jessica was upstairs resting from her adventure in the Great Outdoors.

"I'm home," he called in the most husbandly fashion and was slipping out of his suit coat when she peered over the gallery railing.

"What the—" He stopped dead, one arm still entangled in the coat sleeve as he looked up at her, amazed. "What did you do to yourself?"

"I got my hair cut," she said a little unnecessarily. "Do you like it?"

He blinked. "I hardly know. It's so sudden." He finished taking off his jacket. "Come down here and let me take a look at you."

He put his hands on her shoulders and gave her a good hard look. He tilted his head, examining her, not speaking. She grew apprehensive. What if he didn't like it?

Nervously she looked in his eyes. There was a dancing light in their gray depths. He was teasing her.

When she tried to hit him, he caught her flailing arm and burst out laughing. "Of course I like it. Jessie, it's just wonderful. It looks so, I don't know, so inviting." He reached up and rumpled his hand through the new curls. She shook her head and they fell back into place. "I wouldn't have dared to do that before, but this, I like it, it's really cute."

"Oh, no," Jessica protested laughingly, "not cute. I'm too old for cute."

"Okay." He thought for a moment. "How about enchanting?"

"Enchanting, that's good." Jessica mimicked a Los Angeles record producer. "I can live with enchanting."

"Then enchanting it is." He looked at her again. "It's so different; it'll take some getting used to." He moved into the kitchen and got himself a beer out of the refrigerator. "Why did you do it?" he asked and then offered her a beer.

She shook her head, refusing the beer. "I was sick of taking care of it, and I didn't want to be recognized all the time."

He held the beer can against his lip for a moment longer than he needed to, then lowered it slowly. "Well, good for you."

"Someone still did recognize me," she continued, really quite pleased that Bret liked her hair, that he approved of her getting it cut. "It was the man in the jewelry store, but he said he knew me by my voice."

As she spoke Jessica thought how lovely it was not to

live alone, how wonderful it was to have someone to describe your day to.

"Oh, did you get yourself a ring?" He glanced down at her hand, clearly assuming that that's why she had been in a jewelry store.

Jessica blushed. "Oh, I didn't. I don't know, Bret, but—"

"I understand," he said. "We'll go together."

Jessica was surprised that he did indeed seem to understand, even without her trying to explain. This sensitivity, so very unexpected in him, confused her a little, and she spoke quickly, trying to hide her confusion. "This man in the store, he seemed to know you. He was very surprised that you were married."

"Who was he? What store was it?"

"I don't know." Jessica moved to the counter and flipped through the credit card slips she had put there. "Jensen's Jewelry."

Bret raised his eyebrows, but all he said was "Oh, Peter."

"Do you know him?"

"Just barely. I do know his wife though." Then Bret immediately changed the subject. "Do you want to give me those things?" He nodded to the credit card slips.

"Of course." Jessica handed them to him. "And here is a check." She had carefully totaled up the bills and written him a check on her California bank covering the total. She was quite proud of herself for doing it all in such a businesslike fashion. On the road, she almost never touched money. The road manager took care of all the expenses, and any bills that were hers personally were sent to Nathan's office for payment.

Writing out this check had made her feel like a model citizen, a paradigm of fiscal responsibility.

But Bret just grinned at her and did not take the check.

"Bret," she said in exasperation, "you are being ridiculous. I can't let you buy my clothes."

"Oh, sure you can. It won't hurt you a bit."

She shook her head. "Bret, no, I can't have you paying my bills. It's not right."

"I can't take money from you," he returned. "That's not right either, at least it isn't in my book."

Jessica sighed, having a pretty clear idea what book it was he was reading. "Now, Bret," she pleaded, "you wouldn't go all stubborn and Southern on me, would you?"

"I just might." His gray eyes twinkled. "Look here, Jessie, I can see your point of view—you went out and bought your things planning on paying for them yourself. But you can see mine too—I am a pig-headed, spoiled Southern male who likes having his own way. So I think the way to resolve it is for us to figure out who is going to hate losing most, and we both know perfectly well it's me."

"Well, maybe we should figure out who has the most money," she returned, "because we both know perfectly well that's me."

"Now, now, that was such a low blow that you are disqualified," Bret announced happily, "and I win by default."

Jessica immediately apologized. "You're right; I shouldn't have said that. I am sorry."

"I was kidding," he said in a you-should-have-known-better tone. "I don't mind that you make more than me, not in the least. You make more than everyone. But I'm not going to spend your money, that's all."

"I'm not asking you to," Jessica pointed out, although she would give him every dime she had if she thought he wanted them. "It's just silly for me to spend yours."

"Well, probably," he acknowledged, "and if you were waiting tables and I were parking cars or pumping gas, I'd pool our money happily—"

"We'd have no choice," Jessica pointed out realistically.

He ignored her. "But I can afford it. I think I've earned the right to be silly about money once in a while. Look Jessie, until I stopped and bought some yogurt and herbal tea, or whatever that stuff was, last week, I hadn't spent a cent on you—literally, I don't recall ever taking you to a movie or buying you a cup of coffee—"

"You bought me a beer once."

"Good for me. When?"

Jessica tried to keep her voice cool. "You may not remember, but it was the Christmas before I moved to Los Angeles."

His eyes suddenly darkened. "At the Starlight? I remember," he said bluntly. "But it isn't paying for the beers that I remember."

"Well, you did."

"A beer every ten years or so—you haven't been an expensive wife, Jessica Susan. Now let's go upstairs and see these new clothes."

He sat on her bed, and like husbands and wives everywhere, Jessica eagerly showed him her new clothes, holding up this blouse to her, assuring him that that dress, while it looked like nothing on the hanger, looked great on. In a typically Jessica fashion, she offered to return anything that he did not like, to which Bret, revealing his inadequate understanding of a husband's role, replied that she was a goose and that she should wear whatever she liked.

That night as she lay in bed, Jessica kept thinking, not about her new clothes and certainly not about money, but about the casual remark that had darkened Bret's eyes, a remark that stirred a sweep of old memories.

*It isn't paying for the beers that I remember.*

She had gone home for Christmas nervously that year. The decision to move from Nashville to Los Angeles had been made, and Jessica had a pretty clear idea of what this next career move would entail: a shedding of her sweet, good-girl-done-wrong-by image. She worried about how Amy and Clay would react to it, and she had gone home to try to prepare them.

She couldn't seem to find the right moment. The house was always full; Luke had just gotten married to a local girl and various members of her family kept stopping by just in case the Cavanaughs, now ten in number, got a little lonely. Finally the night before she had to leave, she just flat out asked Amy if she could talk to Clay and her alone.

They both sat through all of Jessica's elaborate explanations, her careful distinctions about exactly what type of songs she would be singing and which she wouldn't. Then Amy simply asked, "Are you going to embarrass yourself?"

"No," Jessica replied, now seeing that Amy had managed to go right to the heart of things, explaining exactly in a few words exactly what Jessica had been trying to say for a half hour. "No, Mama, I am not."

"Then you aren't going to embarrass us. And you know that even if you go up on stage without your clothes on, you are still our girl and we love you."

Jessica would have cried if Clay, trying to herd off female tears, hadn't spoken immediately. "I can't say that I want you to be doing *that*, but look here, Jessica Susan, isn't it Bret you ought to be telling this to, not us?"

Frankly, telling Bret hadn't occurred to her. Even when Clay mentioned it, it didn't seem necessary. Oh, she knew that she and Bret were married, but they just didn't seem to have a lot to do with each other's lives. He always went to great lengths to track her down on her birthday, and some years his call was the only thing that made that day seem special. But other than that, they had no contact. He was home now, having come down from the cold Minnesota winter, but Jessica had only spoken to him casually. With so many people around, there was not much of a chance for a private conversation.

Jessica left the kitchen still on edge. She wasn't sure what was bothering her. Amy and Clay had reacted beautifully—she had thought that their response was the only thing that worried her about these career changes, but clearly she was still nervous about something.

In the hall she found Luke saying good-night to his wife, Judy—to his dismay he had been banished out to the old bunkhouse to sleep with Bret and their youngest brother, Tate, while Jessica joined Judy in the room that the young couple had started to share.

Luke was watching his wife go upstairs, a hard, concentrated look on his face.

"Well, Mr. Luke," Jessica drawled, "how much is it worth to you if I forget to go up there tonight?"

He turned, surprised. He had been so engrossed in Judy he hadn't noticed Jessica come in.

"A lot," he growled. "But not enough to make you sleep out in the bunkhouse."

"Good heavens." She laughed. "I usually sleep on a bus with ten men. It isn't going to hurt me to spend a night in a bunkhouse with my brothers."

Luke looked at her curiously. "Bret isn't—" Then he broke off and just said, "Maybe not, but Ma would sure hurt me if she found out about it."

He started out the door and then turned back to her. "I'm going out for a beer; do you want to come?"

It sounded like a good idea; she was still too jumpy to sleep.

"Where do you want to go?" he asked as they walked to his truck.

"Wherever you were planning." Although Jessica had sung in hundreds of bars and honky-tonks, she had never gone to one in her hometown.

"Well, I was going to the Starlight. Bret, Tate, and the Preston boys"—the Prestons were Judy's family, Luke's in-laws—"are there, but I can't take you there."

"Why not?"

"It's a bit of a rough place; I wouldn't take Judy."

"Luke," she said as she slid into the truck, "remember what I do for a living; I'm not going to see anything that I haven't seen a hundred times. Anyway, I feel like I've barely spoken two words to Bret or Tate the whole time I've been home, and I'm leaving tomorrow."

"Well, I guess between the three of us, we can take care of you."

The Starlight was exactly what Jessica had expected—

dark and seedy, with a long bar, small round tables with
ketchup bottles on them, a jukebox with a little area
cleared for dancing. As she had told Luke, she had
seen it all hundreds of times. She had also seen every
hired hand in the place stop his drinking, his swearing,
his fighting, and listen to her. She didn't sing in such
places anymore, but she felt like they had been her
training ground, where she had learned everything
there was to know about tough audiences.

Bret was leaning against the bar, talking to Cole Preston, his hand curled around a beer. Jessica had also
seen thousands of men standing like this, but suddenly
Bret looked different from all the others as if he were
taller, healthier, cut out of a better grade of fabric.

"I'll get us some beer, and we'll go to a table," Luke
was saying.

But Jessica followed him; she was perfectly capable
of sitting at the bar.

Bret nodded at his brother warmly, but when over
Luke's shoulder he saw Jessica, he straightened and
demanded, "Why the hell did you bring her here?"

"Now, Bret," she answered for herself, "I work in
places like this."

To her surprise, her quick words didn't make him
angry. He paused and lifted his beer. "I bet you don't
anymore," he said lightly, smiling at her. "If those
guys are still booking you in dumps like this, then you
need to hire yourself some new help. Now, let me buy
you a beer because I want to hear all about this move to
California." Bret jerked his head at the bartender and
when the beers arrived, he carried them over to one of
the small tables.

Perhaps because he too had left home—he and she
were the only Cavanaughs not still in Georgia—Jessica

found it surprisingly easy to talk to him. At first they just talked about leaving the South, and gradually Jessica began to confide in him some of her anxieties about the direction her career was going to take.

"Are you going to sing trash?" he asked bluntly.

"Absolutely not." *Trash* was a word Jessica couldn't have ever defined, but she knew exactly what it was when she ran into it, and she knew that although the new songs she had been learning were provocative, taunting, even arousing, they weren't trashy.

"Then what are you worried about?"

"It's just such a big risk."

"Ah-ha." Bret smiled. "Now you are talking my language. I don't know much about this business of different bass lines, but I know all about taking risks." He pulled his chair closer to the table, suddenly more alert. "The first thing to do is figure out just exactly what you have got to lose."

"Everything," Jessica sighed, surprised to discover just how much this had been worrying her.

"That's just not true," he returned immediately. "First of all, you'll never lose the family, and second, whatever happens, you aren't going to starve so you aren't really risking everything."

"Just my career then."

"Well, sure," he said airily. "But people don't have careers to lose if they haven't taken some risks. You took a chance going to Nashville in the first place. So take another chance. Anyway, country-music fans are nearly as loyal as family; they will probably love you whatever you do out in California. So all you are doing is risking making a fool of yourself on the pop charts."

"Is that supposed to be comforting?"

"No, just realistic. But I don't imagine you will make a fool of yourself. You are just too good."

"Bret!" Jessica blushed with delight. "Do you really mean that?" He hadn't complimented her in years.

He shrugged. "Sure, but I am not saying anything you haven't heard a million times. Come on, let's dance." He stood up, extending his hand.

"I don't dance very well." She held back.

"I find that hard to believe," he said, his arm closing around her waist.

"It's true. When there is music and other people start to dance, I usually end up singing, so I haven't had a lot of practice."

"Well, just fake it and I won't tell anyone."

Jessica's excellent sense of rhythm got her through the rough spots, and soon she was able to stop concentrating on her feet and let her body just instinctively follow Bret's.

She suddenly realized that the hand she had been resting on his shoulder was moving lightly against him almost in a caress. It embarrassed her. "This is a nice shirt," she said, trying to explain her gesture away.

"You can get good wool up North. Do you want me to send you one?"

"I don't imagine I would need it in California, but I do like the way this one feels." Her fingertips brushed against the wool again.

"Then we are even because I like the way yours feels too."

"Bret," she said, laughing, "it's just cotton."

"Maybe it isn't the shirt I like." His voice was gruff and he gathered her tighter. She could feel her breasts press into his chest.

Jessica's mouth went dry, and she could hardly even hear the music over the sound of his heart against her cheek.

The music stopped and Bret's hold loosened. He stepped away and smiled down at her. "Do you want to do that again? Get some more practice?"

She nodded; she couldn't speak, listening to the jukebox as its machinery whirled and clicked through the record change. Suddenly some very familiar notes ground out of it, and in a moment Jessica's own voice filled the room.

Jessica's theoretical knowledge of men was vast— she had heard a lot from the ten guys on the bus. So she had a pretty fair notion of why, when Bret slipped his arms around her again, he did not this time hold her so tightly. But her practical experience was extremely limited, and so it was with a certain curiosity that Jessica, after a few bars of her song, pressed herself close to him.

She felt a shudder rack through his body. "Jesus, Jessie, don't tease."

The feel of him had driven all curiosity from her mind, leaving behind only a whirling pool of desire. "I'm not," she whispered.

His hand immediately slipped to the small of her back to keep her against him, and in a moment his other arm closed around her as well, circling her slender body completely until his hand rested on her side just where the swell of her breast began. His fingertips moved against her, feeling her softness.

Jessica sighed.

"Let's get out of here," he said abruptly.

She swallowed. "But I came with Luke."

"And you're leaving with me."

As soon as they were outside, he stepped in the dark shadows out of the neon glare and pulled her to him again, one arm closing around her warmly.

He did not kiss her. He lifted his hand to her cheek, touching it, and then his thumb gently traced the curve of her mouth, moving lightly across her lips, softening them, easing them apart until he could feel the inviting moistness.

She felt as if she could stand there forever in the deep shadow of a Southern night, feeling the warmth of this man against her, his body strong and knowing. This man who was Bret.

He curled his hand around her face, lifting it, as he bent his head to her. His lips moved gently across hers, softly, with a poignant sweetness that denied the urgency she knew was surging through him. It was as if he knew that he was more experienced, more easily aroused, and his slowness was assuring her that he would not leave her behind. Gradually the pressure on her lips increased, tantalizing them into parting, into allowing this first invasion of her body by his.

When one of his arms slipped away from her, she sighed in protest, not wanting him to let her go. But his hands moved to her shoulder, then slipped down between their bodies, fulfilling the sweet promise his teasing fingers had made on the dance floor as his strong hand moved against her, feeling the delicious weight of her through the soft cotton of her shirt.

"Jessie, I want you." His voice was low in her ear.

She couldn't speak, not with his hand touching her as it was, the lazy path of his thumb tracing, treasuring, her body's keen response. She could only nod and move against him, letting that be her answer.

Then he stepped back and turned her face to the

moonlight. "Look, if we go—" He cleared his throat and started over. "Do you understand that if we go home, we can't be together? I am bunking with Luke and Tate; you're with Judy. I want to take you to a motel."

"A motel?" she said blankly.

"Did you think I was going to make you get in the backseat of the car?" he asked gently.

She shook her head; she just hadn't thought about where they would go.

"Is it going to bother you to go home in the morning with everyone knowing we stayed out together? You know how curious they will all be. Although, for what it's worth, we are married."

She couldn't meet his eyes and twisted her face out of his light grasp. "No, it won't bother me."

He lifted her chin with his finger, forcing her to look back at him. "You're lying," he said bluntly. "It would bother you a lot."

"That doesn't matter."

"It does to me," he said crisply.

"Bret, no, I will go with you."

"I know you will, but you don't much want to." Then as he led her back to the car, he said something that she didn't understand. "Don't worry about me. I'm a pro at this."

It was a familiar memory, dark and sweet. And there were times, when she was singing certain songs, when she'd remember how she felt climbing up the farmhouse stairs that evening, glancing over her shoulder to see Bret watching her, an ardent light burning in his gray eyes.

Jessica woke up earlier the next morning than she had in years. When she came down the spiral stairs, she heard Bret moving about the kitchen and then she heard his voice. "Hi, it's me."

He must have called someone on the phone, and she guessed from the familiar greeting that it was someone in the family. Who else would he dare call this early?

But his next words made it clear that it wasn't family. "I just wanted to know what you want to do about that party Saturday. Do you want me to skip it? You know I can't go without Jessie, but I don't want to embarrass you."

Jessica was instantly curious. Although Bret often called her "Jessie," he nearly always spoke about her as "Jessica." So whom was he talking to; what party was it, and why might whoever be embarrassed?

"Only if you're sure," Bret's voice said. "See you then."

He was hanging up the phone as she came into the kitchen. He smiled immediately. "You're up early. How do you feel?"

"Wonderful."

"Well, you look it. I do like your hair."

"I'm glad." Jessica ran a hand through the new soft curls and leaned against the counter, watching him. Her eyes were drawn to his hands as he took the top off the coffee percolator with a sharp tug. They were still quarterback's hands—swift, sure, instinctive—and Jessica again found herself thinking of the one time they had touched her body with passion.

"Do you want something to eat?" His voice was completely matter-of-fact. If the memories of the Starlight bar had disturbed his sleep last night, there was no sign of it this morning.

"You know, I would." Jessica was still surprised whenever she felt hungry. "But let me make it," she said.

"I thought you had forgotten how to cook."

"I have," she said, taking the egg carton from him. "So I am counting on you to be very polite about the results."

He grinned and took the morning paper off the counter. "You expect a lot of a man."

*Maybe that's because I've always gotten a lot from you.*

But she didn't say that.

Jessica managed to struggle her way through scrambling eggs and putting toast in the toaster. "May we eat outside?" she asked. "It looks like a lovely morning."

"Sure," he answered immediately. "I spent enough money on that furniture out there. I ought to use it every so often."

The terrace had comfortable chaises with thick cushions covered in a grid pattern of white and green. In one corner was a glass-topped table on which Jessica set out breakfast. As they ate Bret read the paper and Jessica looked out at the river view that still fascinated her, although her eyes kept drifting back to him—or rather what showed of him from behind the newspaper.

It seemed very married, eating breakfast with him like this in the pleasant morning air, and suddenly she spoke. "Bret, do you ever wonder what it would have been like if I had come to Atlanta with you after I finished high school?"

And, although she would have never admitted it, Jessica was filled with visions, if not of vine-covered cottages, at least of a nice split-level with a two-car garage and a fenced-in backyard.

"That's easy," Bret said, turning a page of the paper. "We would have been divorced."

She dropped her fork. "How can you say that?"

"Because it's true. Now, don't sit there with that

hurt look on your face. I know you would have done everything in your power to be a terrific wife and I'm sure you would have been. No, it would have been me. I was so restless in those days; I wouldn't have walked out on you like the men in those songs of yours, but after a while you would have wished I would."

"Bret, no." She shook her head. "Never."

"Yes. You remember what I was like then. There was something in me that wouldn't let me play it safe. Walker and I were up here, taking risks like crazy people. We loved it; it was exactly what we wanted to be doing, and we could do it because neither of us had any responsibilities. If you'd been with me, I'd have stayed in Atlanta working for someone, and I would have gone mad. A marriage wouldn't have survived."

"But Walker's married," she protested.

"Walker's married *now*. He wasn't ready before. He got engaged during his senior year, but the girl's parents had the excellent sense to make them promise to wait a year, and apparently it didn't take her even close to a year to see that he wasn't ready to settle down."

"He is now?"

He laughed. "Well, Lynn—his wife—sure hopes so. Actually, I think there's a way in which something in both of us is satisfied. We don't have fits everytime we have a scrap of money wasting away in a bank. We used to." He smiled briefly at his once wilder self. "If we hadn't had our chance to be the brash young capitalists for a while, we probably both would have, as my brother once said, wrapped our cars around a pair of trees."

Jessica was too realistic not to see the truth of what he was saying. "So in a way, our marriage, the way it was—"

"Was the best thing that could have happened to me," he finished for her. "I probably would have married someone after college and wrecked her life as well as my own. Being married to you kept me out of making commitments I couldn't have kept."

"Isn't it strange how things work out?" Jessica mused.

"It is," he replied briefly and then changed the subject, obviously not inclined to dwell on such personal matters. "What are you going to do today?"

"I think I shall spend the morning being glad I am not drying my hair." She smiled. "Then I think I may try to make dinner." Until this morning Bret had done all the cooking.

"Well, good luck. Don't do anything fancy."

"I don't think you need to worry about that," she replied. "'Don't hurt yourself' would probably be better advice."

He laughed and started to spread jam on his toast. "Do you feel like facing the world yet? Walker and Lynn have said that I am to bring you to dinner as soon as you are ready to move about."

"Anytime," she agreed eagerly. "I would love to meet them." She was especially interested in meeting Walker Buchanan, this man that Bret was so close to, whom he claimed to resemble. If Walker had been ready to settle down....

"And some friends of ours in their neighborhood are giving a party Saturday night." Bret's voice interrupted her thoughts. "Would you like to go?"

That made her remember the phone conversation she had overheard. As she poured him more coffee, she asked, "Bret, do you have a girl friend?"

He stared at her over his coffee cup. "A girl friend? Jessica, I am thirty, a little beyond *girl* friends."

"You know what I mean, are you involved with anyone?"

"Not while you are here," he said emphatically.

"But before?"

"Yes, if you must know." He put down his cup. "I've been seeing a woman pretty regularly."

Jessica hardly knew what to say. She wished she hadn't brought this up. "Oh, Bret, I am sorry," she faltered. "Have I spoiled things by coming? Were you serious about her?"

"No and no."

Jessica watched him fold the paper back on the stock market quotations. He started to examine them. "Aren't you going to tell me any more?" she asked impatiently.

He glanced up. "What do you want to know? Her name is Karen Jensen. I met her through Walker and Lynn; she lives in their neighborhood. She has an eight-year-old son, and her husband—"

"Her husband?" Jessica nearly spilled her juice. "Bret, is she married?"

"Yes, she is, Jessica, but then"—he looked at her for a moment—"so am I. And she knew that." His voice was crisp, but then softened. "Her husband had walked out on her. Left her for a nineteen-year-old."

Jessica felt a surge of sympathy for this unknown woman. "How awful."

"It was. She's only thirty-four, but when we first got involved, she was feeling very over-the-hill, unattractive, all that."

Jessica glanced across the table at Bret, suddenly aware that if he put his mind to it, he and his smile might go a long way to convincing a woman that thirty-four had a great deal more to offer than nineteen.

"She still feels a little fragile," he continued, unaware of her gaze, "and I hope she doesn't feel like I am rejecting her like he did. Your coming was so sudden I could only talk to her about it on the phone." He was obviously unhappy with the way that situation had to be handled.

"I hope you didn't tell her who I was," Jessica said.

"I don't think I did, but she wouldn't have gone to the papers if that's what you're worried about." For the first time Jessica heard a faintly contemptuous note in his voice. "She has a child and certainly has less interest in seeing this splashed about than either you or I."

"I wasn't thinking of that at all," Jessica said with dignity. With her sure, nearly mysterious sense of other people's feelings, she had imagined the other woman, still wounded because her husband had left her for some young nymph, learning that the next man in her life had left her for Jess Butler, whose public image, whatever the limp-dishrag reality behind it, was quite a sexy one.

Bret just shrugged. "It was her husband you met in the jewelry store, Peter Jensen. He knew I was seeing her; she must not have told him that I was married."

"That man?" Jessica was amazed, remembering how he had first tried to hide his recognition of her and then how he had wanted to give her the earrings. "But he seemed so nice."

"I suspect that he is a perfectly nice, decent sort of fellow who felt forty closing in and made one disastrous mistake."

As she carried the dishes back to the kitchen, Jessica thought about the relationship Bret had described with Karen Jensen. She knew that there were a lot of women who had been rather buffeted by the winds of a permissive society. She had seen some of them show up as temporary girl friends of band members. Their situation was often extremely difficult—their emotions were so shattered that they weren't ready to love again, but their confidence was so shaken that they needed to know that they could still attract some man.

It occurred to Jessica that those women would have been a lot better off if they had met Bret instead of the careless, insensitive, irresponsible musicians. Obviously he felt his marriage kept him from making any sort of permanent commitment to a woman, but he would be able to do a lot for the way she felt about herself, to help restore her confidence so that she could someday love someone else. It was, Jessica thought, probably a pattern for his relationships; he might have helped a number of women in just that way.

Wait a minute, she stopped herself. What was she thinking of? This was Bret Cavanaugh she was thinking about, not some sensitive talk-show host.

No one knew better than she that Bret would do anything to protect a woman from things he understood—poverty, any kind of physical threat or danger. But what would Bret Cavanaugh, quick, arrogant, and competitive, understand about the troubles that afflicted women much more frequently: loneliness, self-doubt, uncertainty?

She had to be careful. She couldn't create another fantasy character and call him Bret. She had done that as a girl, but she was a woman now, and the stakes were higher. Much higher.

# Chapter Six

For the rest of the week Jessica played house. There was no other way to describe it; she knew it and so did Bret. She started to reacquaint herself with a kitchen. The years of eating in restaurants had robbed her of her confidence and dulled her instincts. She looked up a recipe for fried chicken although she had been frying chicken since she was eight, and she obediently measured even the salt and pepper although as a girl she would have no more thought of measuring than she would have thought of wearing jeans to church.

And she cleaned, quite happily wandering around the apartment with a bottle of Windex and a roll of paper towels. It had been so long since she had done any housework that the most wearisome tasks delighted her. Picking up a stack of magazines, sorting out the old ones, dusting the tabletop, and laying the magazines back down in some careful array seemed very wonderful to her, so straightforward and clear-cut, nothing like the dark mysteries of an entranced audience.

Bret checked out a company car and left her his so she could run errands too. She would stop at the dry cleaners, picking up some of Bret's shirts, leaving off more. She would go to the drugstore and buy aspirin, shaving cream, and nailpolish. She would pull the car up to the front of the Red Owl and watch the boy load her groceries into the car.

She knew that her delight with the simple ordinariness of this routine would fade; she assumed that sooner or later she would start to crave the glitter of her own world, but for the moment she wanted to cherish this, to relish it while it all still felt so fresh.

To her surprise, she truly enjoyed living with a man. It seemed silly to find herself particularly liking masculine company because on the road she was with men nearly twenty-four hours a day.

Of course, she thought of the people she traveled with primarily as musicians or technicians; she was conscious of them as men only at slightly offensive moments—when she'd stumble across someone's laundry wadded up in the bus or when another one's face would suddenly harden in a concentrated look and he'd defiantly sling his arm around some groupie and lead her off.

Sharing a home with Bret was quite a different matter. When Jess Butler sat down to breakfast with men, as she did more mornings than not, they were foultempered and disheveled from an all-night bus ride. But when Bret came down the spiral staircase in the morning, he had showered and shaved; he'd be wearing a fresh shirt with a neatly knotted tie and would drape a suit coat over the back of the sofa. And if, like the musicians, he would open the morning paper first to the sports page, when Bret finished with the box scores, he'd then turn to the financial page, checking the stock market quotations, something Cade and the rest of the band would have never dreamed of doing.

Such things reminded Jessica of how different this man was from the ones she worked with, how he had a life in the business community that she knew nothing of. When she'd get his suits ready for the cleaners, she'd find in the pockets the little relics of his day: pink phone messages and white folded programs from luncheons or presentations; business cards, both his and other people's; paperclips that he'd pulled from some report he'd been reading and had carelessly thrust in his pocket; an occasional swizzle stick if he had taken a customer out for a drink; and sometimes strange little pieces of plastic and metal, some with wires trailing out of them, which she supposed were some part of something they made.

It fascinated her. This man looked like Bret, he still smiled like Bret, but he led a life so entirely at odds with the Bret she had known in Georgia.

On Saturday night they drove over to St. Paul. The plan was to have dinner with Walker and Lynn and then go to the party with them. The car swept past the state capital building and the cathedral and into Ramsey Hill, a neighborhood of tall trees and old, large houses.

Bret stopped on a quiet, green street that was lined with shaded lawns enclosed by low iron fences. The houses were all different, some were brick, some stone, some clapboard; each had its own turn-of-the-century charm, but they shared a solid respectable look. To Jessica, the neighborhood almost looked like a movie set. "Give me something 'family,'" the director would have cried.

She sighed. She had been an entertainer too long. She had spent so much time making fantasies seem real that now reality was starting to seem like an illusion.

She wanted to confide in Bret; he'd help her get

everything straight—what was real and what wasn't—but when she spoke, to her dismay, quite different words came out. "Which house is theirs?"

He could only answer the question he had heard. "The white one."

Jessica peered at it through the car window. The huge homes of some California musicians and record company executives had never appealed to her; the sweeping lines of those contemporary structures, however beautiful, did not stir any response in her. But this house—well, to Jessica's country heart, this seemed like a real home.

It was three stories of white clapboard, dotted with dormers and bay windows. A wide front porch led to double doors set with oval panes of etched glass. Jessica thought it lovely; for such a large house it was charming and inviting. She said so.

Bret laughed. "Brace yourself. It's the opposite of my place; it looks great from the outside, but it is a complete mess inside. This neighborhood is on the way back up after having gotten awfully run-down. When Walker and Lynn bought this place last year, it was cut up into five apartments."

As they were getting out of the car, the door opened and a woman stepped out. She was a pretty strawberry blonde, her hair a halo of short curls around her face. She came down the steps to meet them. "Jessica, I'm Lynn."

Then the door opened again and a man came out onto the porch.

She had never met him before, but when Walker Buchanan opened his front door, Jessica's heart went out just at the sight of him. His hair was light brown, a variety of sun-streaked shades, and his features were finely chiseled with an open, welcoming look about them. He looked so familiar, so thoroughly and completely Southern, that for a moment she was homesick.

He started to speak, but as Jessica put her hand on the stair railing and looked up, he stopped, a confused look coming across his face.

Again it was her voice that did it. "You must be Walker," she said, about to introduce herself. "I'm Jess—"

"What on earth are *you* doing here?" He seemed dazed.

She blinked. "I think you invited me."

Then Bret's lazy voice drifted from the walk behind her. "There's just one little thing I forgot to tell you about her, Walker."

Walker glanced at his partner. "Just one *little* thing?" He came down the front stairs shaking his head in apology for his abrupt behavior. "I'm pleased to meet you, ma'am." He put out his hand. "If you were just Bret's wife, I'd give you a kiss, but as it is, maybe we'd better shake hands."

"Nonsense," Jessica said firmly and stood on tiptoe to brush his cheek.

"Would someone please explain what is going on?" Lynn asked patiently.

Walker turned to his wife. "Do you know who Jess Butler is?"

"Sure, you play her records over and over until I am thoroughly sick of them."

"Be careful," Walker cautioned. "You're looking at her."

Lynn shot Jessica a startled glance. "You're joking?" Jessica shook her head.

Walker continued, "And that fellow there"—he

jerked his thumb toward Bret—"he must be Mr. Butler."

Bret laughed and came up the front steps. "Watch your mouth, boy," he drawled.

Lynn was still amazed. "But I thought you had long hair."

"She did," Bret said, greeting Lynn with a light kiss. "But she got it chopped off a couple of days ago."

She looked up at him, shaking her head. "Why didn't you tell us?"

"I said she was a singer working out in California," Bret pointed out.

"Yeah, and made it sound like she crooned in the corner of some cocktail lounge," Walker accused him. "Good Lord, we've gone to record stores and bought her albums together and you didn't say a blessed thing, just let me ramble on—" He broke off, and Jessica saw a dull red color his face. He had obviously said some things to Bret about Jess Butler that he would not normally say to a man about his wife.

Bret laughed. "That's just it, Walker. Would you have enjoyed those records just as much if you knew it was your partner's wife singing?"

"But, of course," Walker said with great dignity that no one believed. "My interest in your music, Miss Butler, has been marked with a purely aesthetic appreciation."

"Well, I for one," Lynn broke in, "am just as glad I didn't know. I was in enough of a tizzy about making dinner for Bret's long-lost wife; if I'd known she were some famous star, I would probably have had to quit my job just to make this one meal. Now why don't we go inside and have something to drink?"

Jessica was glad Bret had warned her about the

house; otherwise she would have had trouble being polite when beyond the beautiful front doors, she found herself walking into a construction zone.

To her left was a staircase elegantly curving past a bay window, but it had no banister and one of the steps was missing. She could tell that she was standing in a front hall, but the wall dividing it from the living room seemed to be missing—only a row of studs marked its place. The room beyond the studs was quite large, but filled with sawhorses, power tools, sheets of plywood, and piles of Sheetrock.

They passed through the hall and another construction site that had clearly once pretended to be some sort of room, and then into what was, Jessica saw with a gasp of delight, the most beautiful kitchen she had ever been in.

It was huge. The counters were butcher block, and reaching to the ceiling were white cabinets with slim brass pulls. It had all the conveniences: a regular sink and a vegetable sink, a microwave, recessed cutting boards, as well as all sorts of engaging details that made it very individual. The stove was six gas burners set under a slab of heavy iron grillwork that, Walker said, had been the radiator cover in an old bank. The wall tiles had been brought from Sweden by some young emigrant bride more than a century ago.

"Is the rest of the house going to look like this?" Jessica breathed, gazing around her.

"Right before they haul us into debtor's prison." Walker laughed. "This isn't cheap, doing this."

Jessica suddenly yearned for something like this. Her California apartment was so anonymous. Nathan and Art were badgering her to buy a house; certainly she had money for this and more.

But she knew perfectly well that a house of hers would never be like this. It was clear from the way Lynn talked about the kitchen she had done an enormous amount of work on it herself, planning it, combing antique stores for tiles she loved, spending time. Jessica wouldn't have the time; she would have to hire someone to do it, and it would come out beautiful and impersonal just like all the other expensive homes of people who were too busy to live in them. It would be like a movie set.

After Walker had given them all drinks, Bret drew him off to the other side of the kitchen. Jessica guessed that he was giving the two women a chance to get to know each other. She remembered that Lynn had mentioned having a job. "What do you do?"

"I am an interior decorator," Lynn answered.

"I should have guessed from this kitchen," Jessica smiled. Then a very promising thought occurred to her. "Did you do Bret's apartment?" The more she saw of his home, the more sure she was that he had had a great deal of help decorating it. His bedroom had made that particularly clear. It was a cool, quiet room, done in shades of gray: pearl, dove, and charcoal. It was impossible to walk in it and not think of his eyes. But a bedroom highlighting the color of his eyes was an affectation Jessica knew Bret was incapable of, and she had to admit that she would be pleased if it were his partner's wife, or any other professional, who had realized that this man should have a gray bedroom.

"Yes, I did," Lynn answered. "Bret simply refused to have anything to do with it; he said he was too busy to care. So I just had to guess from what I knew of Walker's taste, hoping that they were as much alike in this as they are in everything else. I do hope you like it.''

''Oh, I do—very much. It's so comfortable; it doesn't scream out 'decorator' if you know what I mean.''

''I do.'' Lynn smiled. ''Actually I don't do many residences. I am a commercial designer. That's how I met Walker. He and Bret added on an employee cafeteria to their office two years ago, and I did some work on it for them.''

''What are they like to work with?'' Jessica was very curious about Bret's professional self, the side of him she never saw.

Lynn suddenly laughed, and a surprising blush colored her face. ''It's just amazing. I went out there for the first meeting and, let's face it, in my business you don't meet a lot of great men—the two of them just took my breath away. I was wearing my little career-girl blue blazer, and of course, they both had on suits, but somehow it felt like I had walked into a cigarette ad, you know, one of those where great-looking men, the real rugged, manly types, are sitting on horses or around a campfire. Bret sat there with those wonderful gray eyes, calling me 'ma'am' and then Walker, the jerk, started rolling up his sleeves while I was supposed to be talking about the spacing of electrical outlets. To this day he swears it wasn't deliberate. I went right back and told my boss there was no way I could work with the two of them. If that was what all Southern men were like, I couldn't trust myself below Iowa.''

''So you never really worked with them?''

''Oh, no. My boss said that no one had ever heard anything like that about either of them, and anyway, I should learn to handle it. But they were model clients and such complete gentlemen that it got irritating.

They never said or did anything that was remotely sexual—but there was something about them...you just didn't forget that you were female."

"So when did you start going out with Walker?" Clearly these memories were precious to Lynn, and Jessica didn't mind listening. She liked hearing about how ordinary people got together, about romance among people who didn't take photographers with them on dates.

"About the minute I stopped working with him," Lynn answered. "Two hours after their check arrived paying our bill, he sent some flowers. He started proposing about three weeks later, but it took me a year before I was sure that I wasn't swept away by his Southern charm."

They looked over at the two men. Lynn was right, Jessica thought, there was something about them. It didn't matter that at the moment they were standing at a kitchen counter talking about the Dow-Jones average; they seemed to move in an aura of fresh air, as if they had always just come in from the outdoors. Their eyes were bright, their features alert, their limbs strong. The pair would take a woman's breath away.

Walker was suddenly conscious of their gaze. "What are you talking about?"

"I was just telling Jessica how you threatened to stop sleeping with me if I didn't marry you."

Walker turned red. "Lord, Bret, women do tell each other the damnedest things. Those are family secrets, Lynn."

"What do you mean?" Bret asked lazily. "I knew all about it."

"Well, sure you did," Walker returned. "But you don't count."

The bond between the two men was clearly a very strong one.

"Speaking of family secrets," Lynn said to Jessica, "is it really true—this story Walker tells me of your marrying Bret when you were fourteen?"

Jessica nodded. "It is. Does it seem odd to you?"

"Very," said Lynn with a directness that Jessica soon learned was a great part of her charm. "But then lots of things you Southerners do seem odd to me. Why didn't someone call the county and get you in a foster home? And wasn't it strange to have a husband at fourteen? I got one at twenty-seven, and I found it exceedingly strange even then."

"But that's just because you chose such a strange one to begin with," Bret pointed out.

"Well, maybe she did," Walker defended himself. "But you're every bit as strange as me."

"Actually," Jessica explained to Lynn, "I just lived with his family as another sister."

"A sister?" Walker shook his head, musing. He turned to Bret. "Well, then for your sake, I hope she was a skinny, scrawny kid with scraped knees. If that"—he pointed to Jessica—"had been walking around when I was nineteen, my dad would have had to train a shotgun on me every night to keep me away from her."

Bret laughed. "If Jessica had been scrawny, we could have left her where she was."

"Did your father have a good shotgun?"

"Several."

Jessica had never thought about it until this wry interchange, but surely during college, Bret had been like all very young men. Had it been difficult for him, having her mature in his home? Legally he had been entitled to her, and she knew perfectly well, as he must have too, that she had idolized him far too much to refuse him anything that he might have wanted.

But if he had wanted her body, she had never known about it. Had he kept himself under a tight restraint all those years? If so, it was a self-control that she, at least, had never given him credit for.

Confused by these thoughts, by this new version of the young Bret Cavanaugh, Jessica was silent, letting the others speak.

"Shall I put things on the table?" Lynn asked a bit later. "Or do you want another drink?"

"Not for me, thanks," Bret said. "I have to pace myself; I'm driving."

Jessica's mouth must have dropped open because Walker suddenly laughed. "Ah, Bret, here's a lady who knew you when. What is it, darlin'? Did it used to be more than your life was worth to get in a car with him on Saturday night?"

"Yes," Jessica said simply. The Bret she had known had considered himself above such mundane simplicities as traffic safety.

"Now let's not be throwing people's pasts in their faces here," Bret said. "We've all—"

"You aren't smoking either," Jessica interrupted.

She hadn't noticed it, but she had never seen Bret with a cigarette nor had she during her forays with her little bottle of Windex ever emptied an ashtray. Bret used to smoke all the time, even during football season when he wasn't supposed to.

Both men immediately groaned. "It's been over a year," Bret said, attesting to his virtue. "And I still want one sometimes."

"Lynn made me quit before we got married, and I

was going to be fried if I was going to do it alone so I
made Bret quit with me," Walker said.

"Both their secretaries threatened to resign; they
were so foul-tempered for a while," Lynn added.

As she moved to help Lynn carry the food out to the
glass-walled breakfast room off the kitchen, Jessica
shook her head silently. She hadn't been deluding herself this past week; Bret had changed. There could now
be no doubt about it. The old Bret would have never
quit smoking. He was too arrogant, believing that
things like lung cancer only happened to other people.
Even if that Bret had wanted to quit, he wouldn't have
been able to do it. He wouldn't have had that kind of
steady self-discipline.

But this man, the one casually leaning against the
counter, complaining to his partner about the Twins'
pitching staff, still drinking his first gin and tonic of the
evening, this Bret, he had quit smoking.

Dinner was light: fresh trout that Lynn's father had
caught that afternoon, wild rice, a pie made with rasp-
berries that Lynn and her mother had put up last summer. The spring evening was warm and through the
open windows drifted the lazy Southern accents, the
two men's voices deep and drawling, Jessica's a sweet
lilt. They were talking about home, about Georgia—the
red rolling hills of the north country and the light black
soil of the coastal plains where Walker was from. Occasionally the cool tones of Lynn's North Woods voice
would cut through, checking the highest flights of
fancy, reminding them all that they had left Georgia for
very good reasons and that they shouldn't get too senti-
mental about the place. It didn't stop them.

They walked to the party. The Pearsons lived just a
few blocks from the Buchanans in another house that,

like theirs, alternated between rooms that had been beautifully restored and those that still had plaster that had crumbled down to the lathwork and ceilings with gaping holes.

As their host and hostess came to greet them, Jessica noticed Bret look around and then smile warmly at someone. Curious about his warm smile, she was about to follow his gaze. Then a sudden thought stopped her, a thought that pierced like a sharp dart through the evening's pleasant glow. Karen Jensen was here. That's who Bret had smiled at. Karen. The woman he had been "seeing."

This party might be much more difficult than she had ever imagined.

Walker's hand on her arm distracted her. "Now, sweetheart, there's just one fellow in this crowd of Northerners who'll want to meet you as Jess Butler. Do you mind?"

"Not a bit."

Miles Turner didn't need to be told who Jessica was; even with the new haircut he had obviously recognized her as she crossed the room, but he had something to add to Walker's introduction of himself. "I'm a reporter."

Jessica's heart sank. This might be a very difficult party indeed. "Then I'd really rather not talk to you," she said lightly, trying to keep her voice very pleasant. "I'm here on vacation with friends who won't want their names in the press."

Miles smiled. "If you are visiting Walker, then you are wrong. He loves having his name in print, or at least the name of that company of his. But I won't mention that you are here until you want." He was obviously, like many good reporters, willing to risk losing a little story, hoping for something big later on.

Miles covered the music scene for one of the Minneapolis papers, and he knew a lot about Jess Butler's career. They talked about string arrangements and multialbum contracts until Miles finally asked his first personal question. "Are you visiting the Buchanans? My wife and I also live here in Ramsey Hill."

"No, I am staying with Bret Cavanaugh."

Miles looked surprised, and Jessica mentally shook herself. She should remember to refer to Bret as her husband. But before she could explain, a touch on her arm indicated that someone was taking advantage of the lull in the conversation.

She caught a suddenly stiffening expression on the two men's faces as she turned and smiled politely at another woman.

The woman was small with light brown hair, light brown eyes, and a sprinkling of freckles. Not at all glamorous and clearly no girl, she still had a look of good health and clean living about her that was quietly engaging.

"Jessica? I am Karen Jensen."

Karen. Bret's Karen. No wonder the men had grown awkward.

Jessica immediately admired the woman for her courage. It couldn't have been easy to introduce herself. Indeed, several other people were glancing at them, obviously interested in the encounter between the two women. Jessica felt like they were both on stage.

But she had given lots more difficult performances than this one. She looked directly at Karen, meeting her eyes, focusing all her attention on her. "How lovely to meet you," she said in her soft Southern way.

Then it hit her. Bret wasn't just "seeing" Karen. He was her lover. Of course, he was. There was no reason for their relationship to have been an innocent one. Karen undoubtedly felt no obligation to be faithful to a husband who had left her for a nineteen-year-old. Moreover, Bret had not denied it. If their relationship had just been a friendship, Jessica knew as well as she knew anything that he would never let any other impression go unchallenged.

Suddenly she envied Karen. This other woman had given Bret pleasure, had taken it from him. Jessica had not. Karen must know things about him that Jessica, although she had known him all her life, did not. They might be unimportant things, just bits of physical knowledge, how he looked, what he liked, but Jessica found herself wishing that she knew them too.

She realized that neither of them was speaking. Karen's social courage had obviously been entirely used up by her approach, and now her eyes shifted away nervously. It was an awkward moment, very awkward.

But Jessica had been raised in the South, and whatever other limits or failings Southerners might have, most can make small talk under any situation whatsoever. Jessica herself had been in a room full of people, most of whom had safety pins in their ears or little cocaine spoons around their necks, and talked to someone's proper wife about the weather and shopping.

Remembering that Karen lived in Ramsey Hill too, Jessica began to ask about the neighborhood. Karen seemed to know a lot about its history; Jessica listened intently and asked good questions. The conversation was interesting, pleasant, and rigorously impersonal. Neither one of them said one thing about herself.

Jessica was so concentrating on Karen that she didn't notice yet another woman join the small group. But she was relieved when Walker interrupted to introduce her to the newcomer.

"Dana Laird, Jessica Cavanaugh. Dana works down at the public TV station." Walker did not, Jessica was pleased to notice, explain what she herself did.

"Everyone has noticed you and been curious," Dana greeted her.

Jessica was not surprised. The other women at the party were dressed in casual dresses or neat slacks. But she had unthinkingly put on the sort of clothes she would wear to a party some promoter might be giving on the road. She was wearing her best jeans—and Jessica's best jeans were very good indeed—with a hand-hammered silver belt. Her blouse was just a soft drift of white silk, its gossamer folds making the line of her close-fitting jeans seem lean and long. The combination of silk, silver, and denim stood out as an orchid would in a bouquet of daisies.

"We guessed from your accent that you were with either Walker or Bret," Dana continued. "I am afraid my date is going to hope that your last name is Cavanaugh because you are Bret's sister, but your ring suggests otherwise."

Involuntarily Jessica glanced down at the gold band that Bret had brought home one afternoon. "Bret and I have been married for some time," she said quietly, concerned that this interchange would be very awkward for Karen. Dana clearly had no idea how embarrassing her words might be.

"Will you be coming down to answer phones then?" Dana asked.

"I don't understand," Jessica said politely.

Walker explained. Because it didn't air commercials, the Minneapolis public television station had to depend on government funding and listener support. Once a year it raised money by having an on-the-air auction for several nights. Items were donated and viewers called in their bids. Since Cavanaugh–Buchanan didn't make the sort of product that was suitable for the auction, their employees volunteered to man the phone banks one evening during the auction.

"How are you doing getting things to auction?" Miles asked Dana.

"Fine," she answered. "We've done well this year. Except that we don't have anything flashy for the younger crowd, something that would get us a lot of attention and publicity." She turned to Walker, teasing. "I wish you two made video games. We could use some video games."

"Don't you think *we* wish we made video games?" Walker returned.

Jessica suddenly spoke. "Do you have dinners and such with celebrities?" In similar fund-raising auctions out in California people could sometimes bid for the chance to have lunch with their favorite movie star.

"We have some, a few local politicians and sports figures—although that has fallen off a little. A few years ago the governor was on our list, and he was bought up by one of our local . . . well, ladies of the evening." Everyone laughed, remembering the discomfort of that elected official who had, nonetheless, gone out on his date with good humor and grace.

Under the cover of the laughter Jessica quickly asked Walker, "Does this auction matter to you and Bret?"

"It's a good cause," he said softly. "We try to do our share."

So Jessica turned to Dana. "If it will help, I will be glad to have lunch with someone."

The woman's face went blank and Jessica immediately explained, "I am a singer. I work under the name of Jess Butler."

The name seemed to mean nothing to Dana and her face was carefully expressionless. "How about if I get back to you on that?" It was an obvious brush-off.

Miles Turner started to speak, but Jessica interrupted quickly. "Of course. You can reach me at Bret's. I'll be glad to hear from you." She tried to make her voice warm so that the woman could call.

Dana smiled a cool professional smile. Apparently not happy about having to give such a refusal at a party, she excused herself.

Jessica glanced at Miles. "You'll call her Monday?" It was barely a question. More than anyone in the room, Miles probably understood the realities of the world Jessica moved in.

"Of course. Why didn't you want me to explain right away?"

Jessica shrugged. "Why embarrass her in front of other people?"

Miles smiled. "How long has it been since *you* have heard a 'don't call us, we'll call you'?"

"It's been a while," she acknowledged. "And, by the way, I am counting on you to try and keep Bret's name out of this. Jess Butler is doing this, not me."

Jessica was used to dealing with people in this manner. She was asking Miles for a favor; he would do it and someday soon collect one in return.

Only Bret kept giving and giving without wanting anything in return.

An hour or so later Jessica found herself alone on the third floor of the house. The hostess had been showing her around, but had been waylaid by the sight of several empty food platters. Jessica had offered to help her fill the trays, but she had insisted that Jessica go on by herself.

Little work had been done on the third floor, but she had paused there for a moment, relieved to have some time alone. Meeting this many new people was hard work, especially when there wasn't a record company executive at your elbow, introducing you, helping out with the conversations.

But although difficult, the evening had been interesting. She had particularly enjoyed talking to the women; she had so little chance to talk to women anymore. Some were home with children; others had interesting jobs, jobs Jessica had barely even known existed: She had met social workers, art therapists, landscape architects, even some university professors.

In fact, these women and their jobs had made Jessica somewhat uneasy. Although by every possible standard she was the most successful person at the party—male or female—she felt a little threatened, even insecure. These people were all educated; she was not. She had been singing professionally since she was eighteen and she had not gone to college. She often felt ignorant and uninformed, and she worried continually about exposing herself as she had done on her first night with Bret when she had forgotten where the Mississippi started. She knew little about literature and absolutely nothing about science. Her knowledge of American history was limited to the Civil War, and as she occasionally joked, her Georgia high school hadn't gotten around to telling her who won that one.

She shrugged and started toward the stairs. It couldn't be helped. A person didn't get to be as successful as she was without paying a pretty high price. Not having an education was only one thing among many.

As she reached the stairs, she heard Bret's muffled voice.

"Karen."

He had called her by the wrong name. Rigid with embarrassment, Jessica turned.

And didn't see him.

"I've been hoping to speak to you," his voice continued.

Jessica glanced down. There was a good-sized hole in the floor where some pipes had once been. Karen and Bret were apparently on the second floor, their voices carrying up to the third.

"Bret, I don't want to be patronized." Karen's soft voice came up through the flooring.

He didn't answer for a moment. "Of course you don't. Am I doing that to you?"

"You didn't have to hide who she was." Karen's voice was tight with pride. "Did you think I couldn't handle it?"

Bret spoke gently. "Honestly, Karen, I never decided not to tell you; it just didn't occur to me. I never imagined that she would come to Minneapolis. If I had had any sort of relationship with her at all, other than just pleasant conversations at Christmas, I would have told you who she was. But I never thought it would matter. Not even Walker knew."

Jessica knew that she should not be listening to this, but she also knew that she was going to.

"How did you find out?" Bret was saying. "Here?"

"No," Karen answered. "Peter stopped by this

week. He apparently recognized her in the jewelry store. I hadn't told him you were married." Karen's voice was stiff, and Jessica could easily understand her pride, why she had neglected to mention to her husband that the new man in her life was married. "So of course he had to run right over and tell me that you were." The stiffness in her voice became bitterness. "He obviously doesn't think I have a chance competing against Jess Butler."

"I hope you don't feel like you are competing with her," Bret said immediately. "You aren't."

She laughed shakily. "Well, I feel like I am. Part of it is just a normal dog-in-the-manger sort of thing, wanting to be first in your life even though you—" She stopped.

"Even though I am not the first in yours," Bret finished for her.

"Yes," she sighed. "Your taking care of Jessica when she was sick made me realize that if Peter ever thought he needed me, I'd go running. Not that *that* is ever likely to happen."

Jessica was startled with how honest they were with each other. There was no one she could be this open with.

"But it's more than that," Karen continued. "I can't help comparing myself to her. Not only is she so lovely, but look at what she has done. She has this fabulously successful career and isn't thirty yet. I'm thirty-four, and all I have done is to be a wife and a mother."

"Now stop that," Bret said firmly. "Don't let anyone tell you that what you have done is unimportant."

Karen didn't respond. Apparently she had heard that from him before. "And she has to be the most poised person I've ever met. At first I thought that she might be shy because she doesn't talk a lot, but there was this terribly awkward moment with Dana Laird, and she just breezed right through. Maybe selling millions of record albums gives you that kind of confidence. I know that I don't have it."

"But, Karen, how important is that?" Bret asked.

She didn't seem to hear him. "And with me. I just introduced myself because I knew some people would find it a little too interesting if I avoided her. But I had no idea what I was going to say to her. She got everything started, and I forgot who it was I was talking to." A note of amazement crept into Karen's voice. "I liked her. I really did. I talked to her for ten minutes and felt like I wanted to get to know her better. Bret, I don't want to know your wife. Maybe she's the sort of sophisticated person who can deal with that in some terribly civilized manner, but I'm not."

"Now wait a minute, Karen," Bret said emphatically. "Let me explain something about Jessica. Of course, you liked her; she didn't give you any choice."

Jessica straightened. What did he mean? That she hadn't given Karen a choice? What was he talking about?

"The one thing about Jessica—and she has been this way for as long as I have known her—is that the first thing she does in any situation is size up what people want from her, and suddenly she becomes that. She always gives people exactly what they want."

She couldn't believe it. How could he say such terrible, terrible things about her? Did he really think that of her? But he went right on.

"You should have seen her with Walker this evening. He always gets a little homesick this time of year— God only knows how she senses these things—but by the time dinner was done, we were about to raise the Confederate flag and start singing 'Dixie.' It's why she is such a wonderful entertainer. She can tell exactly what an audience wants and she gives them that. I'd bet that's why she hasn't done too much television; she hasn't yet figured out what a camera wants from her. But as soon as she knows that, she'll give that little red light just exactly what it asks of her."

How did he know that? He was exactly right, but how did he know?

"It sounds like you resent this," Karen said softly.

"No, I don't," he answered swiftly. "I just need to keep reminding myself of how she operates. No, 'operates' isn't the right word—I think that it all happens unconsciously; she doesn't know that she does it. It started when she was a kid—you can understand that— she was miserably lonely for a long time and was nearly desperate for affection. Now I imagine that it's the only way that she knows how to relate to people."

"But I don't understand why you think you have to keep reminding yourself of it," Karen prodded.

"Take this week. Karen, when she got here, she was in terrible shape, and my first thought was how much I wanted to make her well and happy. Now, lo and behold, she's well and happy. At least she seems to be; for all I know, she is completely miserable and just putting on an act because she knows that that is what I want. By God, she's starting cooking again because I was fool enough to mention that I liked the way she used to cook. I can just feel myself getting sucked in by this performance."

"What are you afraid of, Bret?" Karen was clearly the sort of person who readily set aside her own interests if need be.

"I'm not afraid of anything," he said a little too defensively.

"If you aren't afraid of something, then why not"— and there was the lightest touch of irony in Karen's voice—"just enjoy the performance?"

Bret was silent and when he spoke, his voice was rueful. "Oh, Karen, I don't know. I guess I feel like I need to protect myself from her, from how easy it is to fall for her act. This show is going to finish playing Minneapolis soon and then hit the road. And this is one performance a man could get used to."

"There's no chance she could stay?"

"In Minneapolis?" Bret laughed shortly. "Good heavens, no. She'd never fit in here."

"You and Walker have."

"No, it's not being a Southerner—it's the whole world she moves in. Do you know anything about the entertainment world?"

"Only what I read."

"Well, it really does seem to be true. It's just so entirely different from Minnesota. We are all so normal and ordinary and unexotic. She's used to attention and excitement; she needs to perform; she needs that audience. And let's face it, the standards of behavior in her world are quite a bit different than in ours. She would never be content here." He cleared his throat. "Speaking of which, I guess I really should go find her and make sure that she is all right."

Jessica quickly turned to go down the back steps, hoping that they would lead somewhere with solid flooring. After all she had heard, she felt a little desperate for something firm to stand on. Bret and his home had this week come to feel like high ground in the chaotic flood of her life. Even that refuge seemed to be crumbling away.

The back stairs, obviously once the passageway for servants, led down to the kitchen, which was crowded with people. Smiling pleasantly at those she had met, she eased her way through the tight clusters, moving toward the far corner of the room where she saw Walker perched on the kitchen counter.

As soon as he saw her, he gestured for her to come over. "I'm taking a break from being charming." He smiled, sliding off the counter. "Will you join me?"

"Of course." But she was still upset and, after a few more pleasant words, retreated into her characteristic silence.

Walker introduced a new topic. "You know, you are different from what I would have expected you to be."

She did not want to hear people talk about her. She had heard quite enough. But it seemed rude to ignore him so she finally asked, "Which 'me'—Bret's wife or Jess Butler?"

"Oh, Jess Butler," he replied. "My expectations of the unknown Mrs. Cavanaugh were simply that she had to be a woman of great sense if she refused to live with Bret. I've lived with him, and I can't say that I thought it was particularly wonderful. I'm having a much better time living with Lynn."

"I'm sure she'll be relieved to hear that," Jessica returned. "I really do like her," she added, hoping to lure Walker into talking about his own wife, not Bret's.

He grinned, but refused the bait. "No, it was the other 'you' I was talking about. I would have thought that big celebrities would always be at the center of everything—very vibrant and up all the time. But then," he reflected, "I suppose by now you get so much attention you don't have to have it all the time."

"It is actually rather pleasant to be ignored."

"Well, if you are expecting me to ignore a pretty lady"—his smile had a warm, innocently flirtatious edge to it—"then you are barking up the wrong tree."

"Now, Walker, behave yourself." It was Bret.

She couldn't meet his eyes, remembering the things he had said about her.

But he continued to speak to his partner. "I've been sent to fetch you. Lynn wants you to go down and look at the Pearsons' new heating system." Bill Pearson had by now joined them.

Walker sighed. "Here I am talking to one of the world's sexiest women and my wife makes me go look at a furnace." But he looked at Bill Pearson eagerly. "Is it this pulse system?"

"It is," Bill answered and then turned to Jessica, smiling apologetically. "You must have noticed that all anyone in Minnesota ever talks about is their heating system."

Thinking of one conversation she had overheard, Jessica wished that were true. Heating systems seemed like a very nice, safe topic.

Then she was alone with Bret. For the first time since she had come to Minnesota, she felt awkward with him.

"Are you having a nice time?" he asked politely.

"Yes," she replied, just as polite. "I do like your friends."

"Well, they just love you," he said abruptly.

She was instantly suspicious. How had he meant that? Was it just a simple compliment? Or was it all caught up with the things he had been saying to Karen about her?

"Especially Walker," Bret continued. An array of bottles sat on the counter next to them, and Bret started to open some tonic. "He thought you and your pretty eyes were the finest thing to show up since, well, since the Bonnie Blue Flag."

The rich blue flag with its single white star was one of the first Confederate battle standards. During the first major battle of the war, Thomas "Stonewall" Jackson, thinking his army surrounded by Federal troops, had peered apprehensively at an advancing column, its uniforms obscured by the dust. His apprehension gave place to relief and elation when a sudden breeze caught and lifted the Bonnie Blue Flag.

"Do you want one of these?" Bret was asking, gesturing to his glass. When Jessica shook her head, he turned and, leaning against the counter, looked across the crowded room and spoke softly. "And speaking of civil wars, I hope you aren't fixing to cause trouble in that direction."

His voice was so light, he seemed so completely interested in the way the ice cubes moved about in the tonic, that it took Jessica a moment to understand that he was talking about Walker.

She drew herself up and looked at him steadily. "That is enormously insulting, both to me and to your partner." Her voice was low, but very firm. "If I weren't a guest in your home, I would insist that you apologize."

He stared at her, surprised as people always were when Jessica finally emerged from her silence to defend herself. His gray eyes went dark, but after a moment, he apologized. "You are right. It was out of line. I shouldn't have said it."

"No, Bret, you shouldn't have *thought* it."

# Chapter Seven

Bret's warning about Walker had only confirmed what Jessica had gathered from overhearing his conversation with Karen. Bret cared for her deeply; he felt a great responsibility for her; he would do nearly anything for her, but his opinion of her was really rather low.

The words had been carried up to her through a hole in the flooring. "She always gives people just what they want." "It's the only way she knows how to relate to people." "I feel like I need to protect myself from her." As she lay in bed, the conversation played back like a stuck record.

She did like to please people, she knew that about herself. A difficult life—and hers was very difficult—was easier when the people around you liked you; that had always been her excuse.

But Bret had accused her of more than that. The woman he had described was empty, without feelings or personality of her own, like water just taking on the shape of whatever container it was poured into: sometimes this, sometimes that, never herself, only what others wanted her to be.

Tears softened the pillow case, and she slipped out of bed to stand by the window, pressing her forehead against the cool glass, looking down at the dark Mississippi.

In some ways, he was right; that was exactly how she had been once. When she moved into the Cavanaugh home, she never felt worthy of this unbelievably good fortune. The contrast between this noisy, loving family and her former solitude had been too striking. She had always wanted to pay them back, and the only way she knew how was to work very hard around the house and to try to be the sort of person she thought they wanted.

When she first started her career, she had been again so grateful, so awed, that people wanted to hear her sing that she would have done anything to please Art and Nathan, who seemed to be the ones making it possible. They wanted her to be sweet and vulnerable onstage, and hardworking, resilient, even rugged offstage. So she had been all that for them. When they told her that she was naturally sensual, that she could sing more provocative songs, that she could change her image, she had done that too.

But she had changed over the years. Working the road, she always thought, must be a little like combat, prison, and any stressful situation where people were forced together for too long in too small a space. The pretenses drop. No one can always be nice when they are sleeping in a bus—not even Jessica.

She had learned that there was something more important than having the people who work for you like you, and that was that they did their jobs. If getting the band to like her meant putting up with them destroying motel rooms, picking up under-age groupies, or coming to gigs too drunk or stoned to play, then Jessica could live with them not liking her. Everyone in Jess's

Boys liked her, but she had worked with people who didn't.

She no longer did everything that others wanted of her. Everyone around her wanted her to start singing rock, but she wasn't ever going to do that. It wasn't right for her and she knew it. She didn't care what other people wanted.

To be sure, the edges of her personality weren't as rigidly defined as in most people. She could slip into roles; she could become other people. But that was something that she did in her work, becoming for three minutes the person in the song. But she didn't do it in life anymore. At least, not very often.

If she did do exactly what people wanted, like letting Walker talk about Georgia during dinner, it was more of a habit than a need. And habits could be broken.

But Bret clearly distrusted this aspect of her nature. It made him wonder if everything she did—right down to taking his shirts to the laundry—was an act, a show she was putting on, trying to turn the whole world into her fan club. Bret's natural arrogance, however much he was now fighting it, wouldn't let him be comfortable as one of the crowd.

And, Jessica forced herself to acknowledge, his reservations about her went deeper than this. "Let's face it, the standards of behavior in her world are quite a bit different than in ours." He had said nothing more, not wanting to expose her to Karen, but Jessica knew exactly what he was talking about. When she had come to Minneapolis, she had been addicted to prescription medications.

She had been inexpressibly relieved to be free of the burden of her addiction. She was so eager to forget how sordid and stained she had felt that she had never bothered to think about how it must have looked to Bret.

He had seen her at her worst. However deeply he had suffered for her, nonetheless he must have been offended. Bret, although not at all vain, still had an athlete's basic respect for his body. He took care of himself. At thirty, working behind a desk, he was as fit as he had been at eighteen playing football and nearly as strong. How repelled he must have been by how she had abused herself.

Undoubtedly he also thought that she was just as careless with her body in other ways. Burning with shame, she remembered what else had happened the first night she had been with him—how she had turned over, offering herself to him, casually, uninterestedly, meaninglessly.

He probably assumed that she was always like that, that she had slept with her entire band and countless others. Many people thought that of her; some of the women in her songs had made similar terrible mistakes. She would have been angry if Bret, like all the others, was just confusing the Jess Butler image with the reality of Jessica herself, but Bret had additional information—the sight of her on her back, white silk slipping off her shoulders, her hands sliding up his thighs.

Bret had certainly not led a monastic life, but if his relationship with Karen were any pattern, he had not been involved in careless, meaningless affairs. He would not expect a woman to be innocent, but he wouldn't want her to be cheap, and he had reasons to think Jessica cheap. If he didn't want to be just one more face in the crowd of her fans, he would even less want to be just one more body to pass through her bed.

Didn't he understand, she thought frantically, that she had hardly known what she was doing? And if she had, it was because she had so hated herself at that moment, that she wanted to be used, punished?

Perhaps he did understand all that. But he would have every reason to think that it had been going on for years, that there had been a long line of men that she had turned to in her self-loathing, in her contempt for herself, that he was just one in that line.

Jessica stared out the window. It seemed like the world below her was full of people who were asleep, sleeping during the night because in the daytime they had the most wonderfully ordinary lives: men who worked on those docks or, if they'd gone to college, in the office buildings; women who baked cookies and waited for the school bus. They would be decent, upright people with useful lives.

It was the daylight world, and she wasn't a part of it. Bret was: He was in the Chamber of Commerce and, at thirty, on his way to being an important force in his adopted city. Karen was: She had a son and she was very involved in the restoration of her neighborhood. But Jessica was not.

She was from another world, where people wore satin baseball jackets, took drugs, and were addicted to the spotlight. How could she possibly fit into Bret's world?

Tormented by these thoughts, she hardly slept that night. She went downstairs early and had just finished making coffee when she heard Bret moving upstairs. She went to the counter and watched him come down the spiral stairs. It was Sunday and he was dressed in well-worn jeans and a T-shirt with faded gold letters that faintly spelled out "Georgia Tech."

Even at his most relaxed, there was still a lazy spring to his walk, and for a moment Jessica thought that in the simple act of walking downstairs, Bret distilled all that was best in American men—all the energy and industry, the lively humor and spirited vitality, that this species was capable of.

He seemed so decent and healthy that Jessica longed desperately to win his good opinion back, but she didn't know how she could. She watched him, admiring the way the muscles in his legs tightened as he moved, the way his shoulders stretched the old shirt, the way—

"Is something wrong with my shirt?" his voice interrupted her thoughts.

She blinked. He was looking down at himself as if something were wrong. "The way you are looking at it," he continued, explaining. "Has it finally rolled over and died? It is a little old."

"No, it's fine," Jessica answered quickly, not about to explain what she had been thinking. "Would you like some coffee?" And while she spoke, she remembered the words he had once said to her in the Starlight Bar. "Maybe it's not the *shirt* I like."

Bret smiled his interest in coffee and ambled over to the door, opened it, leaned over to get the Sunday paper.

Jessica watched him and then went into the kitchen and took one of the hand-crafted pottery mugs off its hook. As she poured the dark hot coffee into it, she heard his voice.

"May I again apologize for what I said last night?"

She turned. He was standing in the center of the living room, looking at the front page of the still-folded paper. But she knew that he wasn't reading it. He just found it easier to talk this way.

She handed him the coffee. "You don't need to." She could tell from his slightly awkward manner, from his bringing it up at all, how much he was regretting his suggestion that she was trying to entice Walker. That was enough. She had never expected him to speak at all.

"Yes, I do," he replied. "I really thought that I had dealt with your being Jess Butler; the posters, the album covers, the things people say, I thought that none of it bothered me, but the first time someone admires you as Jessica Cavanaugh I react like—" He broke off, busying himself putting the coffee and paper down on the end table. Jessica said nothing, and suddenly, swiftly, he looked at her directly, his gray eyes meeting her blue ones. "Look, I'm no good at this, but you do understand? I am really trying. You know how I was brought up, and I am trying to be different."

Jessica understood. She knew what he meant. Country women made it easy for their men to be very self-centered. If the men lived up to their financial responsibilities and put on a reasonable appearance of sexual fidelity, they were thought to be good husbands and fathers. When a woman chose a husband at eighteen, she often didn't dare let herself expect a lot else, certainly not that a man was going to worry himself much about her feelings, her convenience, or her pleasure.

Bret's conditioning had told him it was perfectly all right to say anything he liked to his wife, and that if he did feel a little guilty about it later, he did not have to go to the trouble of explaining himself.

But he was trying to change, to learn how to treat women differently, to see them more clearly. When he reverted to the old ways, as he had for a moment last night, he wanted to apologize to her.

She respected him for it.

Then, looking into his troubled, gray eyes, with the insight she usually only used to understand other people's feelings, never her own, Jessica suddenly realized that she felt more than respect for him. She loved him.

The thought startled her. But, she had to ask herself, what was so startling and new? Of course, she loved him, she had always loved him, and she was sure that if someone had asked, he would have blinked and said, "Well, of course. Of course, I love Jessica."

No, this was new; that familiar old affection had been between a boy and a girl. This time it was different. She was a woman and she loved this man, this man who belonged to a world she could never be a part of.

That afternoon Bret suggested that they go to a park.

"A park?" Jessica said, surprised.

"Yes, Jessie, a park." He smiled. All day he had been like this, pleasant, relaxed, obviously unaware of how confused and jumbled her secret thoughts were. "You remember, they are green and flat—at least the ones in Minnesota are flat—and people go there to—"

"I know what a park is," she interrupted. It had just sounded so odd, to go out to a park for a Sunday afternoon walk. In her world, parks were just convenient places for staging outdoor concerts.

They drove to a park that was by one of the eleven lakes within the city limits. It was a delightful place: Jogging and bike paths snaked through the green trees;

a playground with bright red swings was crowded with laughing children; white sails glided across the blue lake. The spring sunshine was warm on Jessica's arms and face, and as they walked into an open field, she timidly put her hand in his arm.

He smiled down at her. "Are you having a good time?" he asked. "Are you glad you're here?"

She nodded, suddenly unable to speak, unable to tell him just how very glad she was to be with him, living in his home, walking with her hand in his arm.

She wished she could make him understand how beautiful she found the sunshine. She might be a creature of the night, the night with its artificial light might be where she truly belonged, but she wanted him to know that part of her longed for warm sunlit days like this one.

But, of course, being Jessica, she did not speak, and in a moment she felt his arm under her hand tighten. He had stiffened, his attention caught by something else. Jessica followed his gaze. A group of little boys were kicking about a black and white soccer ball. A cluster of parents lingered nearby. Slightly apart from them were two more adults, a man and a woman, exchanging low, but angry words.

It was Karen and Peter Jensen. They were clearly fighting.

Karen's face was tight with pain. Peter put his hand on her shoulder; she jerked away from him and suddenly she was running almost blindly toward the trees.

Bret started to move, then stopped.

Jessica understood. He was forcing himself to remain at her side, putting his obligation to her above his concern for Karen. "Go to her," she said swiftly. "Don't worry about me. Go to her."

She watched vacantly as Bret easily caught up with Karen. He put his arm around her shoulders; she covered her face with her hands.

Slowly Jessica walked to Peter Jensen, who was also staring at the two figures, now dark silhouettes against the line of green trees.

"Peter?" Jessica said softly.

He turned. For a moment he didn't seem to recognize her. "Oh, hello." His face was almost blank, his eyes staring at her in dumb misery.

Jessica pitied him. Whatever he had done, he was suffering for it now. She wondered if he wanted to talk to someone. "Shall we sit down?"

They sat down on an old-fashioned bench with green wood slats and curved wrought-iron legs, waiting as her husband comforted his wife. "This is awkward," he said at last.

"Yes," Jessica replied quietly. "But there are worse things than awkward."

"That's certainly true." Bret and Karen were moving off down a path that disappeared into the trees. "Your husband is a very attractive man," Peter said abruptly.

Jessica could hardly tell him that she agreed. "But Karen does not love him." She knew that from the words that had drifted up to her last night through a hold in the flooring.

Peter shrugged, tilting his blond head back to look at the white clouds. He clearly thought that Jessica was just offering meaningless words of comfort. "Karen says the affair is over. Is it?"

How was Jessica to know? "I'm sure they will want to stay friends," she answered carefully. "But my coming did change things for them."

"Because he doesn't play around when he's got a wife in his home? Unlike some men..." he added bitterly.

Jessica winced at the self-contempt in his voice.

"Do you know what it is like," he continued, almost as if he were talking to himself, "to do one thing that you know is just a little bit wrong, and then without ever knowing how it happened, you are suddenly doing things that are nearly wicked?"

"I understand." Jessica thought of where taking one sleeping pill had led. "I do understand."

Peter blinked at the conviction in her voice. "Yes," he said slowly as if remembering who she was. "Yes, you sing about this all the time, don't you? Husbands who cheat on their wives. But in the songs, the wives always take them back."

Jessica looked across the sunlit grass to the dark mass of trees that hid Karen and Bret. "Is that what you want? To go home?"

He nodded. "I've known for a couple of months."

"And you've told Karen?"

"Just last week. I mean, I couldn't before. He—your husband—was making her happy. I couldn't thrust myself in the middle of that. Not after what I had done to her. But then when you came...that's when I told her."

"What did she say?" Jessica prompted.

"She seemed insulted." Peter's voice had a note of blank confusion. "What she said—it's what we were talking about a minute ago—was that my speaking when I did implied that she had to have a man in her life, that if he were out of her life, then she'd have to take me back...I don't know; I didn't mean it that way." He shook his head slowly, sadly. "A marriage is so precious; you just shouldn't play around with it."

Jessica looked down at her hands. On the third finger of her left one gleamed the wide gold band.

She didn't know why she and Bret were still married, why they hadn't gotten an annulment years ago. And she didn't know what would become of them. Loving him as she did, how could she leave? But being what she was, how could she stay?

But one thing she did know. If ever, by whatever accident or grace of God, their marriage became a proper one, Jessica knew that it was the one thing she would never take risks with.

As the days passed, she and Bret settled into a very traditional routine. He went off to work and she stayed home. She kept waiting to start feeling restless, to get the urge to hit the road, to be out in front of an audience. But it kept not happening.

She kept busy. She read, something she hadn't had the concentration to do when she had been on pills; she explored Minneapolis; she let a needlework store teach her needlepoint; she helped Lynn put in her garden; she even drove one day a week for Meals-On-Wheels, taking meals to senior citizens while one of the regular volunteers was on maternity leave. And she was more content than she had ever been.

To her surprise, her love for Bret did not make her unhappy. In her songs, all forms of love, especially unrequited love, caused great anguish, but, in real life, she was happy to be with him. Even if he didn't return the depth of her feelings, she would still rather be with him than not. For the time being it was, as the title of her biggest hit put it, "Almost Enough."

For the most part Bret seemed happy as well. She knew that in general he was glad that she was there. He would come home at night, his face drawn and tired. He'd set down his attaché case, speak to her, and start upstairs to change his clothes. When she would answer, he would pause at the foot of the spiral staircase and turn to her, listening, his hand loosening the knot of his tie.

He would drift over to the kitchen, and leaning on the counter, he would talk to her, the day-to-day tensions of running a company easing when he had someone to talk to about them. Or he would silently watch her work, lifting vegetables out of the steamer, slicing tomatoes in the salad, slipping a tray of biscuits into the oven. Then when she had dinner on the table, he would look down at himself, surprised that he had not yet been upstairs to change his clothes.

Soon he stopped even bringing his attaché case home. She didn't know if it was conscious or not, but on some level he had clearly acknowledged that as long as she was there, he wasn't going to be working in the evenings.

But sometimes during those evenings, in the middle of moments that were tender, almost intimate, it was as if Bret was checking himself, reminding himself of something. A pale shutter would close over the warmth of his gray eyes, and he would pull away. She wasn't sure what he thought he had to protect himself from—from falling for an act, from growing to need her, to love her.

With the least encouragement she would have gone willingly, eagerly, to his arms. Her body yearned for the feel of his. It was difficult some nights to say good night to him and watch him disappear into his room, or in the morning to look at his half-opened door, hearing him getting dressed in the bedroom that matched the color of his eyes. In the evenings, if they were in the den watching television, he would be stretched out, his feet on the coffee table, his arms hooked across the back of the sofa, exposing the long length of his body. She would long to curl up against him, to feel the warmth of his chest against her cheek.

She felt sure there were times when he responded to her just as strongly. She would see a flicker in his eye as his gaze would linger on her, and then for a moment he'd breathe as if he had been running. But he never approached her.

Almost desperately she wondered why he did not. If what she now suspected about those long, hot Southern summers when he had been home from college were true, then he was used to disciplining his desire. So Jessica would wonder if he were waiting for a sign from her. Certainly that one night at the Starlight Bar, it had been a gesture from her that had unleashed his passion. Perhaps, she would think, he was waiting for her to come to his room some night. And sometimes she would stand at her door, slowly tying the sash of her robe, wondering if she should cross the hall.

But, no, she told herself at other times, she might be fooling herself. He had rejected her on the first night she had been in Minnesota because of the sort of life he thought she led, because of the sort of woman he thought she was. He thought the same things now. He had rejected her once; she couldn't make herself take the risk again.

There was simply so very much that she wanted to say to him, but she didn't know how. So used to the words of gifted songwriters, she felt her own inadequate. If someone would give her the lyrics, if the rhythm guitar would start to lay down a cadence, if the spotlight would switch on, glittering against the mike, perhaps she could have a chance. But as it was, without someone else's words, with the only light being the light fading from his eyes, in these moments of almost terrifying intimacy, she could not speak.

## Chapter Eight

To her great disappointment, Bret did not seem pleased that she had volunteered to be auctioned off for public television.

Dana Laird had, of course, called her the Monday after the Pearsons' party. She had heard of Jess Butler, she protested, but she never listened to country music, and the name just hadn't connected. She was so very sorry, but—

Jessica had been very nice about it.

But when she told Bret, his lips had tightened for a moment. "It's your business, but I thought you liked being anonymous."

Jessica explained how they had worked out the publicity: lots of material about Jess Butler, all implying that she was coming to town just for this. Everyone who knew she was already here would keep quiet about it.

Bret shrugged, apparently not quite believing her. "I was wondering when a private life was going to start getting to you."

But he did ask her if she wanted to answer phones with the Cavanaugh–Buchanan employees. "Lynn is going," he said, "but don't feel like you have to go. We aren't into that 'corporate wife' scene."

"No, I'd like to go."

"Fine. I'll put your name on the list."

As soon as she heard that there was a list of names, she expected another call from the TV station. This might be a small public station in Minnesota but it was television. Surely someone would have the sense to realize that it was a bit of a waste to have Jess Butler sitting third from the left in a phone bank.

It rather irritated Jessica that the call did not come until shortly after eight on the morning Cavanaugh–Buchanan employees were scheduled to man the phones.

Dana apologized for calling so early. "And so late," she added. "But I didn't realize you were coming this evening; someone else was in charge of the volunteers, and you were listed with Bret as 'Mr. and Mrs.'"

Just as Jessica expected, Dana asked her if she would work on-camera, describing items being auctioned and reading off the bids as they were phoned in.

"And I assume you will want me to sing?" Jessica asked.

"Actually, we don't usually have entertainment; it's just the auction."

Jessica thought that sounded rather boring. She also knew perfectly well if people tuned in to see her, they would be irritated if she didn't sing. With open phone lines, some would call to complain. She decided she should go prepared to sing.

It had been years since Jessica had had to organize herself for a performance. She paid people to do it for her. But careers like Jess Butler's weren't built on being unprepared. If no one except Jessica Cavanaugh was around to do Jess Butler's preparing, well, then she would do it.

First, she had to get a guitar. She called Miles Turner, the reporter she had met at the Pearsons' party. He promised that he would get something to the station by evening.

"Not something," Jessica said firmly. "A steel string Martin." She wasn't going to do this with some cheap guitar.

Next she needed clothes. The blouse she had worn to the Pearsons' had been white, and she wasn't sure how good the station's cameras were. Unless a camera had some new technological gizmo, white did not work well on television. The white reflected too much light making the camera "bloom," and the picture lost all detail. Blues and reds, Jessica knew, worked the best on video; they came through the purest, the most real.

But she had no intention of spending the day shopping, tiring herself out, flipping through the racks, and taking her clothes on and off. So she called Dayton's, the big department store. Yes, they had a personal shopping representative, and yes, Mrs. Trent would be more than glad to help Jessica. In fact, when she found out where Jessica lived, she offered to have some dresses sent over.

Apparently someone told Mrs. Trent that Jess Butler was a country singer, and she sent over one very western outfit, a flounced denim skirt with a yoked cowboy shirt and a bright red bandanna. Neither Jess nor Jessica ever dressed like that and they were both relieved that a number of other dresses had been delivered as well.

They were all a bit more ladylike than Jess Butler's

usual performing clothes. As Mrs. Trent had told Jessica on the phone, much of the money in Minneapolis was old money, and the wealthy people dressed very conservatively. But Jessica found two dresses that she thought would do. She decided to take both and change halfway through the evening. On the rare occasions when she had a chance to watch television, she liked it when the women changed clothes a lot.

She decided to start out in the red dress, a crimson wraparound whose skirt was several layers of a floating chiffon. When she moved, the skirt drifted, exposing, for a brief second, the gleam of a shapely leg.

As she was carefully arranging a plastic garment bag over the other dress she heard Bret's key in the lock.

He looked at her for a long moment without speaking. "That's some fancy dress for answering phones," he said at last. His voice was slow, almost sleepy. But there was an undercurrent to it that reminded her of the slow curling of a horse whip. "But then you aren't answering phones, are you, Miss Butler?"

A sudden curl of misery licked at her, the swift response to the bitterness in his voice. She tried to push it aside. She didn't dare let herself get upset, not with this evening's work ahead of her. "No, I am not," she answered carefully. "Did Dana tell you?"

"Oh, no. I found out just like everyone else in the Cities did. I heard it on the radio. It's on every station; Jess Butler is going to be on TV tonight."

She should have called him, Jessica realized sickeningly. She should have let him know. But she just hadn't thought. All day long she had been working, trying to get ready for this evening, choosing clothes, going over guitar arrangements in her head, warming up her voice. She hadn't thought about her responsibilities to him. Jess Butler never had to think about things like that.

He said little to her as they drove to the station. He was not pouting, she knew that. He was not a spoiled child who needed to hear everything first. He was a man, and the publicity, the glittering crimson dress, her professional makeup, all reminded him that this was no ordinary woman he was with. She was an entertainer, and she took her obligations to her fans more seriously than she did her obligations to him.

Jessica knew that everything she did this evening, every wide-eyed glance in the camera, every note picked up by the mike, would remind Bret of the gulf between them, of the complete incompatibility of their lives. But she was going to forget that she knew that.

It couldn't matter that she owed Bret nearly everything she had. It couldn't matter that a most blankly miserable existence would have been hers had he not stopped his pickup that sultry spring night. It couldn't matter that she loved him. None of that could matter. Those were the sort of thoughts that stood in the way of success.

Jess Butler was a pro; she couldn't let personal problems spoil the show.

The auction was a low-key, low-budget affair. There were just two cameras, and little money had been spent on the set. The cyclorama, the eighteen-foot curtain that formed the backdrop for the rest of the set, was old and a little tattered. A three-tiered bank of phones took up most of the space. To one side were the big boards where the current high bid for each item was chalked in and erased as new bids were phoned in. In front of the phone bank were four chairs arranged around a round coffee table where Jessica and the other announcers would sit. Most of the on-camera personnel were from the station's administrative staff, and they were a little startled when Jessica, prepared and professional, had shown up with a second dress and a makeup case and had asked to be shown to a dressing room.

As someone frantically rigged up a soft light in the corner of the electronic workshop and borrowed a mirror from the wall of the ladies' room, Jessica picked her way through the tangle of cables, ladders, used flats, and old equipment that cluttered the stage back to the glass-walled control room where the director and his one technician sat at a console. He leafed through the script with her, showing her what she was expected to do, when her breaks would be. She saw a Martin guitar case leaning against the wall of the booth and told him she was prepared to sing.

She worked hard that night. Under the bright hot lights, she described hot dog cookers, card tables, and snowmobiles. She listened interestedly to descriptions of what marvelous programs public television offered; she read off bids and repeated the station's telephone number until she was more sick of it than she was of her early hits.

She was very good. The other celebrity announcer was a former Minnesota Vikings football player. Jessica chose to react with him, teasing him, interrupting his routine readings of the cue cards with down-home practical questions that made everyone else's performance seem stilted in contrast to hers.

People at home, watching her on their sets, felt like they knew her; her personality made such a fresh, immediate impression. They didn't feel like they were watching something staged; it felt like they were watching a real conversation between a straightforward, frank, funny girl and a former football player whom she secretly found attractive.

But it was an act. She was working. Her own personality was not nearly this open, and if there was a former football player in the studio that she found attractive, it was another one, that one sitting in the middle tier of phones, sitting next to Karen Jensen.

She hadn't expected Karen to be there. She didn't work at Cavanaugh–Buchanan. But apparently Walker and Lynn had persuaded some of their Ramsey Hill neighbors to volunteer, and Karen probably had agreed to come when she could have expected to be coming with Bret. Jessica wondered if it were difficult for her, sitting in the background, quietly answering phones and recording bids while Bret's wife was making such a hit on camera.

Whatever Karen felt, Jessica knew that Bret must be relaxing in her presence. Karen was dressed quietly in a khaki skirt and a blue oxford cloth blouse, and Bret could be sure that a radio station would never know more about her than he did. Even if he didn't want to go home with her, even if he never would again, there must have been a bond there, a closeness he felt with her, an ease and a certainty that he would never be able to feel with Jessica.

How ironic it was, Jessica thought as she changed the crimson dress for one of periwinkle blue. Their situation was the reverse of every country song. In the songs, the wife had to stand by silently while her husband was lured by some glamorous Jess Butler-like creature. But what Jess Butler's own husband probably craved was the stability, the sweet, patient generosity, the dependable everydayness, of just such wives. Karen herself might not be a threat to Jessica, but she was a symbol of the sort of woman who was.

Just as Jessica had expected, people were starting to call complaining because Jess Butler was talking, not singing. She, the director, and the station manager had a brief conference during one of her breaks to plan some songs. They decided to give people ten minutes to call in with bids; the highest bidder got to hear his request.

As Bret had told Karen at the Pearsons' party, Jessica was not entirely comfortable singing to a camera. She had gotten through her occasional guest spots on network shows by doing the taping in front of a studio audience or by lip-syncing to something already recorded. But here there was no audience and certainly no prerecorded material. Well, she thought, all she could do was to try her best—and hope that most people were watching the baseball game or the movie on the network channels.

She would be on camera two. They had marked a spot for her to stand, but she immediately discovered that the riser squeaked, and as the Vikings player was reading her introduction, she hurriedly repositioned herself while the cameraman frantically dollied his camera after her, gesturing to the grip who followed him with an armful of cables. It was not the best way to begin a performance.

Then the football player stopped speaking, and the red light on camera two shone.

Still a little rattled from the last-minute scurrying, Jessica picked the intro to "Lonely and Hurting," looking down at the guitar, postponing the moment of facing the camera. She was glad the bidder had named this song; it was off her second album and was much easier to sing than her more recent material. As she began to strum the refrain she knew she could not put it off any longer; she had to look up and gaze straight in the camera lens, which would be glittering with reflected lights and shapes, and pretend it was a person.

She swallowed and lifted her head.

Bret was there.

He was standing quietly, his hands in his pockets, not much more than a shape in the dark shadows beyond the cameras. As she looked up he stepped forward almost into the bright light, standing so near the camera that she could see his direct, alert gaze. As much as he had resented and resisted what he saw as her efforts to turn him into an audience, he was volunteering now—because she needed him.

Of course, she still sang to the lens, not letting her gaze waver toward him. But it was him she thought of as her audience, and the song suddenly felt very personal; the words were now about what it would be like when she finally left Minneapolis, what it would be like to go back to the way things were, seeing him once a year at Christmas, just two members of a large family.

She sang twice more and each time Bret left Karen's side to stand by the cameraman's shoulder. He didn't speak to her, but he was there for her.

The third song was, not surprisingly, her biggest hit, "Almost Enough." It was a ballad with simple words, but when the smoky depths of Jessica's alto caressed the phrases, it was a song about a woman's desire, her yearning, her need, for the man she loved. And this time she didn't just sing it to Bret; she sang it about him, about her dark longing for him.

As the final notes faded, as the light on camera two died so camera one could take over for a wide shot, their eyes met for a moment, a moment in which Jessica knew her eyes were telling him what her lips could not.

Bret turned away quickly. He touched the cameraman on the shoulder and murmured something. The man took a pack of cigarettes from his shirt pocket and shook one out for Bret. Bret took the book of matches from him, and with a yellow flare that glowed against his face for a moment, lit the cigarette, his first cigarette in more than a year.

Jessica let her gaze remain steady; she wasn't going to let him do this. His gray eyes flashed back, defiant for a moment, but then he leaned forward and with silent apology to the man whose cigarette he had just wasted, he stubbed it out in the white foam cup that was serving as an ashtray.

As the evening ended, everyone, the volunteers, the cameramen, the other announcers, clustered around Jessica, praising her with an enthusiasm that made her blush with pleasure until she realized that Bret did not join in the chorus. Even in the car driving home, their brief exchanges avoided any mention of her work.

Finally she had to speak. "Bret, thank you for what you did. For helping me while I was singing."

His eyes shifted toward hers, his head barely moving. "Anyone could have done it."

"No," she replied. "Only you knew that I needed help."

He shrugged and in a minute reached out and clicked on the radio. The intricate depths of a classical piece filled the car; he had his car radio tuned to the one station that would never play a Jess Butler song.

They pulled into their usual parking space. Bret turned off the car, the lights. Jessica felt a strange tension coming from him. Instead of getting out, he rested his arms on the steering wheel and leaned forward, as if he were looking at something that stretched out darkly in front of him.

"Jessie—" He spoke without looking at her.

"Yes, Bret?"

Suddenly he shook his head abruptly. "Oh, skip it." He jerked open the car door. "Let's go in."

Spring was almost summer, and the night was warm, but Jessica shivered. Her periwinkle dress had just a thin strap that tied over each shoulder. She tilted her head back. In spite of the streetlights she could see a few stars glinting white in the night sky, and she could hear a faint rushing, but she didn't know if the sounds were the Mississippi or just the traffic on the expressway.

Silently they crossed the emerald carpets of the lobby, past the white wicker furniture. The heels of Jessica's shoes clicked on the oak floors.

The ride up the elevator, the brief walk through the brick-walled corridor into the condominium, were wordless.

He flipped on the hall light and Jessica went immediately to the stairs. As always, Bret stepped back automatically to let her climb the spiral first.

He had been carrying her other dress for her, and when they were in the upper hall, he handed it to her, but he let go before she had a good grip and a pool of clear plastic and crimson folds spilled across the wooden floor.

Why had he let it drop? she wondered almost frantically. He could catch anything. What was wrong with him tonight?

She knelt to pick the dress up. As she was groping

through the slippery plastic for the hanger, she heard him speak.

"You know what I was about to say in the car, don't you?" His voice was rough.

Slowly Jessica straightened, clutching the folds of the dress. She stared in front of her, at the line of white buttons running down the front of his shirt. It was a nice shirt. She had been with him when he bought it. It had a tattersall check, a muted blue and brown with—

"Jessica." His voice thrust into her thoughts. "I swore I was going to be the one man who never asked this of you"—he was speaking quickly now—"and, God, I've tried...."

Yes, yes, she knew what he had been about to say, what he was going to say, but she could scarcely hear him over the sound of her breathing, the beat of her heart.

"I want you to come to bed with me."

Her eyes flew to his. The dress fell, and as Bret reached out to catch it she stepped back—away from him.

He laid the dress neatly over the oak railing. "Well?" His voice was almost impersonal now. "Will you?"

"Bret...I..."

How she had waited for this moment, how she had hungered for it. But she had never anticipated it to be like this. She had expected his hands to be warm on her; she had counted on his voice to be low in her ear, not so matter-of-fact, so austere.

She looked at him standing in front of her. He'd jammed his hands in his pockets as if he didn't care what she said. But the sleeves of his shirt were rolled up to the elbow and she could see the tension in the muscles of his arm.

"I suppose you want it wrapped up in pretty paper."
His voice was crisp. "But it isn't pretty. I know you
used to think me some sort of god, but you've got to
face it, I'm just like all those other guys. I want you the
same as they do. There's no difference between them
and me except that maybe I've been in line a few years
longer, that's all."

And she knew that some part of him wanted her to
refuse, to slap him down, to be insulted, outraged. But
how could she? He was Bret, and behind his blunt
words, she heard misery.

She turned and looked out across the banister. The
hall light spilled into the living room below, picking up
the curving shape of a table leg where it stood on the
blue border of an Oriental carpet.

She heard Bret sigh and move closer. His hands
closed around her shoulders; his grip was warm and
strong against her skin. "Do you need to hear it? How
lovely you are...." His breath barely disturbed her
hair. "What a wonderful job you did tonight. And
when you sang, your eyes were like sapphires and a
man knew all he'd have to do was untie this...."

His fingers eased aside the thin strap of her dress and
she felt his head move, his dark hair brushing across
her cheek, his warm lips pressing against the smooth
flesh of her shoulder.

"And your arms...what man wouldn't dream of
these arms pulling him down to you?" As he spoke,
his voice muffled against the curve of her neck, his
hands slid down her arms, wrapping them across her,
pulling her back against him.

She could feel the rise and fall of his chest as he
breathed. When a soft line of kisses trailed across her
neck, she let her head drop, looking down to where his

arms were folded about her. One tanned hand curved upward, slipping across the periwinkle silk, until he reached the soft swell of her breast. An immediate stirring welcomed his touch, a response that he had, just a few weeks before, sought for in vain.

And Jessica felt his body's answering echo.

She turned in his arms, leaning back so that he could see, in her eyes, the light he could not fail to understand.

"Jessie, if this is an act—" His voice was thick. "If this is an act, by God, I don't want to know." With a sharp breath he pulled her to him.

This was the kiss a man gave a woman. The one other time he had kissed her with passion, that winter night in Georgia, he'd been kissing a girl. Now everything was different; there was a certainty about this kiss, a confidence that she was experienced, willing, even an edge of urgent roughness that he didn't bother to conceal. Her lips opened beneath his, and his hands dropped to her hips as if about to shift her slightly, to move her against his leg.

As he thrust open the door of his gray room and, his hand at the small of her back, took her in, as his fingers sought the narrow ribbons that held her dress to her, Bret thought he knew what it would be like with Jessica. She would, he assumed, give a practiced performance, graceful and polished. She would try to please him, ignoring her own needs. She would know exactly what to do and when to do it.

It was not what he truly wanted. He would have preferred the confused sweetness he had seen that winter night years ago, back when she hadn't been so expert, back when it would have still mattered to her who he was.

On the other hand, he thought in a cynical flash, when Jessica set out to please, she would succeed. It would be an adventure worth remembering.

The wisp of periwinkle silk drifted to the floor. She was as lovely as he had thought she would be; her body was a pale, curving shape against the charcoal quilt of his bed. He thought of how long he had waited to have her like this, of the years he had burned for her. And as he first touched her, feeling, as he had so often ached to do, the creamy satin of her leg, the ivory and rose of her breast, for a hard, racking moment, he wasn't sure he could wait any longer.

But a slowly seeping surprise eased his urgency. He had pulled off his shirt before drawing her into his arms, and her hands now moved over his shoulders but her feathery touches were so soft and tentative that he would not have found their delicateness arousing if they had come from another woman's hands. And her caresses did not move downward, to explore him, to work open his belt and jeans, as he would have expected from an experienced woman.

He took her hand in his, guiding it down to his leg, certain that would remind her what a man wanted, and just the thought of her touch slipping between their bodies, just the thought of her white hand on him, shot through him, enflaming his senses as surely as any physical caress. But when he let go of her hand, it fell limply on the bed.

She was clearly aroused, the deep sensuality that charged her voice now vibrated through her body, flushing it with a warm glow, moistening her skin with an easing softness.

But something was wrong. The waves of desire that should have been lifting her, carrying her to a dizzying rapture, were instead pummeling too hard, crashing at her, tossing her like a pebble in an angry tide, grating her across the harsh sands.

Gone was the easy, natural rhythm that underlay every movement she ever made. Her body shifted restlessly, unevenly, not giving in to the regular vibrations that brought a woman her pleasure.

He spoke to her in a low voice. "Jessie, you'll have to tell me what you like."

She didn't answer. And in a sharp coil of pain he realized it was because she didn't know.

What kind of men had she been with? Bret thought with sudden anger. Hadn't any cared enough about her to help her? Hadn't at least one of them cared about something besides his own pleasure? Or maybe pleasure hadn't even been a part of it. Maybe they had all just wanted to say they had had Jess Butler. She would have only been a name to them, barely even a body, certainly not a person. Is this what his family had saved her for—so that she could be used like this?

Suddenly his wrenching anger turned on her. She wasn't fourteen any longer; she hadn't been raped. She had allowed this to happen to her. Didn't she have any pride or self-respect? To have given herself so cheaply, not even getting from those nameless men a certain physical ease.

With Bret's anger came a white-hot flash of desire, a fiercer pain than he had ever known before, more demanding, almost primitive, possessive. He wrenched open his jeans, uncaring that his belt buckle, his zipper, would scrape against her.

A gasp of surprise, a resistance in her body, suggested that he might have been wrong in every respect, terribly, terribly wrong. He tried to stop, but as she moved beneath him, confused by the sudden stillness of him, the feel of her body sent a driving rhythm singing through him, and he thrust himself in her, unable to care that every stroke of his body might cause her pain.

Bret lay on his back, one hand over his face, his breathing still ragged. He tried to speak, "Jessica, if I had had any idea...." His voice was hoarse. "If I had known, it wouldn't have happened that way."

"Known?" Jessica felt confused, disoriented. Had that been Bret?

He sat up, fumbling frantically on the nightstand for the cigarettes that he, of course, no longer kept there. He leaned back against the wall, looking weary, almost as if he hated himself. "You are very inexperienced," he said bluntly.

"Yes."

She had never imagined that it would make such a difference. She wasn't a girl; she knew all about men; she had seen their bodies; she had heard them talk in ways most women never hear men talk; she hadn't felt inexperienced.

But she was. She hadn't known what to do, how to please him. She had always assumed that it was instinctive, but if it was an instinct, she clearly didn't have it.

And she hadn't been prepared for how she herself would feel. The first stirring tightness had been familiar. She'd felt it before. Sometimes, pausing in the wings, listening to a crowd roar their impatience for her, she'd feel an electricity, an energy, that she knew had to be sexual. The current would flash to the band, gripping them with the same fever, and the six of them would perform together in front of thousands an act that, while not physical, was so passionately charged as anything a man and a woman might do alone.

But performing had never deepened the tightness into pleasure. It had only exhausted her enough to drive all sensations from her body.

This had been so unexpected. There hadn't seemed to be a clear road from desire to fulfillment. She had felt lost in a maze, not knowing where to turn or even what it was she was looking for. It was as if her desire was something alien that was invading her body almost hostilely; she knew that she should have been able to turn it into pleasure, but instead it felt like an advancing enemy, bewildering, unceasing, coming at her from every direction, unorganized, diffuse. And she hadn't known what to do.

She had failed in a way that she never had failed before.

Bret's voice jerked at her. "God, why didn't you tell me?"

Jessica knew that she could have never volunteered such information. "You could have asked," she said miserably.

"Oh, come on." Whatever he was feeling was now coming across as anger. "Who would have thought it? I mean, you *are* Jess Butler. Look at those album covers; that's no inexperienced girl in those pictures. There's not a soul on the face of the earth who could listen to your songs and think you didn't know your way around."

Suddenly all of Jessica's confusion and misery were drowned in a surging flood of angry pride. He had no call to be mad at her. She had done nothing wrong. Yes, she had been inept, but it was for the best possible reason.

"Other people might have cause for certain misapprehensions," she said, her voice cool steel. "But not you."

"Me?" She could hear the surprise in his voice. "How am I different from anyone else?"

"You are my husband." Jessica articulated each word with a hard-edged, chilling clarity.

"What nonsense," Bret snapped immediately. "If you've been walking around with some crazy notion that you were saving yourself for me...I didn't think even you were capable of such incredible foolishness."

Jessica gasped with pain at the harshness of his words. For a moment she was afraid she was going to cry. Men hated women who cried afterward; she had heard that from the band. She wouldn't cry; she just wouldn't.

She sensed him move and braced herself for more angry words.

But he spoke gently. "Why are we fighting about this, Jessie?"

She buried her face in her hands. "I don't know." Her voice quivered with a stifled sob.

He touched her hair. "Why don't you go take a shower? You'll feel better and then we can talk."

When she came out of her bathroom, tying the robe that matched another of Nathan's elegant, expensive nightgowns, Bret was in the white guest room waiting for her. His hair was damp; he had showered too.

How sad. What should have been something very precious had left them both feeling dirty, needing to wash all traces of it from their bodies. He stood up as she came in the room. He cleared his throat and spoke. "You do have the prettiest nightgowns of any female I've ever seen."

Jessica blessed him for, well, for being Southern, for not having to start the conversation directly. She glanced down at the fall of shimmering peach. "Nathan bought it for me," she explained.

Bret gestured to the sand-colored wing chair, inviting her to sit down. "You said that about your white one," he said slowly, "that Geer gave it to you. Do you understand how that sounded?"

Jessica started. No, she hadn't thought.

Bret smiled. "Obviously you didn't."

So relieved to see that familiar warm smile, Jessica explained how Nathan had come to send them, glossing over how miserable she had been that night. "He has a lot at stake in keeping me happy."

"So do I," Bret said immediately. "Only it isn't money."

He sat down on the ottoman at her feet and took her hands. "First, are you all right? Physically, I mean. Did I hurt you?"

Jessica shook her head. "I'm fine."

"Then—"

Jessica suddenly didn't think she could bear to discuss what had happened. "Bret, please," she interrupted, pulling her hands away. "Let's not talk about this. You made a mistake, and I admit it was probably a very natural one, but now you know. You were once surprised that I couldn't dance; this isn't that much different. So couldn't we just forget about it?"

He shook his head. "No, we can't. I know it is hard, but we have to talk."

It was hard. They had both been raised in a world where men and women, even husband and wife, did not talk about sex. Whatever uninhibited joys, whatever fumbling disasters, were shared at night, nothing was discussed in the morning.

Jessica and Bret sometimes found it hard to adapt to more modern ways.

But Bret was going to try.

"Jessie," he asked quietly, "does this have anything to do with Cal Winsley? Are you still afraid of men?"

Jessica blinked. She shook her head. "No, Bret, honestly not. I haven't thought about that in years."

He looked relieved, suddenly less weary. "Then why? Surely it wasn't lack of opportunity."

"Well, in a way." She started to speak more quickly. "Bret, I don't think you know what my life is like. I'm on the road nearly all the time. Often I'm the only woman or one of very few, and legally at least, all those guys work for me."

He seemed to understand. "So it is either sleep with all of them or none?" And after she nodded, he continued. "But that can't explain everything. What about when you were in Los Angeles, cutting albums and such? Surely you met other people."

Nervously Jessica plucked at the sash of her robe. Then her words came out in a rush. "Do you know how girls are told boys only want one thing?"

He smiled. "I've heard that. Been accused of it, in fact."

"Well, it's right. They are after one thing, but it isn't sex, at least not with me. There are plenty of men out there who have thought that if I sleep with them, then I will record their songs, sing in their clubs or something."

"And?" he prompted.

"Don't you see?" she asked urgently. "People—

men are always telling me what to do, what to sing, what to wear, what to be like. This was the only thing I had, the only thing I said 'no' about. I did everything else they wanted. I didn't do this."

Bret was looking at her intently, his head tilted, a dark concentrated expression in his eyes.

"I needed something like that," she continued. "Something I would not do. It probably could have been anything; refusing to wear jeans on stage might have satisfied some of the same need. But you know how we were brought up—what girls are told—this was the obvious thing, and I didn't have to do a lot of explaining like I would have with anything else."

"Don't people know?" Bret asked curiously.

"Oh, no." She shook her head. "I think lots of men assume I'm sleeping with every one but them. No one, except now you, has any idea. I mean, it wouldn't exactly be good for the image."

He smiled softly and after a brief pause was serious again. "So this has really been something you've done for yourself, not, as you suggested earlier, out of some obligation to me. Despite that awful crack I made about standing in line for you, I wouldn't want to be put at the head of the line just because of this marriage business—especially if there's been someone you've cared about."

"Yes, you are exactly right; I did it for myself," Jessica answered immediately, knowing that, for the most part at least, she was speaking the truth.

Bret was alert. "No, Jessie, don't tell me what you think I want to hear. We'll never get anywhere with you doing that."

It had been with Cade, her bass player, near the end of her first tour with Jess's Boys. It had been the worst tour she'd ever been on. The band members all hated each other, each member seeing in the others a reflection of his own decision to sell out, to play backup for a female country singer because she was paying steady wages. Onstage they played a tight professional set, but offstage they hardly spoke to one another. The respect that they felt for each other today, the loyalty and affection that now bound them, were still a year away. They seemed sure to break up; certainly nothing Jessica did would make relations among them any worse.

They were in Fargo, North Dakota, farther north than they had ever played. Jessica had been cold all day, cold and dead weary, the normal strains of the road aggravated by the tensions among the band.

After the show she and Cade and some of the crew were in Cade's hotel room, eating pizza and watching the single TV channel still broadcasting that late at night. None of the other band members were there, and gradually the crew left, until it was just Cade and Jessica.

There was nothing unusual about that or that they should both be sitting on his bed, leaning back against the headboard. Working the road was exhaustingly intimate. When Cade put his arm around her shoulders, that too was not worth noting. Casual contact was frequent.

But the weight of Cade's arm was unusually comforting as if it might protect her from all the bitter tensions. She leaned her cheek against his shirt, and when his other arm closed around her, all she knew was that she felt warm for the first time since Oklahoma.

She could have left but she did not, and in a moment, Cade touched her face with his callused, guitar-player's fingers, and turning it upward, kissed her. And

Jessica knew that this was not how a man kissed the woman he worked for.

He pressed her back among the pillows, and the feel of his body was like the strong, steady throb of his bass guitar. Whenever she'd feel lost in a song, it was Cade's bass, not Wayne's lead, that seemed to get her out.

In her exhaustion she might well have let him make love to her except that he lifted his blond head and said, "Jess, I want you to stay here with me, but I hear tell you're married. Are you?"

Jessica nodded.

"Then I need to know if this is going to bother your husband."

She said nothing, but a picture of Bret smiling, swinging off a tractor, filled her mind.

"Then," Cade said, easing himself upright, "I think maybe I should walk you back to your room."

In the morning, facing her difficult life again, she had been very glad. Perhaps her performance would have been better if one of the band was her lover, but her performance was already good enough.

Jessica now tried to explain some of this to Bret.

"He sounds like a decent sort of fellow," he commented at the end.

"Oh, he is," Jessica agreed swiftly.

"You say this was in Fargo? A couple of years ago? I thought about coming to that concert." He smiled. "Maybe I should have."

Suddenly they heard the phone ring. Bret stood up immediately, glancing at his watch, obviously concerned.

Jessica could understand his anxious response—it was very late—but she hated for their talk to be over.

She had never been so open with anyone and she couldn't imagine it ever happening again.

"If you'd come to Fargo," she said shyly, prolonging the conversation for a moment despite the insistent phone, "would your arms have been warm?"

Bret glanced at her over his shoulder. "I think I could have managed something."

## Chapter Nine

Bret had been right. A phone ringing that late couldn't be good.

There'd been a fire at the plant. No one was hurt, and the flames had been contained in the new cafeteria wing, but the rest of the plant was full of very technical, high-cost equipment that could have easily been damaged by smoke and water. He, Walker, and their senior staff had spent three days, checking it all, working as much as eighteen hours each day, trying to get back up to full production as quickly as possible.

Bret had never before resented the demands owning a company placed on him; this time he had. He had wanted to be with Jessica, but there simply had been no time. The first night she had apparently tried to wait up for him, but had fallen asleep on the sofa. She had wakened as he came in, blinking like a soft, sleepy puppy. She had seemed so sweet and warm he had wanted to take her to bed, not to make love to her, but just to have her curled up next to him. But as he had reached for her, he'd seen a careful watchfulness steal into her dark blue eyes, and he knew he couldn't touch her until they had talked.

He had had to put her on hold until things at work

were sorted out. It didn't seem right, but he just didn't see that he had much choice.

But finally all the equipment had been checked, the initial meetings with the insurance adjusters had gone well, and he and Walker had both, quite uncharacteristically, decided to go home at three in the afternoon.

Now as he leaned wearily against the wall of the elevator, he wondered if he might try to get some sleep before dinner. He needed it, but he might sleep through the night if he lay down, and that hardly seemed fair to Jessica.

The elevator door slid open, and Bret stepped out in the hall, reaching in his pockets for his keys.

He was instantly alert.

Coming through the thick walls, the carefully sound-proofed door of his condominium, he could hear music, a melody and a voice he would recognize anywhere, the third song on the second side of Jess Butler's latest album.

Why was Jessica playing her own records? As far as he knew, she never listened to them.

With her back to the door, she didn't hear him come in and she remained where she was, facing the stereo. Her head was bent over the turntable and the white of her neck gleamed between her black curls and the cranberry cotton of her shirt. Scattered around her on the table and the floor were her other albums: the blue eyes and black hair smiling up out of the photographs recorded the history of her growth as a woman, from the sweet and girlish charm of her first album to the direct, more challenging look of the most recent. He had every album she had ever made.

He watched her for a moment, a slender, black-haired shape in white slacks and a dark red shirt. He wondered what she was thinking about. Did she hear the beauty of her voice? Did its magic stir her too?

Then as he stood there, watching her and listening to her song, Bret came to understand why she could sing as she did. Yes, some of her songs were about physical love, something Jessica had proved to know astonishingly little about, but they were about how sex affected the way people felt, how its smoky flames could leave a person restless, lonely, crazy. Jessica, with her amazing gift of understanding, would know how that felt even if she'd never experienced it herself, just as in another song she seemed to understand the pain of losing a child although, of course, she never had.

And as for the physical side of sex, he knew that Jessica would say that was what rock and roll was about. Perhaps her sexual inexperience had been an important part of why she refused to sing rock.

Suddenly she moved, reaching out, jerking, the arm of the turntable. The music became a harsh rasp as the needle sliced across the disc, scratching it.

Bret slipped his keys in his pocket and closed the door. "That may be your voice, but it's my record."

She started and turned. "Oh, Bret, I didn't know you were here." She glanced down to the record still turning around, a silvery gray line now scratched across the black vinyl. "I'm sorry; I'll get you another one."

"Jessie, what is it? What's bothering you?"

"Nothing."

God forgive him, but Bret was tired. He had spent three days with sensitive, delicate equipment; he just didn't have the patience right now for a sensitive, delicate singer.

"Suit yourself," he said briskly. "If something's

bothering you, you are a fool not to talk about it, but it's up to you. I'm going to change.''

By the time he was in the quiet grays of his bedroom, he was already regretting his hasty words. Slowly he unknotted his tie. Undoubtedly she was still upset by what had happened the other night. Their talk afterward had only been about her. The phone had interrupted before he had had a chance to explain himself, to apologize.

He did indeed owe her more than an apology. From the first to the last, he had behaved in a most reprehensible manner.

When they had been standing in the hall, he had been jealous and had tried to camouflage his feelings as a blunt, almost crude realism that Jessica, in her surprising innocence, must have found enormously offensive. And then later when she needed gentle patience, reassurance, someone to steady her and help, he had gotten angry and had taken her almost brutally.

All his life Bret had learned that men were to show only one emotion—anger. When he was hurt, when he had been frightened, he wouldn't admit it even to himself. Any powerful emotion had always come out as anger.

As an adult, he was trying to be different—to admit to more feelings, not to respond to everything with such quick, reflexive anger. But the other night, with the woman that mattered to him more than any other, when he thought she had been misused in the most pathetic way, his concern for her, his grief, had come out as a shatteringly fierce anger.

What possible chance was there for them? When he acted like this? And when she—

"Bret." Jessica's voice was, as always, soft and rich.

He turned. She was standing at the door of his room. None of the tension he knew she felt showed in the quiet repose of her features; the only hint was the shadow that darkened her blue eyes.

"How did the meeting with the insurance people go?"

He pulled his shirt over his head. "Fine. They aren't going to cause any problems."

"That's good," she said politely.

Bret settled the collar of his shirt. "Walker and I still have enough of the country boy left in us that we are always surprised when insurance companies and banks seem to be on our side."

Why were they talking like this?

Then he noticed that she was barefoot, her toes peeping out from under the cuffs of her white slacks. She seemed fragile, so easily damaged.

"Bret, I'm sorry about the record."

"You know that doesn't matter," he said immediately.

She had drifted into the room and was standing by the window, staring out at the river. Without her shoes she seemed very small.

"What was in the song that made you do that?" he asked quietly.

"I don't know, Bret." Her voice had such a distant quality that he knew she was seeing none of the bright, busy scene that lay before them. "I don't know, but some of these songs—they sound like it's so easy."

He was surprised that she had answered him at all; it was so unlike her to explain her misery. "What do you mean, Jessie? What's so easy?"

"That's just it; it isn't easy and I thought it would be."

The husky, almost embarrassed, tremor in her voice,

more than her vague words, told him what she was talking about.

He took a breath and spoke slowly. "I know. It doesn't seem fair that sexual pleasure isn't always easy for women, that it is something to be learned. I think that a lot of women never do really understand their bodies very well and that they mostly get emotional satisfaction from their husbands' pleasure, but that may be it for them."

She was shaking her head as he spoke. "I wasn't talking about that."

He looked at her inquiringly.

"The one thing I always thought about myself was that I would be able to please a man." Her blue eyes met his unflinchingly. Having decided to say this, she wasn't going to be shy or evasive. "I had to believe that or I never could have done the things I have done. I had to be so certain that I never even thought to wonder about it. But I did not know what to do." Her confession, her admission of failure, rang with a rich dignity. "I didn't know where to touch you or how to do it. I didn't know if I was to say things and if so, what. I was completely ignorant. And you—"

"Wait a minute," he interrupted. "You haven't been spending the last three days worrying about *me*? That it wasn't good for me? After what happened... how can you possibly—" He broke off, surprised, disbelieving. But, no, he reminded himself, this was the way she was. "Oh, Jessie," he sighed, "why can't you think about yourself for a change? Why do you always, always, put other people first?"

"I just want to make you happy." Her voice was so low that he had to bend his head to hear it. "What's wrong with that?"

"Everything." Bret's exhaustion flared into impatience again. "That's why messed-up teen-agers sleep around. But you are a woman, and as best as I can tell, there's only two reasons why a woman should sleep with a man, either she loves him or failing that, because she thinks she will have a good time. As far as I know, no woman has ever slept with me because she loves me, but some sure have because they just plain wanted to, and it was simple and clean and a hell of a lot of fun for both of us. I don't want a woman on any other terms. Even you. The other night wasn't a performance. Nobody paid two weeks' allowance for a ticket. Sex isn't one entertainer and one audience. It's two people, both of whom are supposed to have a good time."

Jessica was white; only her eyes had color, their blue depths glowing like a troubled mirror in a badly lit room.

Bret groaned and tried to pull her to him. But the tension in her body resisted him and his hands dropped. "Jessie, I'm sorry I spoke like that, but think of the position you put me in. This business of always trying to please me—and I am not just talking about sex, that's the least of it. Don't you see that I can't ask you for anything, because I know that whatever it is, you will always say yes, even at a complete sacrifice to yourself?"

"But, Bret, what could you ever want from me that I wouldn't gladly do?"

"That's just it. You would do *anything* gladly even if it were...I don't know," he said, obviously casting about for some extreme example. "But say, for instance, I asked you to stay here and have a baby, you—"

"A baby?" Jessica breathed. "Bret, a baby?"

"I am just speaking hypothetically, of course, but if I said, 'Look here, Jessie, I want this,' you'd do it, wouldn't you?"

"In a heartbeat."

He blinked at the sincerity in her voice. "Damn it, Jessica, that's my point. Here you would do something like that just because I asked you, without thinking for a minute whether it would be the right thing for you. You'd tear yourself apart for some whim of mine, turn yourself into a road mother who never saw her child or, God Almighty, you'd probably give up your career if you thought I wanted you to. And you would do it as quickly and as immediately as you would send me your latest album.

"Jessie, don't you see my position? I don't want to use you, but you make it hard not to. I don't ask you for anything, but then I know perfectly well you are trying to second-guess me, trying to figure out what I want and maybe that's worse."

She shot him a surprised, startled look.

"Tell me," he ordered.

"Bret, I've hardly been outside for the last three days."

"What?" He stared at her, baffled. "What are you talking about?"

"Since the auction, I've been afraid people would recognize me."

He tilted his head. "But I thought that was why you did it, because you were ready to be Jess Butler again."

"Oh, no," she sighed.

He moaned her name. "You didn't do it for me, did you? Because you thought it was important to me?"

She nodded. "And I was wrong. Right now nothing is more precious to me than being anonymous, than being left alone.'' Her voice was low, troubled. ''I risked all that to do something that I thought you wanted—without even knowing how important it was to you. As you would say, the stakes were too high.''

He shook his head slowly. ''They sure were. It's a good cause, but it's not that important.'' He slipped his arms around her and this time she leaned against him unresisting. ''In my book there's nothing worth making you unhappy. That's what I really want, Jessie. For you to be happy. I don't think you are, and I don't know how to make you happy so all I can do is try to keep you from deliberately making yourself unhappy because you think you are doing something for me.''

She rested her cheek against the warmth of his shirt. ''Being in Minneapolis is making me happy,'' she said.

''Then stay here as long as that damned contract will let you.'' His hand came up to touch her hair. ''But do it for yourself, not for me.''

She felt his fingers move through her curls. ''All right,'' she murmured into his chest. ''I'll never do anything you like again.''

They stood quietly for a moment. ''Then you are getting off to a rotten start,'' she heard Bret say, ''because your standing here like this isn't half bad.'' She felt the arms around her tighten.

She tilted her head back and Bret kissed her.

It was a gentle kiss, but it lingered on her lips, warm and soft, before flaming to life. She slid her hands up his arms to circle his neck. She felt a trembling, but she didn't know if it was him or her.

''It should be me,'' he whispered, ''not you, who is begging for a second chance.'' Suddenly Bret raised his head and cleared his throat. ''Jessie, I've never been brutal with a woman before, and I am more ashamed of the other night than of anything I have ever done. But if you are willing to take the risk, I promise you that it will never happen again.''

Jessica had to let her eyes, her hands, speak for her. The smoldering beauty of her voice was useless without words, and she could find no words that would tell him of her trust, her faith, her love.

Bret leaned against the windowsill and pulled her to stand between his legs. Slowly he undid the three cranberry buttons along her shoulder and then her shirt was a dark red blossom on the gray carpet. The rustle of the zipper, his hands warm on her flesh, and then her slacks were on the floor too, a drift of snowy white.

Bret eased her toward the bed and his body pressed hers back into the soft quilt. Hesitantly she tried to caress him, but he grasped her hands, bringing them over her head, pinning her wrists against the pillow with one strong hand. He wasn't hurting her, just telling her not to try, telling her that he wanted her to think only of herself. His other hand slipped down the smooth ivory of her leg, lifting her knee, coaxing it outward. She lay across the gray quilt, a slender and fair form, her arms captured above her head and one leg bent. Slowly, his lips never leaving hers, his hand spiraled upward.

Jessica gasped at the intimacy of his touch.

His voice was low in her ear. ''Trust me, Jessie.''

At first it was just as it had been before, with waves of desire confusing her, coming without rhythm or pattern. And whenever it seemed as if these dark forces were about to take a shape, she would be distracted by the gray eyes watching her.

Somehow he understood. He slipped his arm beneath her shoulders, letting her hide her face in the hot darkness of his neck. The rise and fall of his chest against her forced her ragged breathing into a steady beat.

Suddenly his rhythms took over her body. The murky waves became bright, tingling bands, joyous ribbons that she could catch hold. They danced, swirling into an ever-tightening spiral, moving inward, strengthening, concentrating until for a moment, the building pressures seemed too intense, too much, and she wanted him to stop. She stirred restlessly but before she could push him away, before she could acknowledge this second failure, the glowing center glittered and burst, pleasure sweeping through her in spasms of light.

She gasped his name, and when she gripped his shoulder, urging his weight down on her, it was no thought of pleasing him, but only of her own need to feel him against her. He had stopped being an audience, a strange and distant other. He was becoming her lover, her husband, and, finally, a part of her.

Afterward she lay curled up against him, a deep golden glow seeping through her whole body. Her head was on his shoulder, and he had one arm around her, holding her to him firmly. The other was crooked behind his head.

"Bret?"

He rolled his head, lazily looking down at her. "What is it?"

"Thank you."

To her surprise, a dull, almost imperceptible flush colored his face as if he were deeply pleased by her husky tribute, and perhaps even a little embarrassed.

Suddenly she felt very happy, happy to be here with the man she loved, to have been with him, to have learned about pleasure from him. "Now," she teased softly, propping herself up on one elbow, "don't tell me it was nothing, that anyone could have done it."

He grinned. "If I don't tell my customers that other people's products are as good as ours, I am sure as hell not going to tell you that."

She laughed. His body looked wonderful to her, the rounded muscles of his shoulders and arms, the flat ones of his chest, the dark hair lightly covering it all—a picture of masculine strength at rest. She bent and kissed his shoulder, her lips parted against him. "Bret, you are beautiful."

Now he was embarrassed. "Oh, Jessie, I'm not either. I'm just in reasonably decent shape, that's all. Beauty is your department, and you've got enough for the both of us."

But he didn't stop the hand that was moving across him, tracing the line of his collarbone, the length of his arm, the curve of his rib, exploring the curious contrast between warm, firm flesh and the soft tangle of hair. Her hand dropped to the hard plain below his waist, lingering there almost timidly.

"Don't stop on my account." His voice was low.

She'd been curious about him, eager to touch him as he had touched her. His response was immediate, and when she tried to bury her face in his neck again, this time he wouldn't let her. A hand curled about her chin forced her from hiding, forced her to watch the dark lights kindling in his eyes and, in turn, to let him watch her.

Until now she had been most conscious of him as male, a man shaped so differently from herself, but now as she witnessed the passion filling his eyes, she knew that this man—his breath quickening, his pulse insistent—wasn't just a man. He was Bret.

She bent her head and kissed him with a passion nearly as ardent and demanding as anything he had given her.

He breathed sharply. His arms closed around her, pushing her down on her back, pulling her beneath him.

Finally he slowly, reluctantly, eased himself from her, and for a while, they lay quietly, a warm tangle of legs and arms.

He was the first to break the satisfied silence. "Well, well, Jessica Sue," he said softly, "if the last twenty minutes were what you manage in spite of this complete ignorance of yours, then old Thomas Gray was right that 'ignorance is bliss.'"

Jessica was too content to be bothered that she hadn't the faintest idea who Thomas Gray was.

"Do you know what surprises me?" she asked.

He scratched his cheek. "I'm not even going to try on that one. Just tell me."

"How different it is."

"Different from what?" Bret asked, smiling.

"I would have thought that with the same person it would be more the same each time. Is it just because this is all so new to me?"

"That's part of it," he answered. "But this isn't new to me, and believe me, nothing that happened today felt the least bit routine."

"Bret!" Jessica's eyes widened with delight.

"Well, stick around for another thirty or forty years and then maybe things will get a little monotonous." Suddenly his casual tones deepened. "But don't count on it."

She hardly knew what to say. Was he asking something? "Bret—"

The phone rang.

He'd been watching her carefully, but now his glance shifted to the phone and then he slapped his forehead. "Damn, that will be Walker. I said we'd go out with them for a drink and maybe dinner. I completely forgot." He reached for the phone. "Do you want to go?"

"I'd love to." She was enthusiastic. "But aren't you too tired?" He had had very little sleep since the fire.

"I sure should be, shouldn't I?"

Because Jessica and Bret were so late, the bar they wanted to go to was full of the after-work crowd, and so they went across the street to one of the hotels and were seated in the lounge. It had black vinyl tub chairs, a red carpet, and a piano bar. The other customers were tired businessmen.

Jessica kept apologizing for being late.

"You're the one who will have to suffer," Walker said cheerfully. "This is not the sort of place you fancy celebrities usually hang out."

"No, I've worked in hotel lounges. I still do, in fact," she deadpanned.

"You do?" Lynn was surprised. "I thought—"

"Don't listen to her," Bret interrupted, putting his arm across the back of Jessica's chair. "If you compare this to a place in Las Vegas that seats two thousand people, then she still works in hotel lounges."

He was smiling at her, his eyes so warm that she nearly blushed. Surely everyone in the room could understand the message in those gray lights.

But, oh, Jessica thought, what a delicious feeling it was, to be out in public with a man you'd just made love to. The warm flesh a woman had so recently felt against her own was now hidden by his clothes; neatly combed was the thick hair she had laced her fingers through as she had pulled his head down to her body. His public self was all neatly in place.

But still there was an ease in his body, a relaxed stillness springing from physical contentment, and that light in his eyes, shining with memories of what had happened in private.

Jessica reached out and under the table she let her hand drift across Bret's leg.

Their drinks came—surprisingly Lynn had ordered ginger ale—and while they were helping the waitress get the right drink to the right person, the piano player finished his song.

"We've got a request here"—they all heard him say into his mike—"for a song recorded by a woman who was in town last week."

Jessica stiffened, forgetting all her pretty thoughts about private pleasures. She immediately swiveled her chair toward Walker and bent her head so that from the floor, all a person could have seen was a gleam of black hair.

The voice continued, "Now she and I are such good friends that I know she wouldn't mind my singing her song."

The piano started on a thin, plastic version of Jess Butler's "Waiting for You."

Walker and Bret immediately recognized it. "Do you know that guy?" Walker asked.

Jessica glanced over at the piano, taking care not to make herself too visible. "Not that I know of, but that doesn't mean a thing. I meet a lot of people."

"But he said that you were good friends," Lynn protested.

Jessica shrugged; she was very used to being good friends with people she didn't know from Adam.

"Do you want us to go say something to him?" Walker growled.

"Shall we break his head open for you?" Bret offered cheerfully. "We like breaking people's heads open, and we are getting out of practice."

"Good heavens, no." Jessica laughed. Bret was teasing; she wasn't so sure about Walker. "Do you know what he would say if you said one word to him—'Last time Jess and I were together, her husband and his partner, well, they had to beat me up.'" Jessica was imitating a man's bragging voice, "'Yes, friends, it took both of them.'"

Lynn shook her head. "Doesn't that bother you?"

"Not anymore. How does it hurt me?"

"Well, he's sure making a hash of your song," Bret commented. "And I always liked that one."

"Yes," Jessica reflected objectively. "He is. He's not feeling it. He hasn't thought about the difference between waiting and giving up—the song needs to be about taking waiting out to its very limit just before it becomes despair. He's cheating. I mean, I cheat too these days," Jessica admitted honestly, not trying to hide it anymore, "but at least I did think about it once. He's never going to make it out of here unless he starts doing it right."

"The difference between waiting and giving up—that's interesting," Bret mused.

But Jessica was still thinking about the piano player. "And he hates us. You can't hate your audience."

"Hates us?" Lynn exclaimed. "What have we done to him?"

"We are here in a businessman's hotel; there aren't more of us; we aren't listening." Jessica lifted her wineglass and then set it down without drinking. Her voice was suddenly low, impassioned. "He is such a fool; he doesn't know how good little places like this are. He can *see* us; we aren't just some black mass sending out sound. You can really make it good in a place this small; you can get to everybody...and then you can leave. He can go *home*; he doesn't know it, but if he gets what he wants, he won't be able to walk down the street and go home."

The others were quiet, listening to her. Finally Lynn spoke, her clear Northern accent giving her words a ring of truth. "Is it possible that you don't like being as successful as you are? That you liked it better when you were playing places like this?"

Jessica didn't answer.

She felt Bret's hand touch her shoulder. "Memory plays tricks on you, Jessie. Do you really want to be singing again in front of people who don't listen?"

"When I sang, they listened," she said crisply. Then suddenly her words rushed on. "Don't you see that's how you know you're good—in places like this? You've got to make people listen to you; if you're bad, they won't. Anyway, the audiences, I don't know...they are so easy, so cheap. They just like everything. Half are so stoned you could play an old Temptations record; they wouldn't know the difference. The other half feel like they've spent so much money they've got to like it, and they would never admit it if they didn't. It's just not the same anymore." Jessica stared down at her glass.

"Then quit," she heard Walker say bluntly. "If you don't like it anymore, quit."

"I can't."

"Why not?" he asked. "If Bret won't support you, you can clean house for Lynn and me."

"Jessica hardly needs money," Bret answered for her. "But I can't imagine her not performing."

"I don't know about that." Jessica felt defensive. "But I owe the label another album. I've got a contract." The contract now felt like such a burden.

"What happens if you would break the contract?" Walker asked.

Jessica shook her head. "I couldn't do that."

"Why not? Will they try to sue you off the face of the earth?"

"Probably," Jessica said tightly. "Anyway, as Bret said, I've been singing for so long I can't imagine myself without my career."

Jessica now found herself resenting all reminders of her career. A few people did stop her on the street, asking her if they had seen her on TV. She soon learned that if she denied it, they were intrigued, still sure that they were right. But if she admitted that she had done a little work on public television, they were immediately bored and walked on. Her lunch had been purchased by a local hardware store owner for his teenage son and his friends, and Jessica found it so tiring to be Jess Butler for two hours that she came home and slept all afternoon.

How her contract was starting to weigh on her! She couldn't even remember signing it. She had been completely uninvolved in the negotiations with the label. Now she wished she had taken a part; maybe some lucky accident would have prompted her to say, "Hey, guys, let's just sign up for three records, not four."

If she had done that, she would be free now. She wasn't sure what she would do with that freedom. Of course, she longed to stay with Bret although she knew that he believed that impossible. Even now that he knew she wasn't quite the tramp he once thought her, he still thought she didn't belong in Minneapolis. His belief that she wouldn't fit in had been as much psychological as moral. He believed she needed to be on the road, that performing was in her blood, that she couldn't live without an audience. She supposed he was right.

Art and Nathan were clearly thinking that her vacation had lasted long enough. Art sent her cassettes of new songs. She hated them all, some were too political, some too angry, the rest too sad. Why couldn't people write songs about being happy?

Then Nathan called. Jess's Boys were starting some preliminary touring, and they were taking advantage of the publicity she had got from her television appearance and were coming to Minneapolis. Would she sing a song or so with them?

Guessing that this was no offhand request, but Nathan's way of getting her back to work, she felt she had no choice. At least the concert was after Memorial Day; she felt like it gave her more time with Bret.

This was why she hated these reminders of her career—they reminded her that sometime very soon she was going to have to leave him.

As a result, each moment they had together became precious. The sense of how fleeting their time together was gave it a sweetness that they savored.

Because they could make no plans, not even to go boating for a weekend next month, because they could see no future for themselves, each detail in the present mattered. The ordinary dailiness of life, often called "the enemy of marriage," was all that their marriage had and they treasured it. The little things that other couples ignored, Jessica and Bret couldn't.

In the mornings they would have coffee on the terrace and try to figure out who should take the car in for a tune-up. At a restaurant Bret would know without asking what drink to order for her and would later finish her steak. They would stand side-by-side in the line outside the movie theater. At nights she would fall asleep curled up against him and in the mornings wake up beside him. All of these little unnoticed moments that make up the days of the married, Jessica and Bret noticed. The unspoken knowledge that the beauty of their shared life could not last gave those moments a soft bittersweetness.

Jessica had never been so content. Life seemed so easy. The things she hated to do, killing bugs, standing up to auto mechanics, he did easily, unthinkingly. The things that made him impatient, waiting for deliveries, straightening out an incorrect utility bill, Jessica had nearly inexhaustible patience for. They were a team.

She marveled that other couples could move through their days, taking the miracle of happiness for granted. But other couples' lives were not built on the knowledge that one day one of them would again be living on a bus and the other would again find it better to work much too late than to come home to an empty apartment.

Then they learned that Walker and Lynn could afford to ignore these small, daily pleasures because they had a far greater one to look forward to.

Bret was taking advantage of Jessica's presence to do some long overdue entertaining. They had invited

some of the senior people from the company over, and
Jessica had cooked Southern: a country ham and fried
apples; beaten biscuits and red-clover honey; coleslaw
made with real whipping cream, not mayonnaise; a
lemon pie with a meringue that didn't weep, because
as a girl Jessica had learned how to beat cornstarch in;
and a Jefferson Davis pie, an old recipe something like
a pecan pie, but with dates, raisins, cinnamon, and
cream in it as well.

Walker and Lynn stayed after the others had left.
Lynn was helping Jessica with the dishes and the men
were almost managing to stay out of the way. A pie
plate with the last piece of Jeff Davis pie was sitting on
the counter between them, and both were eyeing it interestedly. Finally, Jessica pulled open a drawer and
handed them a pair of forks.

They grinned at her. Bret pulled the pie plate between them, and Walker said, "Nothing beats a Southern girl for making a man happy."

"Don't I deserve a little of your attention?" Lynn
asked as she leaned over and put another plate in the
dishwasher.

"Well, if you're going to get legal about it...."
Walker sighed with exaggeration, but the light in his
eyes as he looked at her was so very warm that Jessica
finally asked, "And when are you all going to tell us?"

She had noticed that Lynn had again had no alcohol,
and while Jessica's California friends tended to be
more creative than fertile, she suspected what it meant.

"Tell us what?" Bret asked casually, more intent on
the battle his fork was having with Walker's over the
last scrap of pie.

"I'm pregnant."

Bret's fork clattered against the pie tin.

Of course, he went to Lynn first, embracing her, kissing her, telling her that she was making Walker a very lucky man.

"Wait until next year," she replied dryly, "when you're sleeping all night and he's not."

Then Bret turned to his partner, saying nothing, just extending his hand, which Walker gripped warmly.

Jessica realized that she had never seen the two of them shake hands before. Upon meeting, they would nod, flash a quick grin, grimace, whatever was appropriate to the occasion. It was as if early in their partnership they had shaken hands and did not need to do it again. But this moment, they knew, was a special one, and in the very limited range of gestures by which men can express their affection for each other, they once again shook hands.

"Cavanaugh, Buchanan, and Kids," Walker mused. "How does that sound?"

"Not half bad," Bret returned. "But why 'Kids'? Are we showing that we aren't discriminating against daughters?"

"That's right." Walker grinned. "We are equal-opportunity nepotists."

Lynn smiled and turned back to the sink. "I just hope you two manage to remember how guilty you felt when neither of you could go in with your fathers."

Bret instantly sobered, but Walker just laughed. "No, this kid will be a Northerner, and Northerners aren't so weird. He will be able to tell his father to go fry himself without a second thought."

"She, Walker, she," Lynn corrected. "It might be a girl."

"So much the better," he replied promptly. "Then these two here can have a boy, and when we are all about fifty," he fantasized cheerfully, "I'll get to shoot Bret's son for messing around with my daughter. It'll be great fun."

The apartment seemed very quiet when Walker and Lynn finally left. As they were undressing, Jessica broke the silence. "They seemed very happy."

"Is Lynn?" he asked. "It's hard for me to tell about her sometimes; she's so uneffusive."

"I think she's thrilled." Jessica noticed how Lynn's lip had quivered when Bret had told her that Walker was lucky.

"Good. I wouldn't like to think she was doing it for him—although he does want it badly enough."

"Oh? You all talked about it?" That would surprise her; men rarely talked about such things.

"Not really, but sometime last year, when we were both starting to wonder why we were working so hard, what the point of building up a company was, I said that it was probably in our blood—since his father worked just as hard as Dad. Walker said, 'It was different for them; at our age, our fathers had children. We don't.' He and Lynn were just about to marry; he wasn't admitting it, even to me, but some part of him was thinking about having a family."

Jessica slipped out of her dress. How had Bret answered that question? she wondered. Had he found a good reason for having worked so hard? Did he ever think about a family of his own? He and Walker were alike in so many ways. Was this one of them?

And she heard herself say, "Do you wish that we were like them?"

"Walker and Lynn?" He was slowly unbuttoning his shirt.

Jessica nodded.

"No, no, I don't," he answered, but they both knew that he was lying.

Jessica had to turn her head away, afraid that she was going to cry.

She felt his arms close around her. "No, Jessie, don't start wanting it." His voice was gentle. "It will only make it harder when you leave." He tilted her head up so that she had to look at him. "We can't pretend that we are like other couples. It would just lead to heartbreak."

"But don't you ever wish—"

"Don't think about it," he interrupted softly. "A person has to play the cards he's dealt. These are our cards. All we can do is play them as best we know how." He looked down at her, his eyes full and dark. "And I don't know about yours, but my hand isn't all bad. Not every man gets dealt the Queen of Hearts."

But they didn't make love that night. Jessica lay at his side, feeling the strength of his arm around her, knowing how they both felt—that what was for them an act of pleasure would feel empty tonight.

## Chapter Ten

Sometimes it seemed to Jessica that everyone, except Bret and herself, were managing to have happy, normal lives. Even Peter and Karen Jensen seemed to be moving slowly toward a reconciliation.

Jessica stopped by Peter's jewelry store to offer him house seats to the Jess's Boys' concert. Surprisingly, Karen was there; she had stopped by to show Peter their son's final report card. Jessica immediately decided that she should call Peter about the tickets later. She did not want it to seem like she expected the two of them to be going together.

But before she had had time to once again ask to see some earrings that she didn't need, another customer came in and Peter moved away.

Karen was still admiring the report card. "We were so concerned about the last nine-weeks card," she said, seemingly unaware of whom she was talking to. "The separation has been hard on him, and it showed in his schoolwork, but now...I just got it in the mail, and I had to bring it in and show Pet—his father right away." A pretty flush colored her face.

Jessica spoke impulsively. "Karen, do you have time for some coffee?"

Karen looked at her, surprised. She fidgeted with the sash of her flowered skirt, but said, "Well, sure, I guess I do."

The two women left the jewelry store together, moving across the Crystal Court to the little coffee shop where Jessica had sat the first day she had been out shopping.

They sat down and ordered.

"Are you going away this summer?" Jessica asked politely. She wasn't exactly sure why she had wanted to talk to Karen, certainly not because she wanted to hear about her vacation plans, but that seemed like as good a place as any to start talking.

"No, as a matter of fact," Karen said, "I'm starting summer school next week."

"You are?" Jessica's cup clattered against its saucer. She had never expected that answer. "College? You haven't been?" It seemed like all Bret's friends had been to college.

Karen shook her head. "No, I got married at nineteen."

"Why did you decide to do it?" Jessica asked interestedly. Then suddenly her questions came out in a rush. "Did you go somewhere and talk to somebody? Did you write a letter? I mean, how do you go about going back to school?"

Karen blinked at this flood of interest, and Jessica explained, "I didn't go either, and I do wish I had. Not just for the degree, but because there's so much I don't know."

"That's why I'm going," Karen replied. "Although I'll be glad to have a degree too. I sometimes feel like I'm the only person on the face of the earth who doesn't have one."

Jessica nodded in sympathy. It was so good to talk with someone else about this, someone else who didn't know what the French and Indian War was about or who Thomas Gray was. "Aren't you scared though? To have to study and take tests again?" She shook her head. "I don't know that I could do that anymore."

"I am terrified," Karen admitted. "I really am, but the counselors at the university keep telling me that 'reentry women'—that's what we're called—do better than anyone else. All I can do is try. After all, what do I have to lose?"

"That sounds like something Bret would say." Jessica laughed.

It was absolutely the wrong thing to say. It reminded both of them that they had a great deal more in common than simply their lack of an undergraduate education. The comfortable closeness they had shared for a moment dissolved into embarrassed silence.

But, Jessica reasoned quickly, she had spoken having completely forgotten what Bret and Karen had been to each other. The past couldn't be changed. Forgetting it seemed like an excellent policy.

"Karen," she said warmly, "why don't we stop pretending that we are strangers, and let's both admit that while we've hardly met, we know a great deal about each other."

Karen had been staring at her coffee cup. Now she looked at Jessica directly. "I'd like that."

"You go first," Jessica invited.

So Karen talked, about how she felt when Peter left, about how hard it was to trust him again. "But I know I would like to because I really do still love him. I know he wants to come home; I wish I could be sure it was for the right reasons."

Jessica sipped her coffee without speaking. If Karen wanted to tell her, she would.

"I don't want him coming home because of Bret, because he's jealous of him. Peter left saying that he was tired of being married, that he didn't want to be married anymore, but I think, on one level, he thought he could get away with it, that he could always come home, that I would be waiting for him quietly like the good girl I've always been. That's what I thought too," Karen admitted honestly, "until I met Bret."

"You see," she continued, "Bret is younger than me, and I'm afraid that that was very important to me— to be able to attract this very good-looking, very successful man who was younger than me. And it really surprised Peter too. I'm a little concerned that he's being like a little boy with a toy he doesn't want until someone else has it. Bret has done so much for me, but mostly he made me see that I don't need him, or any other man, to tell me that I am worthwhile. In fact—" Karen suddenly broke off. "I hope it doesn't bother you to hear this."

Well, it did. Of course, it did. She liked Karen; she felt an almost sisterly intimacy with her, and she was glad that the other woman had found a man who had helped her. But she did wish that that man hadn't been Bret. She couldn't help feeling that way.

But those feelings weren't going to change what had happened. And Jessica knew from the women in her songs how jealousy, anger, and resentment can poison a person. She should just concentrate on how much she liked Karen and not think about why their liking each other was a bit strange.

So Jessica smiled at Karen and shook her head. "No,

when you were involved with Bret, he and I didn't have much of a marriage."

"What happened between the two of you? Why did you separate?" Karen asked. "Was it just your career?"

Jessica looked at her curiously. "Didn't he tell you about how we got married?"

Karen shook her head. "No. I'm afraid we always talked about my problems, not his."

So Jessica told her. What it had been like to grow up alone, with nothing to do after the school bus dropped her off except clean house, sing, and watch her stepfather get drunk. How when Cal Winsley arrived, Jessica had, in her innocence, been glad to have another person around. And how slowly she had begun to notice the way he looked at her. How he had started to touch her, standing so that she would have to brush against him when leaving a room. How it had frightened her. How Bret and his father had taken her away.

"So you and Bret have never had a home together?" Karen asked slowly, a little dazed by what she had heard.

"Not until now."

The waitress came, offering them more coffee. Both women refused, but they made no move to leave.

"So how do you like being a housewife?" Karen asked.

"I adore it."

Karen looked up, a little startled at the fervent tone. "Does that mean you are staying?"

"Oh, no. I do two hundred and fifty concerts a year, and the country circuit tends to be in the South and the West. I couldn't work out of Minneapolis."

"You are going on with your career?" Karen asked.

Then she quickly apologized. "That's a stupid question. Here I am wishing I had a career, and I act surprised that you aren't giving yours up."

"Actually I don't have any choice." Jessica explained about her contract. "And even if I weren't under contract, it wouldn't work. As Bret keeps pointing out, I'd just get restless and want to be out on the road again."

"*Bret* keeps pointing this out?" Karen asked.

"Yes." Jessica didn't understand what Karen was trying to say.

The other woman looked at her intently. "Forget what Bret thinks; what do you think?"

"Well, of course, he is right."

"No." Karen shook her head. "There's no 'of course' about it. Look, Jessica, I may be very wrong, but if you've known Bret since you were a girl and if he's done as much for you as you say, you must have simply idolized him once."

Jessica acknowledged the truth of this with a tight smile.

"He's a very wonderful man, but he's still a man—he's human and he is wrong about things. Maybe he's wrong about this. He might be right; I don't know, but it seems to me you're making a terrible mistake if you automatically assume that he's right."

The waitress laid their check on the table with a meaningful glance at the other tables rapidly filling with the lunch crowd. Feeling a little guilty for having taken up a table for so long, they paid and left.

As they were walking toward their cars, Jessica smiled at Karen. "I'm glad we talked."

"Me too," Karen answered. "And, Jessica, if you decide that Bret is wrong, why don't you come to school with me? We can copy each other's homework.''

The next two weeks slipped away in a delicious haze. It seemed to Jessica that time was measured out, not in hours or minutes, but by colors: the lemon sun in the morning sky, the scarlet geraniums blooming on the terrace, the yellow-white blossoms on Lynn's green squash plants. And suddenly, without Jessica ever knowing where the days went, it was the evening of the concert and she was outside, waiting with Bret next to the brick warehouse for Walker and Lynn to pick them up.

It was a warm, lovely evening. The sun was low in the sky, coloring the world with a gentle golden light that was soft, invitingly leisurely.

''I love that it stays light so late,'' Jessica mused dreamily.

''You can thank the government,'' Bret replied. ''It's daylight saving time that does it.''

Jessica sighed, breathing in the pure Minnesota air. ''Isn't that the most lovely idea? That you can save daylight. Like money—put it in a bank and get it out when you need it.''

Bret smiled down at her. ''Would you get interest on it?''

Jessica slipped her hand through his arm and rubbed her cheek along his sleeve. ''Yes, they would pay you in marigolds.''

His arm moved, trapping her hand against the warmth of his side. ''Only a Southerner would think such a pretty thought.'' His voice felt like a caress.

Although she was going to sing, Jessica had decided she would sit out front with Bret, Walker, and Lynn. She was only going to sing a song or so; she could go backstage near the end of the set. So when they arrived at the theater, all four of them picked up their tickets and moved down to their excellent seats on the aisle of the fifth row.

Walker and Lynn stopped to talk to some people they knew, but Jessica, afraid that she might be recognized and mobbed, didn't want to linger in the aisle. She nudged Bret; he took her arm and they quickly moved to their seats.

It was fun to be a part of the audience, Jessica thought, to be a part of the expectant eagerness, to be one of the audience waiting to be entertained, to be talking, laughing, waving to friends until the lights went down.

Thinking of people waving to their friends reminded her of Peter Jensen. Had he used the tickets she requested for him? Had he brought a date? Curiously she glanced over her shoulder.

He was with his wife, his arm across the back of her chair.

He noticed her immediately, smiled, and then touched Karen's arm. They both stood up and began to make their way out to the aisle, excusing themselves to the other seated people.

"I think Karen and Peter are coming to talk to us," Jessica warned in a low voice.

She saw a muscle twitch in Bret's cheek. She knew that he would find this meeting hard. It certainly wasn't that he dreaded meeting Karen; she suspected that they were still good friends, having managed to retain an affection for one another despite the ending of a love affair. It would be Peter he would find it hard to meet.

One part of him certainly believed that Karen had had every right to act as she had done, and that part of him knew how much she had gained from him, knew

that if her troubled marriage became strong, it would
reflect the confidence she had gained from him. Part of
him knew that.

But another part of him, the old-fashioned Southern
part, was telling him that none of this mattered, that
the issue was terribly simple, that none of this modern-
day talk changed a thing. That voice whispered to him
that he had done Peter the greatest wrong one man can
do another.

Jessica knew that voices like the one Bret was now
hearing were the heritage she and he shared. Their
Southernness was something they would carry to the
end of their days. It would always be a part of them,
sometimes giving them strength, sometimes torment-
ing them. Their background had taught them the old
ways, forcing on them a high standard of behavior and
manners that no longer applied to most people's lives,
a standard they'd never quite be able to live up to.

Jessica had been addicted to pills; Bret had had an
affair with a married woman—these guilty secrets
would always be with them. But their feelings made
them who they were, just as the land that had shaped
them had, in its own history, a fearful stain.

In a moment Karen and Peter were in the aisle. Bret
stood up. And amid all the bustle and noise of the
crowd, with people hurrying down the aisles, ushers
peering at tickets, and sharp hums coming through the
speakers, in all this confusion, Peter put out his hand.

Jessica knew that in shaking Bret's hand, Peter was
trying hard to say something to Karen. Jessica was just
grateful for what it was also saying to Bret. Nothing
Peter could have ever said would have done so much to
ease Bret's guilt as did this gesture.

Jessica immediately apologized for not getting up,

saying that she didn't want to call attention to herself. "But, Karen, tell me, how's school?"

"Yes," Bret said immediately. "Jessica told me you were going back. That's wonderful."

"It really is," Karen agreed, her brown eyes sparkling. "I just can't believe how terrific it all is."

They chatted about her classes for a moment, with Jessica listening almost enviously. Then Peter spoke, "Did you two hear that there's a house for sale in Ramsey Hill?"

Jessica gasped. In Ramsey Hill... that lovely old neighborhood where Walker and Lynn, Peter and Karen, Miles Turner and his wife, lived. So many of the people at the party that night had been from Ramsey Hill; they had all seemed like such pleasant, interesting people, just exactly the sort you would want for neighbors.

"It's quite a good deal," Peter was saying, "because most of the major work has been done—the wiring, the plumbing, the insulation—but nothing cosmetic so they can't get as much for it as they could if it were tidier. But if you've got the money, it could be a very comfortable place in six months."

Jessica started to speak, but Bret interrupted. "Thanks for thinking of me, but my partner already told me about it. It is a wonderful house, but I just don't need that kind of space, and I don't want to buy it as an investment since I'm sure the neighborhood would rather see a family move in for good than just have renters there."

"That's certainly true," Peter agreed.

"Thanks for thinking of *me*," he had said. "*I* don't need that kind of space." Not *us* and *we*. Jessica was suddenly depressed. But of course, Bret was right, she thought soberly. *He* didn't need a big house. And why should the two of them buy a house together?

Peter was speaking to her. "Is there any chance that you'll be singing tonight, Jessica?"

His simple words were a mistake. They set off a flutter among the people sitting nearby, and Jessica immediately had to turn and start signing autographs.

Out of the corner of her eye, she saw Bret give a quick signal to Walker. He hurried down the aisle, and each partner took one of her arms in a warm strong grip. Their accents went more Southern and with frigid politeness they got her out of the rapidly swelling crowd and hustled her to the stage door.

As the steel door closed behind her, Jessica looked around. It was a familiar world, a well-known jumble of equipment, lights, and excitement. A lot was happening. Security people were checking passes, the laminated cards that showed whether a person had a right to be backstage. Roadies were doing last-minute checks of equipment, the younger ones strutting across the stage, self-conscious in front of an audience. The opening act was gathering in the wings, almost ready to go on. As the houselights went down for them, a young stagehand touched Jessica's arm. "Excuse me, miss, but you can't be back here without a pass."

Jessica had not put on the pass the stage door manager had had waiting for her; she never bothered with passes during her own concerts. But now she extended this one to the boy. It was stamped "Full Access" and had "Jess Butler" inked across it in black.

He blushed and hurried off, but in a moment returned with a folding chair, which he put in the wings for her. He had apparently alerted the Director of Artist Relations who came up and introduced himself, offering to bring her wine, beer coffee, juice, whatever she wanted. Smiling, she refused. How odd it seemed to have people scurrying around her again, trying to make sure that she had everything she needed—as if a regular supply of diet sodas was all she needed in life.

As the opening act began to play, Jessica saw, in the dim light of the backstage, a thin female form among the crew. It was Sally Daniels, Cade's girl friend. Jessica hurried over.

"Jess!" The two women embraced.

"Are you on tour with them?" Jessica whispered.

"Just for a week or so," Sally whispered back.

"Are you having a good time?" Jessica kept her voice low.

"No, I hate it. I haven't seen the sun in four days."

Jessica smiled. She remembered.

"But, Jess, you look just marvelous," Sally said. "What have they been doing to you? Besides scalping you?" She looked carefully at Jessica's shorter hair. "I really like it."

"Do you?" Jessica was pleased. "So do I." She touched her hair.

As she lifted her hand, the stage lights caught the gleam of her gold ring.

"What's this?" Sally grabbed her hand.

"You knew I was out here seeing my husband." How right that sounded. Two months ago she would have never referred to him as her husband.

"I take it you're getting along?"

"You might say that." Jessica's blue eyes shone in the dim light.

"Then what on earth have you been doing in California?" Sally demanded in a furious whisper.

"Would you give up your career for a man?"

"No," she admitted. "But I'd sure do it for myself if running my professional life made me as sick and miserable as you were two months ago and *not* running it made me look as happy as you do now."

Karen and Sally—two very different women but both saying the same thing. Stay with him. If only there weren't that contract telling her she couldn't.

Jess's Boys were starting to gather in the wings. Jessica didn't speak to them. She didn't want to break their concentration. She sensed a tenseness in them, an electric nervousness that they had never had playing with her. Of course not, this time they were doing it for themselves.

The lights came up; the musicians bounded out onstage, bundles of nervous energy moving to the rhythm of the crowd's thunder. Stan swung onto the stool behind his drums; the others strapped on their guitars, and Jessica heard Wayne calling out the familiar count, "One, two..." and then the electric current vibrated through the pickups, the wires, the cords, through the amps and the speakers and then out across the crowd as music.

Jessica leaned forward in her chair, her shoulder moving to the beat.

They were good. More than good. Their music was difficult—they were changing time signatures in the middle of a song, from four-fourths to three-fourths and then back again, and changing from major to minor keys and then back. Cade's bass was carrying a second melody while the lead and rhythm guitars were chasing each other, blending, dancing.

The more she listened, the more impressed she was. They were tight, rehearsed, electric. She wasn't hearing the sort of simple, catchy melody that would make it to the top of the AM charts; their work might be too sophisticated for that kind of success, but the critics and the rest of the music business would be impressed.

"Jess..."

It was Art, her producer and now the producer of Jess's Boys.

They embraced quickly. "I didn't expect to see you here," Jessica whispered.

"I thought I'd better come check up on you," he returned. "Do you like them?" He jerked his head toward the stage.

"They're marvelous," she said, her voice full of soft enthusiasm. "You've done a terrific job."

"I didn't do a thing. It was all them. They don't seem to understand a producer's importance quite as well as you do."

Which, Jessica guessed, meant that the band didn't let Art tell them what to do as she always had.

"By the way," he continued, "I like this new look." He tilted his head, examining her hair. "Maybe the top should be shorter, fewer curls, you know, a slightly harsher look. That would fit the new Jess."

Jessica looked at him suspiciously. What new Jess? Clearly plans were already being made for the new album. Oh, well, she sighed, someone was bound to tell her about them sooner or later.

The band was just finishing a song, and Jessica turned back to the stage to listen. It was a carefully thought out ending, much more intricate and satisfying than the boring easy fades typical of country music.

"Are you ready to go on?" Art's voice was low in her ear.

Jessica saw Wayne step up to the mike, holding up a hand to quiet the crowd.

"What do you mean? They've only been playing for twenty minutes."

Art didn't answer.

Onstage Wayne was starting to speak. "We used to play for one very pretty lady..."

The crowd's roar swallowed his voice.

"You all know she's here. Do you want her?"

From the black mass of the audience came a cry, a thunder of noise, luring her onstage. An enticing spotlight danced over to the wings.

Suddenly she felt like singing, like giving these people what they were calling for. She wanted to entertain them, to make them forget their ordinary lives, their routines. She would share with them the energy that was vibrating through her. She stepped into the spotlight and let that hot white light encircle her.

She was Jess again.

A stagehand had moved a mike to center stage and without quite knowing how she got there, she was in front of it. As she acknowledged the crowd she touched the shaft of the mike, the cool glisten of it feeling as familiar as the sound that was pounding the floorboards of the stage.

In the shouts and claps she heard that treasured affection, a crowd liking her, wishing her well, wanting to hear her sing.

She glanced over at Wayne to name a song, thinking to do something simple—she hadn't sung in weeks—but he was already counting out the beat. They must have already chosen a song.

It was "Write When You Get Work"—the song about a man coming North to find a new life. Thinking of another man who'd come North, Jessica was glad that they had chosen it—even if the man in this song was different in every way from Bret.

Then her ear was suddenly alert to another difference. The intro sounded wrong, and it was more than just the whine of a steel guitar being replaced by the growling saxophone. Everything was faster, louder, punchier. The drums were fuller, the guitars more alive and electric.

It was rock and roll.

She glanced over at Cade and saw his eyes immediately slide from hers. It had all been planned, she thought in alarm. This was the "new Jess" with shorter hair, singing rock and roll, and they were forcing it on her.

She felt trapped between the wave of sound coming from the thundering audience and the unfamiliar beat coming from the band behind her.

And she was furious. They had no right to force her like this; she wouldn't do it. She'd just drop the mike and walk off. No one could expect her to sing so completely differently, without a rehearsal, without even a warning. She wasn't going to do it. She simply wasn't.

Then the pride came, the stiff, stubborn Southern pride; it didn't replace her fury; no, it fed on it.

If anyone could do it, she could. She'd sing it their way. Not for them, but for the audience—the people who paid their money, drove in from the suburbs, parked their cars, waited in line; she would do it for them.

Jess let her hand slide down the mike, pulling it toward her. Her throat tensed, tightened, and she began to sing.

It was a different song. It had to be. The same words,

in which Jessica had always seen heartache and loneliness, the pain of living apart from your man, the anguish of knowing that he was a failure and that there was little you could do to help him, those words became anger—anger at him for leaving, bitterness that he was pretending to be what he was not, and with the thundering drums and a harsh, relentless bass, a beautiful bittersweet country song became rock and roll.

The audience loved it. They were young, and the driving beat hit them, mining for the energy lurking in their restless depths, an energy that they poured back to her, their vitality echoing across the dark hall onto the lit stage, flooding the performers with a sharper light, hotter and brighter than electricity.

As she finished, the band crashed into another song, not giving her a chance to quit. In song after song she searched for the darker side of the lyric, finding in the pounding rhythm the power of the night. There wasn't time for sensitive coloring, for careful interpretations and phrasing, for squeezing meaning from each syllable; it was all a rushing, relentless stampede.

Heartbreak became bitterness, reproach became anger, gentle words of love became sharp sarcasm; the songs now described an uglier, more powerful world.

Only once did she falter. Someone had chosen the songs carefully, songs where she could instinctively find their darkness, but when the band broke into the opening of "Almost Enough," she panicked.

To her the song had always been about a woman's yearning for her man, a soft, sweet, aching misery—just the way she had longed for Bret before they had become lovers.

She glanced frantically at Cade. His body was half turned to her, the inlay work on his guitar catching the bright lights. This time he looked back at her steadily, but there was nothing in his glance to help her.

Desperately she signaled to Wayne to repeat the intro. But she knew it wouldn't help. She was going to freeze, failing in front of thousands of people, in front of all her new friends, in front of Bret.

Bret. The bruising beat of the bass brought back memories of that dreadful night after the auction, and with her sure, sharp intuition, she surged through her own humiliation, her own sense of failure and shame about that night and wired directly into the anger he had felt, an anger that had, in him, burned with passion.

He had regretted that moment more than anything he had ever done, she knew that. He was still struggling to forgive himself for it. She knew how it would sear at him to be reminded of it.

But she was going to use it. She didn't have any choice.

After two encores, long past the point where someone was going to have to start paying union employees overtime, they finally quit. The crew, the reporters, the hordes with backstage passes, mobbed the wings, and Jess felt Art's arm go around her, and she was led, dragged, through the crowd back to the hospitality room.

People were kissing her, congratulating her, touching her. Noise and sweaty bodies swirled around her, and she couldn't keep any of it straight. There was too much excitement, too much exuberance.

"Hey, Jess," she heard someone call. "How was it to be singing again?"

"Wonderful," she heard herself answer.

And it had been. It had been wonderful—the crowd,

the music—there was simply nothing else like it. There could never be anything this intense.

It was wonderful.

But not worth it.

Suddenly she felt weary. Wide awake and yet exhausted. Stretched thin as if she had given everything to the crowd and had nothing left for herself.

It wasn't worth it. It just wasn't.

"I bet you wish you were getting on the bus with us tomorrow." Roger's shout trailed past her like a fading train whistle.

No. She was relieved. Tonight she would go home. Home to Bret. She wouldn't be able to sleep, but it wouldn't matter; she wouldn't have to take pills. In a day or so she would be back on schedule, sleeping at night, getting up with the daylight. She was deeply, profoundly, grateful that she was not getting on the bus.

Jessica leaned against the cinderblock wall and closed her eyes, letting the noise swirl around her.

The sound of a throat clearing. A touch at her arm. It was Miles Turner, the reporter she had met at the party in Ramsey Hill.

"I know you are tired," he said, "but you owe me."

"I know," Jessica said pleasantly. "Start asking."

He pulled out a notebook. "Why didn't the band warn you that they were going to play rock?"

"Because they wanted to make me mad; they thought it would sound more like rock if I were mad."

"And were you?"

"Yes."

Miles's eyes widened as he scribbled frantically. No wonder, she thought. They both knew what she was giving him and how extraordinary it was. Her words were hard diamonds of truth that would glitter sharply amid all the muck and platitudes that reporters usually heard from entertainers.

He had expected her to deny that she hadn't been warned, and perhaps three hours ago, she would have lied unthinkingly, but now she wasn't going to bother.

"So what's next?" he asked.

"I don't really know." The pressure to do a rock album would be enormous after tonight, but she didn't want to do it. The thought of it depressed her.

Her throat hurt. Many female rockers had had voice lessons since earliest childhood; some had even had operatic training. Their vocal cords were stronger than hers; they could scream without hurting themselves. But her throat hurt.

By now Art had fought his way through the noisy mob. He wasn't going to have Jessica talk to a reporter alone.

Jessica introduced them. "What's next?" Miles repeated his question.

"Well, what we'd like is for Jess to do a live album."

"A live album?" Jess blinked in surprise. A live album recorded an actual performance. Country musicians rarely did them, but apparently she wasn't a country musician anymore.

"Yes," Art continued. "Jess's Boys have concerts scheduled in Detroit, Milwaukee, and Chicago. If Jess could go and sing with them, we could put together a live album. Her fans will be very eager to hear the new interpretations of her old songs," he added a little pompously.

Jessica guessed that she should be grateful she was in on this conversation; otherwise she probably would have learned about all this from Miles's column tomorrow morning.

"I don't suppose that this has anything to do with contracts, does it?" Miles asked. "As in Jess owes the label an album and legally the band is still under contract to her?"

"Why, no, of course not," Art said, fooling no one. "It's just that Jess and the boys *want* to do this album."

"Well, I don't know about Jess and the boys," Miles said with mild sarcasm, "but Jessica sure looks like she wants to do it just terribly bad." Jessica was again leaning against the wall, her eyes closed.

But before Art could continue to deny any deviousness, Jessica finally understood what Miles had said. "Wait a minute, Art." She was instantly alert. "Even if the band gets equal billing, will this finish out my contract?"

"Sure, but that's not why we would—"

"Then I'll do it," she said with decision. "Let's do it and get it over with. Call me tomorrow with the dates, but I want a decent amount of rehearsal. And get me plane tickets. I am not riding the bus. Now call me a car. I'm going home."

Art looked at her, astonished, but he signaled to one of his assistants.

Miles's look was just as curious. "You changed your mind in a hurry. I could have sworn that you didn't want to do this."

She kept her voice low; she didn't want Art to hear. "When I start explaining, I'll explain to you first."

"I couldn't ask for more," he said.

"You sure couldn't."

It was dark as Jessica slipped out the backstage exit into the waiting limousine. Night had long since fallen, making Minneapolis look like any other town, a place of closed shops, neon signs, and streetlamps. This was the world she had known—the world of night and artificial lights—but she didn't belong to it anymore.

She sighed, sinking into the deep cushion of the limousine, resting her black curls on the butter-soft leather headrest.

She was out. Three, maybe four concerts, and she was out. She wouldn't be under contract to anyone; no one would be under contract to her. She could quit.

And she was going to. She knew that with more firmness, more certainty, than she had ever known anything, that this was absolutely the right thing to do.

She remembered what she had been like when she got to Minneapolis, exhausted, unable to face a day without pills, incapable of making even the littlest decisions, and now she was a normal human being, capable of functioning in the adult world. She didn't want to go back.

She loved singing, and she had loved performing—back when her audiences were small, when she hadn't been a name. Of course, she would miss it, she would miss it terribly, but she would not miss the road nearly as much as she would miss the daylight if she went back out on the road.

# *Chapter Eleven*

A thin glimmer of light under the apartment door told her that Bret was still up. She was glad. She had so much to tell him, so very much. Her hand trembled and her key scraped against the lock.

Only the brass chandelier over the table was on. It cast a yellow pool of light that softened into shadows in the corners of the large room. Sitting at the table, a bottle of bourbon at his elbow, a glass in his hand, was Bret.

He looked up as she entered; the flat look in his gray eyes checked her eager step, filling her with caution. Wordlessly he hooked his foot in a chair, pushing it back, inviting her to sit down.

As she sank into the chair she saw a record was turning around and around on the stereo as if someone had picked the arm up halfway through, but hadn't bothered to switch the turntable off. The album cover lay on the speaker, facedown. It was her very first album.

"So you can sing rock." His voice was flat.

"Yes."

"Is it too arrogant of me to assume that perhaps I had a part in this new understanding of anger and passion?"

"Bret, I—"

He interrupted. "Are you leaving with them tomorrow?"

"Not exactly, but there are concerts in Milwaukee, Detroit, and—"

"Then don't come back."

Jessica's heart stopped. She stared at him, her eyes widening. "Bret, what do you mean?" she asked. This wasn't what she had expected; this wasn't what she wanted.

Slowly he twisted off the cap of the bourbon bottle and splashed some into his glass. He tilted the bottle toward her, offering her some. She shook her head.

"You heard me," he finally said. "It's been fun, but we knew it wouldn't last so we may as well get on with our lives."

"Fun?" she gasped, numbness giving way to pain. "Is that all you can say? That this has been 'fun'?" How could he speak like that? How could he be like this? Didn't he care?

His lips tightened, and when he spoke, the blank matter-of-factness had left his voice, leaving behind honest, raw anguish. "No, it's been more than fun, a world more." He buried his face in his hands. "God, how I wish you had come a few years ago. This was exactly what I needed then—for you to breeze in here for a few weeks at a time, forcing me to lighten up, to work less, and then for you to move on, letting me get back to work. But I want more than that from a woman now, a lot more, and you can't give it."

He was now looking straight ahead, staring beyond the light into the soft shadows. "I have never envied another man before, but when we walked out to the parking lot with them afterward, I envied Peter Jensen and, God help me, I envied Walker too. I don't want Lynn, and truly I don't want Karen, but I do want a family and a home."

Jessica could hardly see, tears were blurring her sight so, but she felt his hand close over hers, lifting it until his lips brushed against it. His voice was as gentle as the kiss. "The Queen of Hearts may be the loveliest card in the deck, Jessie, but a pair of deuces will beat her every time."

"But what happened to playing the cards you're dealt?" she whispered, hardly able to speak.

"Oh, I am." He let go of her hand and picked up his glass. He tilted it, letting the amber liquid swirl against the sides. "I'm folding. You know how to play poker. Sometimes your hand is so weak that you just pitch it in. I've been sitting here, taking a good look at my cards, and they aren't good enough." He set down the glass, the bourbon in it untasted. "Tonight I saw what an audience can give you, and I know I can't compete with that. I'm just one man, and I've got too much to lose if I stay in this game."

Jessica shook her head, miserable, confused. "Oh, Bret, what do you mean?"

"It's simple really. I've just decided that the stakes are too high. When I played football, I took risks with my health, playing crazy even if it invited injury. Up here we—Walker and I—risked money, and I honestly think that if the country needed me, I'd risk my life for her. But, Jessie, even in a war a man has a chance. I don't with you. It's my heart that's on the line now, and I've decided I'm not going to risk it, especially when I know I'm going to lose. Every minute you stay will make it harder for me to let you go, but there's no way you'd ever be happy here: what you need isn't here.''

Jessica could not sit there anymore, listening to him. He was saying too many things; something was wrong with them all, something very, very wrong, but she couldn't tell what. She slipped out of her chair, moved across the dark apartment to the windows. She stared out across the terrace to the river below.

What was she going to do? She wasn't going back to singing, she knew that, but when she decided that, she thought she would come to Bret. Now he was telling her to go.

Where would she go? Nowhere, not the apartment in California or the farmhouse in Georgia, felt as much like home as did here, this Minnesota warehouse. And what would she do? For years and years, people had always planned her life for her, but when she finished this next album, Art and Nathan would be out of her life, no longer telling her what to do.

She felt empty, empty and alone, without purpose or direction, with no hope of happiness or occupation. Her misery was nearly complete.

Some lights moved on the river, a boat that had people in it, people with somewhere to go.

And then what had always saved Jessica saved her again. Her pride.

It told her that she was wrong. She wasn't bereft, empty-handed. She had herself and she had the money that she had made. It might not be a royal flush, but it was enough. And not "Almost Enough"—it *was* enough.

She was going to college. Yes, that was it. She was going to get an education. Maybe here, maybe in California or Georgia—she wasn't sure yet, but she knew that she was going to go. She didn't know what she would do after that, but she wouldn't be the only woman there who didn't know what she would be doing in ten years. Jessica Susan Cavanaugh wasn't going to sit back and wait for someone to tell her what to do.

She would do what she wanted.

What she truly wanted was to stay here with Bret and go to school. And suddenly she wasn't so sure that she was going to let him tell her that she couldn't.

He hadn't understood what had happened to her tonight. Of course, he hadn't. As usual, she hadn't tried to explain herself. She had accepted misinterpretation as her fate just as twelve years ago she would have accepted Cal Winsley's hot breath as her fate.

But everything was different now. She was going to explain herself. Without being forced to, without being prompted, without anyone asking her a question, she was going to speak.

"You're lying, Bret Cavanaugh." The words, so crisp, so unlike her, jerked Bret's head around. "You're lying. It's too late to talk about risking your heart." Her voice rang with confidence. "You already love me."

A sharp clatter rattled through the apartment. Bret had knocked his glass over, a clumsiness that was ututterly unlike him.

Slowly he slid his arm across the table, letting his shirt sleeve soak up the drops of spilled whiskey. "Yes, I do." His voice was again flat and tight. "So I guess I'm not folding. I've played my cards as best I could, and I'm ready to pay up like the gentleman I occasionally am." He picked up the glass and placed it next to the bottle, aligning the two objects carefully. "I don't know if this makes you feel good or not, but when I walk in that door, remembering what it was like when you were here, it's going to be the highest price I've ever paid for anything.''

Jessica sat back down across from him. ''Why are you so sure that you lost?''

''Tonight—that crowd, the audience, they loved you, and rightly so . . . you were wonderful. I couldn't believe how good you were. I kept thinking that you must be rattled because you weren't expecting them to play like that. But it never showed, not for a moment. You were more alive, more vibrant, than anything I've seen, and I can't believe that you can get that anywhere else.''

''I can't,'' she said firmly. ''There'll never be anything like performing, but I am not going to do it anymore.''

And carefully she explained, telling him how she had felt after the concert, telling him about the live album, telling him that all her obligations would be over. ''Bret, I love you. I want us to buy that house in Ramsey Hill, make it into a home, have children, and be normal people.''

He was shaking his head. ''No, Jessie,'' he said slowly. ''I can't let you give up your career for me.''

''I'm not doing it for you,'' she said, her rich voice giving the words soft emphasis. ''I'm doing it partly for us, but mostly for myself. And, anyway, you don't really have anything to say about it. You can make me leave your home, but you can't make me go back on the road. I'm going to college, and if I don't do it here, I will do it somewhere else.''

''College? Jessie, what are you talking about?''

''I'm talking about going to school. I never went,

you know, and I'm going to. I'm going to go and find out who this Thomas Gray is."

"Thom—" Bret stared, unable to follow her logic. "Why do you want to know about him?"

"Because he is wrong. Ignorance isn't bliss. I hate being ignorant. You don't know how awful it is. You know who he is, don't you?"

"Sure, but, Jessica, this is insane. You can't be talking about giving up your career because you don't know who some poet is." Bret rubbed a hand over his eyes. "You just can't take that big a risk."

"That doesn't sound like you, Bret," she said softly.

He threw her a little, half-ironic smile. "Not sounding like me can only be in its favor." He picked up the bottle again.

She watched him pour himself another drink. What could she do? How could she make him understand that this was what she truly wanted, that she wasn't doing it because of the things he had said when she walked in the door? That must be what he was thinking, that this was just one more extravagant effort to please him.

She had her body. If she played it that way, in the wordless mysteries of the night, she'd win every time—she could make it impossible for him to tell her to leave.

But no, she told herself, that wasn't how marriage worked. Marriage was a daytime thing. Minds and hearts mattered more than bodies. She was going to have to say something, say something that would make him understand.

And she couldn't do it through music; there wasn't a band behind her or a spotlight around her. She had no lyrics. It had to be words, her own words.

She looked at him, the top few buttons on his blue shirt were undone, exposing the dark hair of his chest. The shirt fit snugly across his shoulders, still the broad shoulders of a quarterback—

"Bret," she spoke swiftly, her voice urgent. "Why did you give up football?"

He looked up, surprised. "What does that have to do with anything?"

"Everything, I think. Cade says you could have turned pro. Could you have?"

He shrugged. "Probably."

"Well, did you quit because you hated it."

"God, no. I loved it."

"Why then?"

Bret ran his hands over his face and got up, walking toward the counter that divided the kitchen and living room. "It's so complicated. The game itself is wonderful, but it's three hours a week, sixteen times a year. And that wasn't enough to build a life around, especially when it meant having someone own you and having it all be over at thirty-one. It just didn't seem worth it."

"Do you ever regret it?"

"Yes," he said bluntly. "When I'm watching a game and someone throws a terrific pass, I can't help thinking that it could have been me." His back toward her, he rested his hands on the persimmon counter. "And then it hurts. But, in general, I'm glad. It was the right thing to have done."

Jessica came to stand next to him. "Then don't you see that it will be the same? Performing is wonderful, but the cost is too high; you remember how I was when I got here—I'd be like that in a month if I went out on the road again." She slipped her hand in his arm, feeling the warmth beneath his shirt. "Of course, there will be times I will regret it, but not nearly as much as I would regret leaving you."

His gray eyes were starting to lighten as if he were now finally understanding. His next words, she knew, were one final protest. "But, Jessie, how can you be sure? How can you know that in six months you won't go crazy and flit off or that when you are forty, you won't really regret giving it all up? How can you be sure?"

"I can't be. But, Bret, the future is always a risk." Jessica spoke with a certainty, a confidence, she had never felt before. "A person is lucky to be sure of the present. And one thing we know is that we are in the same places in our lives. We want the same things now and we want them for keeps. And to get them, yes, we will have to take a gamble, we will have to take a risk, but, oh, Bret, isn't it—aren't we—worth it?"

He turned, his arms closing around her, pulling her against him. He kissed her, a long, hard kiss, until a slow rhythm began to beat through both of them. She moved against him, treasuring the feel of his body, but in a moment he stepped back.

He ran a hand through his hair and cleared his throat. "I'm not sure that we have time for this," he said, his voice a little gruff.

"What could possibly be more important?" Jessica whispered, her hands stealing up his arms again.

He captured her hands, stopping their journey. "If we are going to buy that house, we—"

"The house in Ramsey Hill?" Jessica gasped and her eyes shone. Suddenly it seemed as if it were all really going to come true. "Are we really going to buy it?"

"Only if you like it." He smiled. "I've got pictures

and all the information. Walker gave it to me and I just couldn't throw it out. So we need to sit down and look at it and decide what kind of offer we want to make."

"Whatever they're asking," Jessica said immediately. "Let's offer them whatever they are asking. Or more."

Bret grimaced. "You *never* do that, Jessie. But we do need to get our bid in first thing in the morning since I guess we'll be leaving for Detroit pretty soon."

"We?" She didn't understand.

"If you're doing those concerts, I'm coming with you."

"Oh, Bret, I'd love that," she sighed. It would make everything so much more bearable if he were there with her. "But you don't have to; I'll be all right. It's for such a short time; you'll hardly notice that I'm gone."

"Oh, I'll notice."

The tightness in his voice told her everything, told her why he was coming with her. "Bret, I'll be back. I really will. You don't have to worry."

He ran a hand over his face. "You just have to understand, Jessie, how much I love you, how much I—" He faltered, his voice breaking, it was so charged with feeling. Then he recovered and spoke with his usual crisp decision. "I'm coming with you."

She understood. It wasn't really that he didn't trust her, but for the first time in his life he didn't want to trust his luck as he had always done before. He wanted to change the odds; he wanted to be sure.

Building a life with her was the first risk that had ever frightened him, but Jessie knew that, with her at his side, as both his partner in the game and his reward for winning it, this risk he would take. It was worth it.

His arms closed around her and in a low voice he spoke to her with words of love and longing, words of hope and trust, words he'd never dared use before tonight.

And in the morning, the sun, as it always does, swept across the United States, first touching the eastern seaboard, then glittering across the Great Lakes, sweeping the prairies and the forest, and, finally, as if this were the sole reason for today's journey, flooding one gray-walled bedroom in Minneapolis with bright, sweet daylight.

# Readers rave about Harlequin American Romance!

" ...the best series of modern romances
  I have read...great, exciting, stupendous,
  wonderful."
                              –S.E.* Coweta, Oklahoma

" ...they are absolutely fantastic...going to be
  a smash hit and hard to keep on the
  bookshelves."
                              –P.D., Easton, Pennsylvania

"The American line is great. I've enjoyed
  every one I've read so far."
                              –W.M.K., Lansing, Illinois

" ...the best stories I have read in a long
  time."
                              –R.H., Northport, New York

*Names available on request.

# Enter a uniquely exciting new world with

# *Harlequin American Romance* T.M.

**Harlequin American Romances** are the first romances to explore today's love relationships. These compelling novels reach into the hearts and minds of women across America... probing the most intimate moments of romance, love and desire.

You'll follow romantic heroines and irresistible men as they boldly face confusing choices. Career first, love later? Love without marriage? Long-distance relationships? All the experiences that make love real are captured in the tender, loving pages of **Harlequin American Romances.**

What makes American women so different when it comes to love? Find out with **Harlequin American Romance!**

Send for your introductory FREE book now!

# Get this book FREE!

**Mail to:**
**Harlequin Reader Service**

In the U.S.
2504 West Southern Avenue
Tempe, AZ 85282

In Canada
649 Ontario Street
Stratford, Ontario N5A 6W2

**YES!** I want to be one of the first to discover **Harlequin American Romance.** Send me FREE and without obligation *Twice in a Lifetime.* If you do not hear from me after I have examined my FREE book, please send me the 4 new **Harlequin American Romances** each month as soon as they come off the presses. I understand that I will be billed only $2.25 for each book (total $9.00). There are no shipping or handling charges. There is no minimum number of books that I have to purchase. In fact, I may cancel this arrangement at any time. *Twice in a Lifetime* is mine to keep as a FREE gift, even if I do not buy any additional books.

_____
**Name**                    (please print)

_____
**Address**                                    Apt. no.

_____
**City**               State/Prov.        Zip/Postal Code

_____
**Signature (If under 18, parent or guardian must sign.)**

# HARLEQUIN
# PREMIERE AUTHOR EDITIONS

## 6 top Harlequin authors—6 of their best books!

**1. JANET DAILEY** Giant of Mesabi
**2. CHARLOTTE LAMB** Dark Master
**3. ROBERTA LEIGH** Heart of the Lion
**4. ANNE MATHER** Legacy of the Past
**5. ANNE WEALE** Stowaway
**6. VIOLET WINSPEAR** The Burning Sands

Harlequin is proud to offer these 6 exciting romance novels by
6 of our most popular authors. In brand-new beautifully
designed covers, each Harlequin Premiere Author Edition
is a bestselling love story—a contemporary, compelling and
passionate read to remember!

Available in September wherever paperback books are sold, or through
Harlequin Reader Service. Simply complete and mail the coupon below.

- - - - - - - - - - - - - - - - - - - - - - - - - - - - -

**Harlequin Reader Service**
In the U.S.                              In Canada
P.O. Box 52040                      649 Ontario Street
Phoenix, Ariz., 85072-9988    Stratford, Ontario N5A 6W2

Please send me the following editions of **Harlequin Premiere Author Editions.**
I am enclosing my check or money order for $1.95 for each copy ordered,
plus 75¢ to cover postage and handling.

☐ 1      ☐ 2      ☐ 3      ☐ 4      ☐ 5      ☐ 6

Number of books checked_____ @ $1.95 each = $ _____

N.Y. state and Ariz. residents add appropriate sales tax      $ _____

Postage and handling                                                         $ _____.75

I enclose $ _____                                    TOTAL $ _____
(Please send check or money order. We cannot be responsible for cash sent
through the mail.) Price subject to change without notice.

NAME _____
                                        (Please Print)
ADDRESS _____ APT. NO. _____

CITY _____

STATE/PROV. _____ ZIP/POSTAL CODE _____

PA-S

Offer expires 29 February 1984.                                    30856000000